The Search for M

Studies in Austrian Literature, Culture, and Thought
Translation Series

Doron Rabinovici

The Search for M

Translated and with an Afterword by
Francis M. Sharp

ARIADNE PRESS
Riverside, California

Ariadne Press would like to express its appreciation to the Austrian Cultural Institute, New York and the Bundeskanzleramt–Sektion Kunst, Vienna for their assistance in publishing this book.

Translated from the German *Suche nach M.*
©1997 Suhrkamp Verlag, Frankfurt am Main

Library of Congress Cataloging-in-Publication Data

Rabinovici, Doron, 1961-
    [Suche nach M. English]
    The search for M / Doron Rabinovici; translated and with an afterword by Francis M. Sharp.
        p.   cm. — (Studies in Austrian literature, culture, and thought. Translation series)
    ISBN 1-57241-088-4
    I. Sharp, Francis Michael. II. Title. III. Series.
PT2678.A2325 S8313   2000
833'.914—dc21

                                                        00-025928

Cover design:
Art Director, Designer: George McGinnis

ISBN 1-57241-088-4 (paperback original)

Doron Rabinovici

Photo courtesy of Suhrkamp Verlag
©Anita Schiffer-Fuchs

Tonja

The café, his favorite, had been renovated a decade after the War. There was nothing any longer reminiscent of the walnut paneling or of the alcove where the proprietress had once held court behind her cast-iron cash register. The walls were white-washed; one side gleamed like a mirror. The room had gained in width. The new chair covering was green artificial leather. A square clock above the entrance told the time. The shades of the wall lamps and floor lamps were made of perforated metal and light poured through them like through a sieve. One of the glass facades looked out onto a magnificent boulevard of the former royal capital. The other faced a square and a monument to a world-famous anti-Semite.

An autumn day in the year 1963. Rain drummed against the glass that extended almost to the ceiling, its shadows flowing over the linoleum floor and the tables. The waiter in black crossed the room. The café was overcrowded. There were passers-by who had fled the weather, students from the academy, women's groups with little pinned-on hats, officials from the tax office and taxi drivers having a frankfurter with mustard. The bridge club was playing in the back room. But he didn't have any time for cards and only wanted to rest for the time it took him to drink a cup of coffee before he kept an invitation for the evening.

He had scarcely found a seat when a waiter in a tux took his order. He gave the attendant his umbrella, silk scarf, coat, and hat, took from his vest a pack of cigarettes as well as his Ronson lighter.

A short glance into the mirror on the way to the newspaper rack: he inspected his image and straightened out the handkerchief in his jacket.

"Doctor," Rudi Kreuz called from his window seat, "How's business?"

"Don't shout it out to the whole world," he answered softly and looked around.

The gangling, scrawny Rudi Kreuz stood up, his back bent and shoulders sunken – he bent forward and whispered: "Careful doctor, they *nabbed* Waldser yesterday."

"Nabbed?"

"Waldser," Kreuz repeated.

"There must be a mistake, Kreuz. I'm not Waldser."

Kreuz waved his right hand, let it flutter off and said softly: "Times have changed, Doctor. I'm aware that you're doing well."

"That's quite true."

"For that reason alone we have to let everything come out. Economic miracle, right, Doctor? And times have changed. . . "

"You're confusing things a little, Kreuz. Maybe those are your problems, but not mine. Besides, a cool head. Everything is for sale, Kreuz – even me. Nothing is keeping me here."

Kreuz smiled: "Why Doctor, you're leaving us again?"

"How do you mean that Kreuz? Again?"

"I was just thinking."

"Oh, I see. Well, if you were just thinking," muttered Jakob Scheinowiz. He smiled bitterly and turned away.

Kreuz called after him: "Goodbye, Doctor. No offense!"

Scheinowiz continued on, stared straight ahead and wasn't anxious to meet any more acquaintances. All of a sudden, however, he caught sight of the familiar face of an old man with white hair and a stubbly beard. His once correct wardrobe seemed to have grown with time and dwarfed his body. The shirt collar – hanging loosely without a tie – and the cuffs – threadbare and frayed – dangled around his throat and hands.

The old man smiled and stumbled toward him. Scheinowiz, his eyes to the ceiling, already knew that he would hear the same old story. Just like every time he met him, he would be mistaken for someone from the old man's past.

The old man greeted him and said: "The printing shop, you know – you shouldn't have sold it. I told you at the time that was the crucial mistake. It was after that when the whole disaster started. I advised you not to sell but you didn't listen to me."

Jakob had often contradicted him and made clear that he had never owned nor sold a printing shop, but his clarifications

remained pointless. The old man had only understood them after
he had repeated them several times. Even at that point he had
remained incredulous and, at their next meeting, had totally forgotten them.

For several weeks now Scheinowiz had no longer even put up
an argument. He grimaced as if he were annoyed with his supposed
error, nodded several times and patted the old man on the shoulder
with "You're right" and turned away.

The other man commented: "That's what I told you. You
shouldn't have sold out. The printing shop."

When he sat at his table again savoring his mocha he scanned
the headlines: "Madame Nhu distrusts Kennedy's government"
and "Women vote for the first time in Iran." The government party
captured all but two of the two hundred mandates.

Since it was already too late to show up on time for his
invitation he stayed seated, read an article about Krushchev and
ordered another coffee.

After the waiter had served him, Scheinowiz paid his bill,
gulped down his coffee and ran to the checkroom.

At the door he opened his umbrella.

A few blocks and one staircase later Rita Fischer opened the
apartment door for him. She said: "*Git Jontef*, Jakov," and: "It's
nice that you came after all," and: "*Schana Tova*. How are you?"
Before he could answer, she cried out: "You're drenched!"

Scheinowiz returned the traditional greetings but remained
silent and kept his distance.

Those passwords – because of their effusiveness – those
phrases connected to the high holidays could be amusing, yet they
were also moving because they caught him up in the festive mood.

He chose the more extravagant, more orthodox phrases. When
he uttered these words he seemed to gain an easier entry into a
world to which he had not been entitled for some time. It was a
world in which he had perhaps never lived, or maybe always as a
stranger. It seemed to him he had a secure right of domicile here,
yet at the same time he realized that only he could prove himself
as not belonging – no one else could do it for him. In this way on

a few evenings during the year he subjected his mockery to the mimicry of belief.

Scheinowiz said: "It's raining. Am I too late?"

"No, not at all. We're just sitting down to eat," answered Rita, her smile just a bit too polite. "But I am the last one," he asked.

"You know we aren't going to talk about that today. We'll wait until the last one is here from his *Schil*. They were finished in the temple quite early."

Scheinowiz didn't mention that he had tried to compose himself in the café.

Of the thirteen other guests he knew twelve: four married couples and a few children. Rita Fischer immediately began to go into raptures about the newcomer: "She's from Cracow as well and has been in the city for just a few weeks. She's living in Tel Aviv. An educated, charming woman. You'll like her. Shall I introduce her to you?"

Scheinowiz shook his head: "Rita, don't tell me that you were planning a *Schiddach*. You know how I hate these arrangements. That doesn't suit you at all my dear."

She blushed and was annoyed at the obstinacy of her friend, who seemed more and more peculiar lately. "I wasn't planning anything, Jakov. Tonja is simply very nice and I wanted to introduce her to you."

"Just don't," he said. "I'll choose my own acquaintances."

He would really have liked to have walked out on the spot because he didn't want to get wrapped up in intimate arrangements. Scheinowiz was also convinced that marital bonds were for mere beginners – out of a basic concern with population statistics – or, at most, for people at an advanced age who needed mutual security.

He still amused himself with love affairs, affairs that had long since begun to get laborious, however, and threatened to wear him out. These were attachments to reasonably tolerable women in whom he could escape himself.

Many of his other acquaintances had married as soon as they had been liberated from the camps. He feared such marriages of dual suffering. They seemed a sham to him. They had found each other in great deprivation and come to terms with it.

He didn't believe that what an individual had lost could be kept and wondrously replenished by another. All the individual losses were simply doubled in both parties.

Yet it never would have occurred to him to condemn bourgeois normality. He recognized the right to indemnity, but didn't want to claim it for himself. And he knew that for many offspring were the only hope for victory over obliteration, a hope that he totally denied himself. He no longer wished to have hope.

Leon Fischer greeted him loudly. They had been friends in Cracow and the host admired his guest's education and former academic career. Scheinowiz could now claim nothing at all of this career, a career wrenched from the anti-Semitic conditions in Poland, the quotas and restricted university entry for Jews. Neither did he try to glory in his former titles nor did he try to affiliate with any university. He didn't wish to find his way in the world, but just to get by in its daily routine and to evade it.

Leon Fischer switched to Polish: "You've heard? Waldser..."

"That was to be expected," he answered and: "You have to be careful with Kreuz. Just stay away from doing business with him."

"What does Kreuz have to do with it?"

Scheinowiz retorted: "Kreuz is an informer."

But Fischer contradicted him: "He's much too dumb for that."

"That makes it even worse since then the idiot gains nothing by it. He talks too much. Just don't do business with him."

Fischer shook his head. "Since when have I done business with Kreuz?"

Leon Fischer had gotten respectable and had put on weight around the hips. The suspenders under his suit were taut and his skin had a fishy pallor. The once youthful scamp with the noticeably curved lips had swelled up to a new form. The soft smile – weightless and capricious – which had once set off his face, now seemed chiseled into his cheeks as if only a trace of his carefree nature were left.

Fischer said: "What I'd like to know is whether Maria-

Theresia is still in the picture."

Scheinowiz mumbled: "Her name is Marie-Thérèse."

"Well, Marie-Thérèse then. What's her story?"

"What should it be?" and then: "No, that ended a long time ago."

Fischer judged that "Wonderful," but Scheinowiz responded: "My involvement now is rather tricky. Don't ask me. Let's talk about something else."

"Again?" Fischer asked.

Scheinowiz confessed: "A voice student. Twenty-nine years old."

Fischer's glance pinpointed him. Scheinowiz, shrugging his shoulders, explained: "I don't know myself what I find in her."

The host replied: "You don't know what you find in her? I ask you then, don't even bother looking. You are fifty-three and have already gone through enough. . . You drink and smoke too much, don't sleep enough and are making yourself sick with your craziness. Get hold of yourself, Jankel, or you'll lose all control."

"You're exaggerating again beyond all bounds, Mr. Chairman," Scheinowiz replied in German and took his cigarettes and lighter from his jacket as Rita repeatedly called them to dinner.

The guests, already assembled in the dining room but standing around indecisively, were shown to their seats by Rita. The room was illuminated by a chandelier, the parquet flooring hidden under an oriental rug. The windows were draped in velvet and the walls blossomed in blue; the table setting was opulent. The rows of utensils framed the porcelain china.

Scheinowiz had scarcely been noticed up to now. He had entered from the hall while everyone was directing their attention to Rita and the seating arrangement. He was quietly greeted by individuals as if small talk were forbidden during the seating.

He gloomily noted that he had been seated at a distance from his good friends and right across from the new woman. Leon Fischer was a long way off and Scheinowiz sat next to Rita's end of the table, surrounded by the most boring people there and their children.

As he was thinking how he could quickly make his exit, Tonja came into his view.

Tonja had immediately taken notice of the Polish male voice in the hall. The tone of voice and manner of speaking were familar to her; she had once lived where these sound patterns were endemic.

She had seen the last guest come into the dining room. As she took her seat she started to smile at him, but his look turned her smile into a nod, silent and brief.

The stranger stared at her in apparent anger, as if he despised her or as if he were desperately trying to figure out who she might be or as if he thought he knew her. She seemed eerily uncanny to him. Tonja tried to remember whether she had not already met the man. She examined his once blond hair and his bluish gray eyes. His face was creased, appeared to grimace, and was disfigured by a scar on the left cheek, yet not at all ruined.

A memory gradually surfaced in her mind.

Rita Fischer was satisfied. The *Krepplachsuppe* was served, her husband had poured the kosher red wine and Anna, the maid who was helping out today, passed the bowls around. Rita was able to sit down with her guests for a while.

Smiling, she soaked up the praise for her cooking. The guests talked about their absent daughters and sons, about prospects for the future, their studies and about language courses in Israel.

Then she looked at Tonja and Jakov. Their eyes had become locked on each other as if they were alone in the light shafts of two spotlights. His stare relentless and imperious, he didn't allow Tonja out of his eyesight. "I'll choose my own acquaintances." Rita Fischer was satisfied.

Later, as the conversation heated up, there was talk about a court case against a Nazi war criminal and about an acquittal. A tribunal against the victims was being set up. The judiciary was protecting the murderers, while politics protected their henchmen. In this Catholic country everyone owed each other absolution just as long as the other in the particular case didn't confess anything.

Scheinowiz said simply: "Everyone is silent about something else," and then, again looking at Tonja, stopped talking.

The group continued to talk, especially about the Jewish community and its complacency. The complaint was aired that nothing was happening and that no one took part in the associations. Berger announced that the leadership generally lacked energy, the community a semblance of order. The others smiled skeptically. Scheinowiz said curtly: "We are representatives of a grand tradition – each is more lethargic than the other."

Afterwards, when everyone else had retired to the drawing room, Tonja and Scheinowiz stayed at the table. Her face, uncompromising and elegantly proportioned, was made up and slightly powdered. Her hair, combed backwards toward the nape of her neck, was colored dark brown. She touched the tip of her tongue to her upper lip and said in Polish: "Just so we don't sit here until tomorrow. I think I'm the one. . . "

He shot back: "It's you? Tonja . . ." Her last doubts vanished as she gently nodded and he added: "Tonja, if it *is* you, then it's me as well. I thought. . ."

She said: "I also believed that they had killed you. You were picked up in one of the first raids," and then added: "Aren't you going to ask about our daughter?"

Scheinowiz stared down into his coffee, was silent for a moment and whispered: "I didn't dare. What's become of her?"

"We survived together. Gitta is married and has a child. She's doing well."

Scheinowiz remained silent. Tonja continued: "She hasn't forgotten you. We never talk about you but I think she's still sorry that I left you. Henryk never became her father."

He cleared his throat, opened his pack of cigarettes and asked: "And Henryk?"

"He was murdered in camp."

"And why did you leave me?" he questioned.

"That's a long time ago, more than twenty years," she replied, adding: "You were a dreamer. Besides, I was in love with Henryk. I could have grown old with you but I wanted to stay young."

He didn't let up: "Aren't you sorry?"

She smiled: "That I've gotten old? No, I'm not sorry about that." He laughed bitterly and lit up a cigarette: "I've always wished you'd come back to me."

She asked whether he didn't know why they had been seated together, now that they were both unattached. A soft smile crossed her lips as she sat up straight and chided him: no, he shouldn't talk about miracles or dreams. He tried to tone down his enthusiasm and she repeated, he mustn't throw the past in her face again. If he wanted, they could easily start from the beginning again.

Scheinowiz suddenly realized: "It won't work." When she didn't understand, he added: "I can't. I had wished you'd come back because of me. – Try to understand. If you've only come back by chance, I have to be grateful to the Nazis that they've eliminated my competition."

After a few moments of silence she declared in an icy voice as if she were trying to overpower a pungent aftertaste with a sorbet: "You're right, things can't work out because you're still the same. Still a dreamer. You don't understand a thing."

He replied: "That's right and you haven't changed either, my dear. You've never understood, never loved me."

She turned down his wish to see his daughter anyway: "I don't want that. For me as well as for her you're a figure from the past which we don't discuss. She remembers you as a loving father, as the husband of her mother. Disturbing this memory would destroy it."

As he continued to claim his rights – "Gitta is my daughter, Tonja" – she asked him calmly, but firmly, to leave. Scheinowiz stayed seated, however, lit a cigarette and broke out abruptly in a broad smile. He looked at her for a long time and said in a friendly tone: "Tonja, do you know the difference between Jews and the English? The English leave a party without saying any farewells. Jews say their farewells without leaving."

Tonja Kruzki sat motionless without laughing. She fished the mirror out of her purse, opened it, craned her neck and rubbed her lips together. She then fastened the mirror back together and put it away. Finally, she looked at Scheinowiz again – as if she had forgotten him in the meantime – lowered her eyes and said: "You were always a perfect gentleman. Choose the English version and go, please."

After Scheinowiz had disappeared, Rita Fischer looked into the dining room. "Where is your dinner partner?"

"He had to go home," Tonja explained.

"Is that so? I thought you two were enjoying each other."

"No, we were totally incompatible," Tonja said sprightly and was about to stand up in order to avoid any further conversation.

Rita was amazed: "Strange – I thought you two had so much in common and so much to talk about. Jakov comes from Cracow, you know. . ."

"Jakov," Tonja blurted out, "did you say Jakov?"

"That's right, Jakov. A doctor twice over, Jakob Scheinowiz. A friend of my husband," the hostess emphasized. All at once she noticed that Tonja seemed different.

Tonja's eyelids fluttered as she folded and refolded her napkin, drumming with it on the table. "Was he married? Was Jakob Scheinowiz married, Rita? Did he have a daughter?"

Rita called to her husband so loudly and sternly that he rushed over in an agitated state. Leon Fischer, his cheeks turning red, said: "Yes, Jankel was married. But that was decades ago, Tonja," and more emphatically: "He lives alone. – Where in the world is he?"

He had to leave, Tonja said. She took some pills from her purse, swallowed them with a drink of water and asked about the name of his wife, her fate and whether Scheinowiz had children.

Leon Fischer recounted: "Hannah, Hannah Scheinowiz, a beautiful woman. Their daughter's name was Chava. Hannah left him even before the war." He nodded and his voice became softer: "Because of someone else. She and her daughter were both put to death. – Did he go without saying goodbye?" He shook his head and sighed: "You should have known him earlier. He studied in Vienna and Berlin at the beginning of the thirties. He has twin doctorates. Was a specialist in German literature and an assistant at the university in Cracow. Later he became involved with the social services in the ghetto. – Why do you ask? Do you think you knew his wife?"

Tonja Kruzki shrugged her shoulders, finally answering no and inquiring softly: "Leon, don't you think that Scheinowiz somehow resembles my Adam?" Leon Fischer hesitated, shot Rita a worried glance, shook his head and said: "Jankel Scheinowiz and Adam Kruzki . . . ? No, not at all. I knew both very well. No, no, not a bit."

She still sat at the table not making a move to get up and her eyes glazed over. How could she have mistaken this stranger for Adam? All at once he no longer seemed to resemble him. She wondered if Scheinowiz had taken her for his wife or if he had intentionally fooled her. For a moment it seemed as if this man she had never married might – under other circumstances – have become her husband. She wondered whether Scheinowiz could have been her lover and spouse.

Leon Fischer had returned to the other guests in the drawing room while his wife sat down next to Tonja. She said: "What's the matter? Have you changed your mind? – If you want I can get you his telephone number."

"No," Tonja Kruzki replied and got to her feet so she could leave the dining room. She stretched her neck and threw back her shoulders. "It's too late for that."

Jakob Scheinowiz stepped out onto the street. The rain had stopped. The traffic had dispersed in the night with only a taxi now and then rushing past. A limousine turned the corner.

The sidewalk was empty. Scheinowiz saw only patrolman Huber – nicknamed the Swede in this area – on his beat. Jakob passed by his favorite café. It had been long closed and, behind the front windows, completely in the dark. Outside, in front of the place, the garden chairs were in chains.

A disdainful smile spread across his face as he muttered: "I'll get to know whomever I please." Had he made a fool of Tonja to get revenge for Rita's presumptuousness or merely to punish Tonja for what had been done to him – and her? Had he misled her since she reminded him of Hannah, her pride and disloyalty? Or maybe because Tonja had survived while Hannah. . .?

As Scheinowiz turned into the pub next door to treat himself to a schnapps, he ran into the old man from the coffee shop: "Listen, you know what: I saw your wife today. I'm certain of it – let me tell you, your wife. . . she's living, she's here."

Cursing, Doctor Scheinowiz grabbed the old man by the collar and screamed: "Now just you watch out. Do you want to throw me into total confusion? You've been mixing me up with the printer Kruzki for months. And not only you . . . Maybe I have taken part in this game and probably I took it myself too far today. But that's it with this masquerade. I know who I am – do you understand? It may be that this Kruzki was not unlike me – maybe in many ways. But I'm Jakob Scheinowiz – right? I, Jakob Scheinowiz, was a Germanist and philologist and an assistant at the university in Cracow. Jakob Scheinowiz! Do you understand? Jakob Scheinowiz!"

The old man pushed Scheinowiz away and said: "Let me go! Do you think I don't know who you were? I know exactly who you were – but whoever you were, you are certainly not that person any longer."

Dani

In the heat of a summery afternoon he lifts him up, sets the boy on his thigh and brushes the hair off of his forehead with the inner part of his hand. Little feet wrap themselves around his hairy legs and the child's arms flutter around. Slowly he falls off to one side, flailing his arms and loses his balance. The man grabs the boy with his left hand, rescuing him, and looks into his frightened face with raised eyebrows and rounded lips: "Oops!"

The man the boy calls Papa leans back in the sofa, stretches out on the checkered wool blanket and lifts the boy up to him.

Dani's legs are raised from the straddling position until he lies stretched out face down on his father's chest.

When the father tosses him into the air Dani shoots up like a rocket. His legs draw him back down. For a moment the boy seems to hover over him, weightless and floating upwards to the ceiling.

All of a sudden he's drawn back down. He tumbles as terror flashes through his mind – but then, he can fly in his Papa's arms.

The adult lies on his back with Dani on him, twirling the hair on his chest that flows from beneath the white undershirt. In the summer Dani's father wears loosely knit cotton, in the winter coarsely pleated underwear. Every weekend, as soon as he wakes up, Dani runs to the double bed, slowly at first, then crawling quickly and quietly through the heavy pile of blankets forcing his way in between the two whales who are his parents. He snuggles up to his father, clings to his mother and pushes them slowly apart. Avoiding the bristly chin and sour breath of the man, he gravitates toward the shallow breathing and softness of the woman. As it heats up between the two bodies he turns away from the heat and toward his father. He is still lying on his back and sleeping, but Dani prickles with restlessness and he crawls down to his navel.

Every Sunday here in the darkness of the blankets and sheets, Dani lifted his father's undershirt and poked his index finger into the circular hollow of his belly where overnight pieces of lint had been trapped. Dani was certain: this white matter originates in this fold, this opening, this trap for bits of fabric. Papa's navel is a factory that nourishes his underwear, a mill that spins out clothing like cotton candy in a rotating drum.

In the heat of a summery afternoon he lies face down on his father who clasps his body with one hand and holds up the newspaper with the other. Dani smells the thinly rustling paper of a newspaper delivered via airmail, its sweetish printer's ink as well as the darkly tinted skin of this huge, just showered body. The heavy fabric of the sofa, its undulations held taut by metal springs, sends out sticky particles into the air. The scent of alum that his father uses in shaving floats past him. On Sundays the boy watches his father. While lathering the soap with a shaving brush, the man smears a dab of foam on the boy's face and responds with raised eyebrows and rounded lips – "Oops!" – to Dani's laugh.

Dani, in short cloth pants and checkered shirt – his frizzy gray socks tossed to the floor – lies on top of his father and looks around. The windows are wide open and birds are chirping in the yard. In the empty glass there are the sticky remains of lemonade and crumbs – a fly buzzes against a window pane.

The man and his son could stay on each other for hours. When Dani wakes up many dreams later he's amazed at the power of his father's hand. It doesn't fall asleep, and even when father dozes off, it stays calm and supports him during the nap. His father holds his head without getting tired and without letting it slump.

Dani begs: "Papa!" and rubs his feet together. He squeals: "Paapaaa!" and thrashes about with his legs. The forty-year-old asks: "What?" The fly buzzes through the room.

The boy lets out a scream: "Papa" and, laying his paper aside, the father grumbles: "What's the matter with you, Dani? Is something wrong? Isn't Papa holding you tight enough?"

"Sure" Dani whispers, casting his eyes down, sticking out his lower lip and picking his nose with his right thumb. The father sees him. He whisks the boy's hand from his face and threatens him with raised index finger: if he keeps doing that, a trunk would grow out of the middle of his face.

"Papa," the boy now says quietly, wiggling the toes of his feet together: "A story." The father is silent and chases off the fly with a wave of the newspaper. "Papa," Dani pleads in a whiny voice. The man resigns himself, throws the paper over the boy onto the floor and sinks deeper into the sofa. "Once upon a time there was a little boy and his name was Dani."

"No," the four-year-old shrieks as if his throat were on fire. "I want a real story." Papa says: "A real story. Lie still and listen. Once upon a time there was a little boy and his name was Dani."

One nursery school and two school years later, Dani no longer wanted to lie for hours on his father's belly. Although the boy had a frail, rather lean figure and seemed to be too small for his age, he had become too heavy for the man – and not merely because of his weight. The lad could be unbearable. "He's so restless," his father sighed. Dani tried to escape his parent's hugs and he became flushed when his father put his arm around him.

Even as an infant he had rebelled against nursing and as a small child, he had spit out everything that his mother had tried to force between his teeth. Only his grandmother had known how to feed him. All she needed to do was to pinch his cheek, look him sternly in the eye and, as his mouth opened up, he quieted down.

After she had had her second heart attack the grandmother had given up her own apartment and in no time had moved in with her daughter. The two women had survived the ghetto and the camp together. At the point when the older woman's health deteriorated, she wanted to be close to her child who herself had become a mother. She wanted to be near her daughter, her only ally against death.

They enjoyed a relationship of harmonious silence. A report in the evening news was enough – whether it was a Nazi trial, a portrait, obituary, or eulogy that erased the important years of military service or that waltzed serenely over the bumpy spots – to short-circuit their facial expressions. The air seemed heavy with memory. When the women looked at each other like that, there was a chirping in Dani's head and he thought he saw tiny specks buzzing between them as if gnats were flitting about in the light of nocturnal headlights.

If someone complained on television about deprivation during the war and about the dire straits afterwards when peace broke out, his mother erupted in bitter laughter. His grandmother shook her head, nodded toward the screen and said: "Poor things . . . I feel so sorry for them."

Father either left the room at such moments or turned to another channel. His family, supported by non-Jewish friends, had gone underground for years near the city limit of Warsaw. The youth, who was later to become Dani's father, had learned to remain motionless for days – lying or sitting – while living closely packed together, body on body. Shortly before liberation the neighbors had heard a child's laugh, had become aware of the regular grocery deliveries and figured out who was supporting the family's supply line. Jam-packed in their hiding place during those last weeks, the family members realized that the neighbors must have become aware of their presence and even suspected they had known for some time about their secret dwelling yet had not betrayed them. So they felt a bit more secure and no longer spoke just in whispers.

He had survived. His parents, younger at the time than he was today, had been murdered. Gone too were his brother Samuel and sister Ruth together with all the children in their religion class as well as the teacher.

At certain moments Dani's father switched to another channel. He then sat still with his arms around his son. He was a rock. He was a coffin.

The father's past lay in the darkness of his silence. It was as if he were still hiding in that hide-out on Warsaw's city limits; as if he remained motionless, saying nothing, not complaining – only about his back pain. He described the medical reports and told about the bone damage, the distortions of his spinal column. He showed his son the X-rays of his body in which the stigmata of his lack of motion as a child were etched.

On the transparencies all soft material that the rays had penetrated appeared in black while the bones cast white shadows. Together with his father Dani could clearly distinguish all the lumps that had not been illuminated. During those moments in front of the television set, when all the talk died down, he heard his parents' omissions, the individual words, the shorthand code, the pauses and the grim silence. All the fade-outs were recognizable by the glaring contrasts just like on the medical photographs. What remained unspoken was not disguised or covered up like in the families of his classmates. No one indulged in reminiscences of denials here. What his parents didn't want to remember and what they avoided talking about was something they couldn't forget.

One look from his mother was all Dani needed to understand why he shouldn't wear a black leather jacket or jackboots.

Only his grandmother sometimes talked about that time, looked back on a past that had grown old and revealed episodes of the persecution to her grandson. In addition she told him how weakened and skinny she had once been and explained why both his mother and father were afraid of confining spaces. She impressed on him the need always to eat copious amounts of food and to pay attention to his outward appearance since it could come in useful for him in a time of need. He shouldn't tie his future to any country but ought rather to stay mobile. In no case should he send his father pajamas for his birthday. She asked whether he wanted to put him into striped blue material again, whether he wanted to cause him sleepless nights and whether Dani had eyes in his head.

When Dani asked his father questions about that time, the adult brushed them aside and if the boy wanted to hear a tale from those days, he said: "Once upon a time there was a small boy whose name was Dani." His son then turned away glumly.

His father could never bring the fairy tale about Dani to its conclusion because his son always refused to listen. Dani's story seemed to be the only one left to his father. All his daydreams were wrapped up in it and were of no interest to the child.

The man said: "Once upon a time there was a small boy whose name was Dani," and the boy's mother answered his few questions very briefly. "Standing," she explained: "in cattle cars." She cut him off and derailed him before he really got going in order to shake him off and silence him. His grandmother didn't tell much that was coherent, but some things in great detail. She said nothing about the larger picture, yet everything about the small evils that stretched into the present. His father told him: "You've grown big and strong. Once upon a time there was a womanizer whose name was Dani." But his grandmother chimed in: "You look like your Uncle Danek with your black curls and blue eyes. He was the handsomest man in the whole city and when he walked through the streets, all the women dropped their handkerchiefs so that this lady's man could go his way only with incessant bowing." His mother, however, simply whispered: "Who told you about Uncle Danek?" and then: "Shot. In the woods."

Dani recognized his parent's former suffering, but knew nothing about it. It seemed impossible to him that his father, mother and grandmother had all gone through these horrors and survived these crimes; improbable that they had all experienced the things which he had heard talked about.

At the age of eight, much earlier than his classmates, he knew about the crimes of mass extermination, and didn't at all doubt that they had taken place but secretly doubted that Papa, Mama and Grandma could have been there. This was a puzzle to him that did not seem entirely dissimilar to the many sexual secrets. His mother had basically.explained human procreation to him, but that he could have come from such a union of his parents – that they actually slept together – he could not and did not want to imagine such a thing. As soon as he asked his mother about the geography of the female body, the anatomy of her suffering, the names of the concentration camps as well as those of the sexual organs, he immediately forgot it all. Eagerly and coyly he then was forced to obtain certainty until she finally admonished him and banned any further inquiries.

"Stop pestering your mother," his father said. Dani stopped talking. He was a scrawny and pale beanpole, had scarcely any friends and read books. Even his grandma had become powerless to do anything about his emaciation. She could no longer gorge the boy and just shook her head when he went, scantily clad, to the bathroom in the morning. She said: "He looks like. . . he's so skinny. . . I don't want to say it, but. . . "

"Well, don't say it then," the father interrupted her. And she became silent.

His only playmates were Peter and Manfred, the sons of the building custodian. They were small, stocky fellows whose pranks, tricks, traps and thefts he accompanied as if awe-struck. Peter was four years older than Manfred and Dani.

If one of these crimes became known in the building, the

tenants called for the brothers. Their names were sighed, shouted and cursed. If suspicion fell on one of the two, the third member of the alliance immediately volunteered himself. Dani announced: "It was me. I'm guilty. I did it." His confessions aroused delight, laughter and admiration, although nobody believed them. This attestation to friendship, however, attracted general regard and the unanimous praise of everyone. Dani said: "It was me. I'm guilty. I did it" and the misdeeds of Peter and Manfred Schaunder were forgotten. All the outrage was forgotten because the tenants were delighted with Dani who, of course, could not have clipped the dog; who certainly could not have gotten into a fight with fat Traude; who could by no means have been guilty of plastering shut the Wybyral family's front door. Not Dani, whose father seemed to be proud of him in these moments and whom Manfred and Peter had grown fond of. He was the accomplice of their guilt. At the beginning they ridiculed his confessions and mocked the boy from the second floor, but they were amazed at his knowledge and had to admire his quickness. Dani could run faster than the older and stockier Peter. He scampered to the lead in every prank, but never away from a confession. Scarcely had the misdeed been discovered, the guilty party sought and the suspicion directed at his friends when Dani hesitated, came to a stop, turned around and said: "It was me. I'm guilty. I did it." The main reason for the friendship between Dani and the brothers was, however, an ability which woke in him when he met the two for the first time alone on the staircase. It was an ability, that once it had been aroused, would never again fall dormant, an ability that would cause Dani many sleepless nights and the loss of his liveliness. He saw the brothers coming up the stairs and was startled by what he immediately knew: "You're planning to plaster up the Wybyrals' door."

Peter slowly nodded and said: "Do you have something against it?"

And Manfred said: "How do you know that?" But the older brother calmed the younger one down with a nod.

Peter said: "Are you with us?" Dani trudged up the stairs to the Wybyrals, but didn't raise a finger. "Just stand there. You don't have to do anything. We need you for something more important," Peter whispered and the silent partner just watched and ran along with them to the ground floor as soon as the entryway had been sealed tight. From this day on Dani accompanied them on their illicit escapades without taking part in any of the actions. He was able to anticipate the deeds of the two other boys, tell them in all detail what was planned and which prank awaited them. They called him the "thought reader." Dani was for them both the accessory to their most secret wishes.

Peter was the ringleader of the trio. He admired Dani, the passive one, who knew in advance what was to be done, even though it hadn't been said aloud. Peter merely asked: "Do you know what we're doing today?"

Dani: "You're planning to saw off the jaguar from Stumms' hood."

Manfred then added that the air was to be let out of the tires as well. Dani was drawn to their misdeeds and slipped into the conspiracy of silence. He was enthusiastic about the brothers who pursued their passions without any pangs of conscience. He never lost his way in the darkness of their secrets. He saw their plans in the silhouette of unspoken remarks, since silence was part of his family's oral tradition. But Dani never knew if he were capable of prophesying their wishes or if he had given rise to them. He didn't know if he was the prophet or the pilot of the group and if he hadn't been the one to give the go-ahead for their misdeeds. It seemed to him that he had ordered them to do everything for which they were called to account, even though he didn't doubt his abilities to summon up things hidden and out of sight. Yet he feared the thought that they might never have gotten in touch with their innermost desires if he hadn't given voice to them. The fact that he did nothing while they committed their petty crimes was not sufficient for his acquittal but rather forced the confession from him: "It was me. I'm guilty. I did it."

When he was fourteen Dani's classmates began to rebel against their parents. They colored their hair, wore tattered clothes, smoked up a storm, asked their fathers unpleasant questions, played hooky from school, and, under fraudulent pretext, stayed out overnight. They found out about an uncle's rebellion or about *that* cousin, or about the clan's notorious outsiders.

In Dani's family there were no more black sheep.

Direct unpleasant questions at one's own father? The Jewish boys of his age group from religion classes tried it sometimes: they played Maccabees, minor reincarnations of David. They threw stones, sang the songs of the Jewish resistance movement and of the Israeli state; they knew how to slip into historical costume and, when the need arose, to slip out of it again. Dani was different. He was not capable of rebelling against papa and mama. To protest against them meant to abandon them, to leave them alone once and for all in this foreign place.

Quite to the contrary, the boy didn't want to disappoint his family: certainly not his grandmother who seemed to try to see in him the return of her murdered relatives. Nor did he want to disappoint his father who longed for a new, different, and fitting story as well as a son not burdened by the past. This son should be filled, moreover, with the legacy of tradition: Once upon a time there was a boy named Dani . . . Nor did he want to disappoint his mother who was afraid that she might overwhelm the child with her own childhood or that she might fail – with every word, every syllable, every look.

Dani could not fulfill the various expectations. He was supposed to be a boy like all the others in his class, yet he was not allowed to forget his roots. It was up to him to prove his equality as well as that of all Jews to the others. He was expected to keep pace in German – even to be better than all the others – and to study Hebrew at the same time. He was required to know the names of poets and philosophers whose words he could not believe or trust. To acquire something alien as his own without alienating himself from that which he felt most deeply: this was his impossible task. If someone praised him, he was unable to be happy about it and simply saw himself overestimated. His grandmother remarked: "Just like Uncle Marek, who could remember everything that he had ever heard. That's why no one dared to ask him anything. He could calculate exactly how often his answer had already been heard and when he had been asked the question." But he was skeptical of her praise, pulled away from the hug and distrusted displays of affection. He believed that he didn't know how to satisfy the demands.

In school he was just mediocre. When he occasionally brought a good grade home from school, it was rarely the best one. If it did happen to be the top grade, he was ashamed in front of his classmates; he believed he had succeeded at their expense.

If the teacher asked: "Who wrote *Der zerbrochene Krug*," or "Who hurled the spear at Siegfried," Dani stood up and said: "It was me. I'm guilty. I did it."

At home his parents were worried. His father shook his head, sighed, and no longer seemed to be proud of his little boy. His grandmother complained: "I don't know where he got that. Certainly not from our family." His mother would then grimace off to one side, raise her eyebrows, lean up against the wall and look into the distance out of the window. Even Manfred Schaunder, Dani's most faithful admirer, would light up a cigarette, look past the boy from the second floor and say: "Even if I had done it, I'd never admit it. What does this Siegfried mean to you? It's just not any of your business who shot at him."

Dani's father began to slouch over the years and seemed drained of the dreams which he had nourished for his son. The dreams that had once blossomed in him and given off the fragrance of optimism, now dried up, became twisted and made him stiff as a board. The man who had once been able to lie motionless for hours now took on a rigid posture even while standing. His shoulders caved in, his back buckled.

His bearing was like that of his sixteen-year-old son, a tall and lanky lad who also resembled a question mark. Even the father's speech changed – his voice became strained and faded with his expectations. It deteriorated into a singsong that was mis-interpreted by some as Yiddish but stemmed in truth from doubt about his own existence. Every one of his remarks curled its way into a question as if the melody of his words were following his bent and twisted spinal column. If he wanted to say: "I'm satisfied" – period – it came out: "I'm satisfied?" – question mark. "Berger is an honest man" became: "Berger is an honest man?" Due to his insecurity he lengthened the very last syllable and it took an upward spiral. If he wanted to know at a restaurant whether a certain dish could be prepared, he asked: "You don't have veal cutlet," period.

The waiter replied: "Yes we do. One veal cutlet?"

He ordered: "I want veal cutlet?" – question mark.

"You do not want it?"

"Did I say I don't want it," period.

"What *would* the gentleman like?"

"Bring me the veal cutlet?" he demanded impatiently.

His father's confusion even went so far that he began to mix up the punctuation in his business letters. But his profits just increased. In agreeing with a suggested offer, he wrote: "You're asking 6.7 for one ton? That's fair?" The price was promptly lowered.

His father's professional advancement was closely tied to his disappointment in his son since, as the slender youth's mediocrity became increasingly evident, the family head became increasingly prudent and cautious in every negotiation, every contract, every business deal. Thus he became more and more alienated from Dani.

The boy was sitting in the kitchen after lunch, thinking about the test he had failed when the old man plodded in and asked: "You're not doing well in school." Dani gave him a dirty look and blurted out: "You know Papa, once upon a time there was a little boy and his name was Dani," but his father had already done an about-turn and had disappeared.

His father continued to grill Dani about his accomplishments. And, as the boy resisted the inquiries more and more vehemently – refusing to divulge anything at all – the old man clung even more doggedly to his daily sentence: "You're not doing well in school."

For the most part Dani's work did receive a barely passing grade, although not always. At year's end he found himself at the mercy of the Latin teacher's discretion and forced to take an examination. His family's fear that he might fail depressed rather than motivated him and paralyzed his ambition and resolve. When he did pass it, however, his parent's joy was not enough to cheer him up.

During that school year everything seemed to have turned against him. He was no longer the model son of the building. Instead, all the tenants now registered their astonishment at the successes of Peter Schaunder, a twenty-year-old university student majoring in information technology. These either cast all of his earlier pranks into oblivion or, more often, cast them into a new light. If Peter Schaunder had once been notorious for his impudence and bad manners, everyone now praised his ability and cleverness. The bad boy had not turned into a good boy, but rather a serious student.

After his grades had come and Dani wanted to travel to a Muslim country in the Orient with Peter and his university friends, it was only with difficulty that permission could be wrested from his parents. The neighbors' counsel and recommendation were necessary in order to allay his father's reservations, his grandmother's fears, and his mother's opposition. "The Schaunders' Peter will keep an eye on Dani. He's so grown up already," the Wybyrals gushed. When it was settled that Peter would watch out for his friend as well as his own brother Manfred, and since Dani's parents had to stay in Vienna all summer – his father couldn't leave his office and his business – Dani was allowed to join the eight other boys.

His mother packed his suitcase full, stuffed extra things into a large bag and the whole family drove him to the airport. They went along with him to check in his luggage and as far as passport control. And, in front of all his friends, they gave him numerous pieces of advice. "Put your money in the hotel safe?" his father ordered.

His mother said: "Don't get cocky. Take care of yourself." Only his grandmother was quiet, since she felt weak and tired at the moment.

The vacation started for Dani only afterwards when the boys rushed into the duty-free shop and bought cigarettes and alcohol for the coming weeks. When Dani didn't want to go into the shop with his bag, a friend of Peter's – a quiet giant with a hurt look and a short, bristly hairstyle who was also majoring in information technology – told him: "Go on in. I'll look after your things."

When their flight was called, they hurried to the exit. Dani was the last one up the stairs to the plane since the lock on his stuffed bag had burst open and he had had to put it down on the apron and force it shut. On board they drank champagne to their trip together. Peter remarked knowingly: "There's nothing better than alcohol."

Only Martin disagreed: "Do you really think so?" but he shut up when his friend gave him a dirty look.

A shroud of humidity and noise enfolded them on their arrival in the Middle East. In the baggage-claim area they immediately attracted attention as they laughed and caused a racket. A customs officer screamed at them unintelligibly as he gave them the once-over. These tipsy students seemed suspicious to this overweight man with a mustache, and he was looking for the most insecure one, the one whose bad conscience would catch his eye. At that moment he caught sight of Dani who promptly got red in the face, lowered his eyes and jammed his thumbnails between his teeth. The officer straightened his cap and detained the boy who obeyed without any resistance. He took Dani by the arm, pointed at the suitcase and then toward the counter.

In the heat of the summer afternoon a uniformed official orders Dani to the side and has him open his bag. The official examines his toiletries kit, searches through his underwear and socks, ferrets out a little packet and puts it on top of the clothes pile. Dani no longer pays attention to the movements nor his unfolded pants nor his rumpled shirts but stares only at that small box, his eyes fixed on that small packet of condoms. All of a sudden Dani senses the looks and hears the whispers of his companions; Peter Schaunder mutters something to his fellow student Martin and Dani feels the tension going through the group. He feels the blood rushing to his head, the pounding in his temples, and it's as if he's caught up in a rotating motion, as if he's become a small boy again. The thought occurs to him: I'm being tossed by my father and hurled through the air like a boy. Papa lets his son fly and soar until his head is whirling. I tumble head over heels until gravity takes over, pulling me down to a crash landing. Terror strikes at my heart as I hear Papa say: "Once upon a time there was a little boy and his name was Dani . . ."

But Grandma suddenly interrupts him: "I don't know where he got the rubbers – not from our family anyway."

As the official is cramming the things back into his bag, Dani's fingers slip past his, picking up the condoms and he says: "I don't have any contraceptives in my luggage. I'm not guilty; I didn't do that. Those don't belong to me." The official, who understands not a word of German but who now is alerted, pauses while taking the packet and opening it. All the while he scrutinizes the boy who pleads: "It wasn't me." With a censorious expression in his eyes he tears open the foil and white dust floats down onto Dani's undershirts and swimming trunks, trickles into his shoes and between his books. At that, the official grabs Dani by the collar and, while screaming at him in a foreign language, begins to shake him.

Just at that moment, however, Peter Schaunder jumps in and declares in English: "Let him be. He's innocent. I am guilty."

At the hearing Peter maintained that he had smuggled the drugs into the luggage and that the boy had not known anything about it. Nor had anyone else been aware of the stash. While Schaunder was immediately taken into custody, Dani – after several hours of interrogation – was put on a flight home. It was only on the return flight when he began to realize that Peter had taken all the blame, that he had stood up for him and had been put in jail in his place. All of a sudden he also knew who had passed off the packet to him. He recalled that Martin had kept an eye on his bag and that shortly afterwards the lock had been cracked open.

To Dani it was now clear that Peter Schaunder had not merely confessed innocently but now sat behind bars because of Dani's thoughtlessness. If he had kept his mouth shut in front of the official, Peter would still be free.

At home in the kitchen, his father and Dani sat across from one another. His mother had driven his sick grandmother to the hospital. The Schaunders had flown off to come to the aid of their son. His father asked: "You don't know what something like this means in these countries." He said: "For smuggling drugs you can get the death penalty?"

Dani whispered in a choked voice: "It was me Papa. I did it. I'm the guilty one."

But then, for the first time in his life, the father smacked his son in the face and yelled: "That's enough now?"

It cost a semester and diplomatic efforts for Peter to be released and deported. But Grandma Tonja never came home.

Arieh

How was that night different from all the other ones? Years later he would still ask himself this question and wonder why his life had taken that turn at the time.

A day just like all the others: his mother's grumbling about the disarray in his dresser, the lecture at the university, the swimming pool, the work at the café on the equations together with several people he didn't know, the exchange of words with his father about the car. In the evening he slipped into his sneakers, hurried past his father's room and his mother's greeting down the stairs three steps at a time – sliding the final stretch down the railing – and landed in front of the house door.

Meeting with the clique, the race to the river island and the camp fire with his Jewish friends was nothing unusual. His mother had kept ties with friends from her youth, even though loose ones, and Arieh had grown up with their children. And he occasionally turned up on nights when they met for parties. Although his family was not a member of the community, he tried to keep contact with the Jewish students in order to find out what had been withheld from him at home, something that displeased his father. He wanted to learn those ciphers and code words into whose secrets he had not been initiated. He wasn't interested in doing community work within an organization but rather in enlightening himself with the help of the Jewish youth. Let others lead discussions, give lectures, raise money, put on festivals or edit newpapers. This didn't concern Arieh. He hardly noticed it and sometimes even made fun of the fanatics' diligence and the arguments among those on the executive committee.

In the light of a summer fire Tanja laid her head down in his lap, adjusting it until he felt a tremor between his legs. At the same time, he was leaning back on Dani who was talking to Dina who was lying next to Roni. The others were warbling along to the twanging of a guitar, all entwined together. Arieh let his fingers glide across Tanja's face. The song trickled away into discord as he kissed her, all the while thinking of Karin, whom he had broken up with only days before. It had been on Karin's initiative since she had accused him of not looking after her and he hadn't been able to reply.

All of a sudden Tanja extricated herself in order to join in a conversation that had flared up among the rest of them. A unit of rowdily intoxicated men, uniformed and armed with helmets and clubs, had attacked some young people in a suburban night spot. Shouting insults, they had dragged one man apart from the rest, called him a nigger bastard and slashed his face with a shattered bottle. Unimpeded by the others, they had stomped on him, twisted his knee like a chicken neck until the ligaments gave way with an loud snapping sound. At that point, they turned to the rest of them, charged through the jumble of chairs and limbs without meeting the slightest resistance. The one who had dared any opposition and called for them to stop, had been silently beaten. They disappeared just like they had come.

"On an estate just outside of the city" Dani answered when someone asked where they held their paramilitary exercises. And Tanja said "nothing" when Dina wanted to know what the police were doing about it.

Arieh had heard about all the precautions for their own

protection and that Jewish organizations might be targets of such attacks. He wasn't surprised that such groups got off scot-free in this country, even found sympathy and support in parts of the judicial system and from the police. War criminals were not brought to court and everything recalling the crimes once committed as well as actions provoking persecution and mass murder was deliberately ignored rather than prosecuted. Guilty parties were just not to be found in a country that claimed to be without blemish. The police pretended to have those radically subversive organizations under control by giving free rein to their leaders and supporters. The press scarcely took note of their crimes because they were afraid of waking sleeping dogs with their reports. While the state did nothing to stop its enemies, it believed it had them in check.

He knew his father's contempt for these indigenous traits. When Arieh heard about incidents in Jewish circles that filled the others with terror, he slipped behind a protective wall and pretended to be unaffected. The attack on the night club in the suburbs didn't amaze him. Arieh took care of the problems of those nearest him and wasn't concerned about their worries. He was occupied with the same thing but in a different way. He was looking for the source of the danger and wanted to confront it directly. He had joined the clique to become acquainted with his origins but this evening for the first time he felt the desire to get all the way to his roots. He wanted to take up battle with the arch-enemies of these roots.

A thought, expressed only in an undertone, startled Robby. Arieh had said that a crime would have to be attributed to such people so that the government would be forced to act. How would he go about finding out who they were and outwitting them? Didn't he think the enemy would see through him and get their bloody revenge? Dani remarked that he probably thought he could solve the problem like an exercise in a math class.

"Exactly," Arieh replied as he pressed the nail of his left thumb into tip of his fourth finger like he always did when he pondered something. "This question resembles an equation with several unknowns." It was not only the others who were amazed at this remark, but also Arieh himself was surprised at how far he had dared to go out on a limb and exposed himself to ridicule. And also that this thought just wouldn't let go of him as it pressed for an experiment and a proof.

What made this night different from all the other nights? Right after breakfast with Tanja he set out on his search, from then on neglecting everything at the university, sacrificing his swimming and even forgoing his weekly training in hand-to-hand combat. This was a discipline in which Arieh, a black-haired student with a delicate build, had never had much success anyway. He simply didn't believe in solutions with one blow. He wasn't able to find clarification with his fists. He was mostly a failure at violence.

Jakob Fandler, his father, had given him lessons in Taikwondo as a child. "Nobody who hits you gets off unpunished, Arieh, do you hear? No one hits you," the old man had said. When Arieh asked if his Papa had ever been beaten, he only answered: "No one hits you, do you hear?"

But his mother, twenty-five years younger than her husband, said three days later: "Look at his back, the scars."

When Arieh said: "I don't know anything about you, father, not who you are or who you were," Jakob Fandler laughed.

"Who I was will be on my gravestone. Have a little patience, son." Then he pulled a lighter and case from his vest to light up a cigarette. His father kept his past obscure, shedding no light on the shadows in which he raised his son. His son groped around in this darkness, feeling a kind of animosity which the old man held toward him that the boy could not explain. Deep within Arieh there was a mysterious guilt, a guilt about which he knew nothing but which clung to his being and very presence. Jakob Fandler did not find any joy in Arieh's successes at school and in mathematics. It seemed to Arieh that his father begrudged him any success and that his occasional failure just confirmed the old man's displeasure.

Jakob Fandler had his son dropped from religious instruction, never stepped foot into the synagogue, and stayed away from all festivals, celebrating only *Pessach* at home with his family.

"*Ma nischtanah ha lailah haseh mi kol ha leiloth,*" the boy sang. "What made this night different from all the other nights?" And his father, true to the *Haggadah*, told about the exodus from Egypt, about the trek through the Sinai desert as if he had experienced everything himself.

Arieh had soon made inquiries, found out the meeting places of such gangs and sought them out. He had decided not to try to find the whole group at once. He wanted to track them individually and bring them down one at a time. It seemed to him that, similar to dealing with a complicated equation with several unknowns, he first had to think up a partial result that stood in a functional relationship to the rest of the variables. He wanted to begin with one person who, together with the others, formed a whole. He decided that this person should be the one who called out nigger bastard as he flung himself on the first victim.

Arieh knew neither the name nor the face of his opponent. Unlike when he did his calculations, a textbook was of no use here. Yet without knowing how he could find a solution, he felt a rippling sensation in his joints and temples that had filled him while working with mathematics as he blindly found his way along new paths to his goal – with the nail of his thumb pressed into the tip of his ring finger.

That young man who had struck first had entered his consciousness and lodged in his innermost self. Ever since he had been on the lookout for the culprit, he had been seized by a revulsion that he had never known or even fantasized. He was filled with an aversion to himself that alienated him from Tanja as well as Karin, a reaction that stimulated their interest.

He fell into a state that at first made him nervous, then began to scare him. His search for the culprit became an addiction. At night he dreamed of the attack he had heard about. He saw the silhouette of the attackers and parts of their faces as if he had been there. He heard the cries and the whimpering of the injured, the chairs and the bones being broken. It was not the first time in his life that a passion to track down another person had taken possession of him, a passion that dominated his thinking, his feeling, his movements and robbed him of sleep. Even in school he had been overcome by a similar change, a change resembling an allergic reaction to the person he intended to find. At the time he had taken a pocket calculator along with him to school and placed it on his desk. With its help he had shown off by demonstrating the formulae with which the speed of a space ship could be determined. He had appeared in front of the ringleaders of the class with his tricks, in front of the girls whose admiration every male pupil sought to elicit. He had dedicated a special show to Anja. He had amazed Klaus, always the center of the whole class, to such a degree that he suffered an attack of his tick, a nervous cough like a voiceless burping. "Can you – show me – how that works, man," Klaus had asked.

"Sure thing," Arieh had answered, but he had repeated it in such a rapid and involved way that Klaus never would have been able to follow it.

In the next few weeks he had sometimes left the calculator in the room during recesses. One day the display area and the buttons had been coated with super glue and ruined. That was the first time he had made up his mind to catch a wrongdoer. The provocation that took hold of him extended into his sleep and forced him to dream incessantly of Klaus. Arieh had awakened in the morning with an urge to cough as if a clock were ticking in his throat, as if its one hand had stuck in his neck. He had looked at Klaus in class as they stood opposite one another. They alternately cleared their throats, back and forth, mimicking the oscillation of a metronome from one mouth to the other. Neither spoke a word until Klaus suddenly bolted with a shriek on his lips and Arieh in hot pursuit. Arieh fell on the stairs. His thigh fracture helped him forget his calculator and, after Klaus had visited him in the hospital, they became best friends for the next few months.

He still remembered the metamorphosis. A few years later he had experienced something similar. Anja had been unfaithful to him and confessed her cheating without wanting to reveal the name of the rival. Once again he was seized by the desire for the hunt, to find out who the mystery person was. Once again he was able to intuit who that person was, to pick up his trail and to approach him. His compulsion to buy a certain fragrance, to change his hair style and clothes was irrestible until he recognized that he was mimicking Anja's dancing partner, with whom she had opened the school dance.

It was precisely this ability, this passion to pick up the scent of his prey that was again aroused in him as he sought out the gang which had committed the assault. He could think of nothing else. On the next day he was compelled to look for the pertinent night spots and inquired where he might encounter the criminals. Without knowing why, he decided to observe one particular meeting point of such groups from the opposite side of the street. He stood in the shadows of a tree, pressing himself against the wall of a house when a Turkish family came past him. Grimacing, he bought a newspaper, taking care not to come into contact with the Arabic peddler. Afterwards he wiped off his hands with his handkerchief. He was overcome by nausea, a reaction whose source he couldn't identify.

An hour later Arieh saw a man leave the pub. Wearing a leather jacket and boots and carrying a helmet in his left hand, he went up to the newspaper vendor, picked up a paper, wiped his hands off with a handkerchief and grimaced. At that very moment Arieh understood whom he had sought and had found at the core of his being where the source of his disgust was located.

Intoxicated by his success Arieh lurked along behind his enemy until he knew building, apartment and address: Herwig Wernherr. He drew up a balance sheet. He knew how to draw close to a culprit prior to an encounter by simply following a guilty scent.

Without being able to say it, he *felt* that it was Wernherr and not someone else who had dislocated the victim's knee and torn the ligaments. This thought consumed him. Like Herwig Wernherr, Arieh now always wore leather gloves. He was intent on bringing

Wernherr down, but all of a sudden he lost sight of him. His only other interest now was for electronic gadgetry, computers and cameras. Arieh almost began to believe that he was neglecting his real design until he realized that this curiosity was again merely a sign of the hunt, a sign that he was taking up Wernherr's tracks in these peripheral matters.

He dialed Wernherr's number and an answering machine – something still out of the ordinary in the early eighties – played a march. Two days later Arieh had cracked the remote control code and was able to tap the device, to erase messages and alter its operation and settings. He had also gathered that a new operation was on the agenda. Wernherr had to be ready to take care of a delicate job on call. The urgency of the instruction was unmistakable and when Arieh erased the code word at just the right moment, the signal that should have brought a response from Wernherr, he plunged the entire group into consternation. Wernherr didn't show up and the nocturnal entry into the publishing office of a cadre party which placed all its hopes in distant China went awry. But Arieh's plan to defame the ringleader Wernherr in the eyes of his group failed. Wernherr simply bought a new device.

In spite of this Arieh didn't give up on his plan, but rather supplemented the knowledge about his adversary. He realized that with his previous hunches, hunches that stemmed from his hypersensitivity, he had merely sized up and sidestepped Wernherr. So he made new inquiries. Wernherr's parents had never drawn political attention: they had gone along with National Socialism and profited from the aryanization of an apartment. His mother's brother, however, had been incarcerated after the war because he had distinguished himself as a concentration camp supervisor. But he soon had been released and, in spite of his crimes, had been acquitted in a court proceeding. This uncle, Heinz Czehofsky, grieved for his career in uniform and envied all of his earlier party comrades who now were considered democrats. The entire family remained defiantly self-righteous. Even as a schoolboy Herwig had collected devotional objects of the dictatorship, the army and the party organizations and had found company among like-minded people. His speeches were crowd pleasers since he was capable of anything under the sun. Although Herwig Wernherr had a network of supporters he was only able to rope a few stalwarts into his operations. This reliable nucleus that could be called on for criminal actions gradually dispersed as its members finished their studies while Wernherr just got older.

Jakob Fandler took uneasy note of the changes in his son. It was as if a stranger he had known for a long time and then banned from his life, had suddenly shown up and moved in with him. He had already noticed Arieh's disgust and his obsessive washing weeks ago. Then it was his restlessness and after that the electronic devices he dragged around. Now it was the new literature his son had that scared him, a literature about the community of the masses, racial doctrine and the compulsion to erase the past, to undo the mass murders and to declare the crimes to be myths. When Arieh returned home with boots and a crew cut, the old man was seized with horror by the sight of his own child. In spite of all his love he had secretly harbored an inexplicable anger toward him – as well as toward himself – for a long time. And his mother Ruth said: "You look like . . . " But his father suddenly interrupted her: "It's better to wear boots than to be stomped. Let everybody know: If somebody's doing the stomping, it's us. Leave him alone!"

But on the next day after a restless night Jakob Fandler stormed into his son's room and demanded to talk.

A walk along the canal. Jakob Fandler was in pinstripes, his cane in his hand and slightly hunched over. Arieh had on boots and a leather jacket. His father coughed softly and asked: "Why this costume Arieh? What kind of an act is this?" And one bridge later, since the young man remained silent: "Are you trying to find yourself in others?" And ironically: "Do you want to find yourself by hiding out in other people? Are you listening Arieh? What do you know about yourself, about me, about your family? Do you have any inkling about yourself, about who you are Arieh?"

His son screamed out: "You're a fine one to talk! I hardly had put on this jacket that reminded you of everything you wanted to forget and you bring up the past that you never told me about. Never! Haven't you always told me that identity in its final form is nothing more than an inscription on a gravestone?"

His father stayed calm and smiled. He replied: "None of our relatives, Arieh, none of them has a grave marker. None of them, do you know that? As long as you live, the last word hasn't been spoken. As far as I'm concerned I had already survived my death sentence before you were born. . . "

"But I've asked you. Why haven't you ever talked about yourself, never answered me, Papa?" Arieh whispered.

"I was afraid it would poison you. It was probably a mistake. I simply thought: not you, Arieh, not you." But his last words exploded into a cough, a cough due to an untreated bronchial infection and too much smoking that had plagued him for months.

"My name was Jakov Scheinowiz. I had two doctorates and was an assistant in German Studies in Cracow." He was telling about his family, his wife and child, who had all been murdered. "She was six when they dragged her away, fourteen years younger than you are now. Her name was Chavah – my daughter. . .," his father stammered.

Arieh asked: "Then I have a sister?"

But then the old man screamed at him as if the brother were responsible for the murder of his first-born: "No, don't you understand? She's dead! Dead!" They stood across from one another. "What do you know about it?" Jakov said.

Arieh answered like an echo: "What *do* I know about it? What all have you kept from me? Papa, is it my fault?" All of a sudden his father took hold of Arieh's shoulders and embraced him.

They continued on and his father told about the Cracow ghetto, about his escape and disappearance under the assumed name Fandler. He told about his detention and the camps. He talked for hours, yet only in sketchy terms, explaining his silence about the worst things: "Another time about that. . ." For the first time in a talk with his father, Arieh was seized by an excitement that he felt when he discovered the formula with which the unknown could be named.

After liberation, his father continued, he had come to this city where he had once studied and had become the businessman Scheinowiz. "I'm not Fandler nor was I ever Adam Kruzki."

"Adam who?"

"Adam Kruzki. He was a printer who was murdered in the ghetto. In the sixties, just before you were born, his widow confused me with him and I . . . simply let it happen. Just after that, still haunted by this mean trick, I changed my name to Fandler again. I broke all my ties to friends and married a young Jewish woman, your mother, Arieh. You came along a year later."

They came to the next bridge. His father said: "I am Jakov Scheinowiz, Arieh."

"And who am I, then," Arieh Fandler asked.

"That's your business. You must decide that for yourself. I'm Jakov Scheinowiz and tomorrow I'm going to write letters to the community, to the camps and the Red Cross. You should know what happened to your relatives and where they were murdered. Listen, Arieh, do you know I once learned in the *Cheder* the old axiom: "If you are you because you are you and I am I because I am I, then you are you and I am I. If, however, you are you because I am I and I am I because you are you, then you are not you and I am not I." And, although Arieh had been extraordinarily impressed by these words – or maybe just because of them – it suddenly occured to him how he could bring down Herwig Wernherr. He would insinuate himself into the confidence of his enemy under a false name, since Arieh *was* another person and would never find his true identity as long as Wernherr remained undefeated.

The next morning Jakov Scheinowiz drafted his letters while Arieh began the practical work of putting his plan into action. Although his father's words were on his mind, he still was unable to abandon his plan. He got the means to set it into motion at a pharmacy. He followed Herwig Wernherr from his home that evening, sat down beside him in a bar, nodded to him and greeted him. After that he ordered beers, flaunted them and clinked glasses; he discussed women, how to come on to them, and clapped Herwig on the shoulder three times. He called himself Volker when questioned, then told the anti-Semitic joke about the ash tray, about Volkswagen. Arieh broke into a laugh, hiding his horror and hatred. He treated to another round of drinks while Herwig Wernherr, a numb expression in his eyes, was already wobbly. It was easy for Arieh to slip the tablets into the glass. Afterwards he dragged the staggering Wernherr through the streets.

The frail Arieh, who was by nature somewhat clumsy in practical matters, already had the feeling that things were going too easily. When they came past Arieh's car, he took a bucket with brushes out of the trunk. He then stumbled on with Herwig. Stopping in front of a jewelry store, he put down the fully inebriated and partially dazed Herwig and painted an awkward "Bite the dust, Jew!" on the wall. Arieh knew that the business didn't belong to a Jew, but that didn't matter for his plan. On the contrary, Wernherr was to be caught red-handed committing a crime that sprang from sheer lunacy. Now they were at the heart of the matter: Arieh pushed Herwig Wernherr against the window pane, a pane that was harder than he had imagined. Ramming the loudly babbling Wernherr against the glass, he tried again, but the window merely cracked and the alarm went off. Panic stricken, Arieh grabbed him by the collar and ran with his head three times into the glass, until Wernherr plunged into the display with blood streaming down his face. Arieh was just able to stuff a few pieces of jewelry into the leather jacket and boots before he heard the police siren. He fled to his car and left the scene unnoticed.

The next day the newspapers reported a mysterious break-in and burglary attempt with a fatality. At that moment Arieh Arthur Fandler realized that everything had gone wrong and that he – who couldn't perform one successful Taikwondo kick, leap or throw – had killed Herwig Wernherr. Had it been an accident? No, he had taken deliberate action spurred on by his animosity. Would he be able to hope for understanding from the system of justice in this country? Would someone exempt him from the act of homicide? Didn't everything look like a planned act of revenge?

Arieh – Volker, that is – that man who had drunk and caroused with Herwig Wernherr in the bar, had been seen and described in detail. An artist's sketch had been produced. The security agents first of all looked for suspects among those of similar persuasion. Then they searched for clues among those at whom "Bite the dust, Jew!" had been aimed, among the members of the Jewish student body. Maybe somebody had noticed Herwig Wernherr together with a man named Volker. In the course of the investigation it occurred to one of the criminologists that it might have been a deadly act of revenge. He began on his own to look for the perpetrator in the ranks of those whom Herwig Wernherr had hated. The official also held numerous prejudices against them.

While his father's words bothered Arieh – but if I'm Arieh because Scheinowiz is Jakob, then I'm not Fandler nor can I be Scheinowiz – the investigation, proceeding by successive eliminations from a list – when Barazon is the next suspect because Axelrod is not guilty – had drawn close to his name. Precisely because his name was Fandler.

The meeting with Dani Morgenthau in the streetcar was a coincidence and their conversation just a way to pass time. Dani reported: "The police are interrogating every one of us. They even have an artist's sketch." Mentioning "ANR" and "NDP" in passing, he continued: "And the jeweler isn't even Jewish." Moreover, "somehow my sympathy with that Nazi has its limits. The commissioner seems to believe I'm guilty, as if I had pushed the guy through the window. It's as if I – rather we – were in a way taking revenge for his hatred and just maybe the policeman is right. . . " Dani asked: "Are you sick? You're so pale, Arieh!"

It was all resonating in him: the suspicion of murder, the investigation of his fellow students, Dani's self accusations which it seemed could only be aimed at him, his father's words. If I'm the perpetrator because I'm not myself and the perpetrator is a dead man because I *am* myself, then I'm the murderer as well as the victim. And, if not I, then who and if not now, when?

Something had to happen. He had gotten carried away and another one of his plans had gone wrong. With his thumb nail on his ring finger, the thought of escape began to take shape. He had never traveled in Israel nor had he gone around with his hat out for contributions toward reforestation nor had he been able to get enthusiastic about the country's language, songs, or dances, but it seemed to offer his only chance for rescue. He packed on the same day, plundered his savings, and booked his trip for the next morning.

A feeling of elation in the airplane. Liberated, he would first head for a kibbutz and then study mathematics. If all the others were somewhere else, he could finally be alone with himself. He would go his own way, hunting and tracking no one, avoiding no one. For the first time in weeks he felt whole again.

That day Jakov Scheinowiz found two letters in his mail box. The first one was from his son who wrote that he had emigrated to Israel in order to be able to answer all those questions his father had imposed on him – far from the diaspora, his own alienation and his parents.

It was only hours later that the old man, the corners of his mouth drawn, depressed by coughing fits and Arieh's revelation, was able to read the second letter. It was the answer of the Jewish community to his inquiry. Skimming the salutation and the first paragraph, Jakov Scheinowiz read: 'We are able to supply you with information regarding one of your relatives, but at somewhat of a loss about how to tell you. Your mother Lea Scheinowiz survived the war. She came to this city in the sixties and was in our community. Esteemed Mr. Fandler, how were we supposed to have known about you? How could your mother have found you? You were living here but under another name and not as a member of our community. Your mother lived for a long time in the same city as you and died here five years ago." The letter closed with words of regret and sympathy.

Jakov Scheinowiz's whole body trembled. He left the apartment without words or his keys and wandered for hours through the streets, his eyes glazed and his breathing heavy. He found his way to the café that had once been his favorite spot, but which he hadn't entered for twenty years. Coughing, he began to stumble between the tables, repeating to each of the strangers: "My name is Adam Kruzki," and then, more to himself: "The printing shop. I shouldn't have sold it." When the waiter spoke to him, he collapsed.

The plane landed and when Arieh looked out the window he saw to his amazement that palm trees actually did grow in this country. Then he was hit by the heat, the smells and people shouting as if they were making up for centuries of silence; the static of voices from the radios carried by men in uniform, their machine guns, the honking taxis and the two men fighting.

In the kibbutz Arieh had taken the name Scheinowiz, had settled down and met Navah. For the time being he decided to stay in the country and take out citizenship. He couldn't escape the military draft and had to undergo psychometric and medical examinations. In an interview he made known his interests in mathematical problems, breaking codes, and solving for unknowns. The talents of the new immigrant pointed him toward the intelligence branch. When Arieh made known his preferences to the examiner who was supposed to be determining his aptitudes, it left behind the impression that he was applying for a job in espionage even though he had not talked about it directly. This aroused mistrust in an organization whose profession is suspicion.

After several days of tests an old man suddenly appeared. His hair was graying, his clothes gray, very proper and smartly pressed and the collar of his shirt was turned out over his sport coat. He approached Arieh Scheinowiz as if by mistake, smiled through an icy gaze and asked Arieh in German: "Excuse me, but do I have the pleasure of speaking with Arieh Fandler. . ."

"How do you know that?"

"I . . . figured it out," he said and smiled, but the coldness in his eyes remained unmistakable.

His pronunciation had a North German strain which fades over the years. His words sounded preserved as if they came from another time. "We have made inquiries, Arieh," the man explained. He immediately began to interrogate him about the students of the diaspora organization, about his activities and then abruptly about Wernherr's gang. There were still some open questions, the man believed, and laid down the artist's sketch in front of Arieh that had been made according to the details supplied by the bartender. Denial seemed pointless. Arieh asked: "Who are you?"

"Call me Teddy." Arieh saw no way out. He told him what he had done and about his strange abilities: how he had tracked Wernherr down, pursued and attempted to eliminate him, and finally killed him.

Checking Arieh's statements took weeks. He was also forced to give experimental evidence of his rare ability to ferret out guilty parties. Police files were carted in. After several cases had been presented to him, Arieh came down with a fever, began to limp and developed a speech impediment. But he laid all of these changes aside when, with his help, one criminal after the other had been exposed. One day the old man asked him to come into his room and said: "We have a suggestion for you. You do have something special, a unique kind of intuition, a hunting instinct. . ."

"I didn't come here because of that," Arieh insisted. "Quite the contrary. My intuition is a kind of allergy, a symptom, a hypersensitivity for which I'd like to find a cure here. I want to serve my time in the military and then study mathematics. I didn't intend and don't intend to search for anyone here – only myself."

The old man burst out laughing. "This is not a health resort. This state wants you precisely because of your allergy, Arieh. It wants your hypersensitivity. You're a bloodhound. You need to love your symptom like yourself. You, Arieh, can find the guilty person. I know what I'm talking about. People like you I can pick out of the crowd, because I'm the one who finds such special talent, who discovers such rare gifts – just like the one in you. I can make something of you, Arieh. Be happy about your good luck. You'll earn a lot of money because you'll be highly valued. Enjoy yourself," and the old man's eyes again turned to ice.

When Arieh continued to hesitate, avoiding the offer of the secret service, Teddy said in a quiet singsong voice: "Just listen well, Arieh. Every time you want to visit your mother, you'll have to be afraid that the affair with Herwig Wernherr will some day come up again and that you could be arrested or run into trouble. Or? I don't intend to blackmail you, Arieh. We won't betray you or extradite you, but . . . you scratch our back and we'll scratch yours . . . It's your choice."

So it happened that Arieh Arthur Fandler – or was it Arieh Scheinowiz? – became an Israeli secret agent. Only years later would he ask himself the question why his life took this turn at the time. How was that night different from all the other nights?

Yilmaz

In the arcade at one thirty in the morning Franzi Kranz received a wallet that his Danuta had lifted from her last suitor in the bushes near the amusement park. At the same time, Herbert Zander, a man in early retirement since his accident three years ago, arrived in front of the gate to his house. Ten seconds later and still breathing heavily, he was rummaging in his pocket for his key when he noticed that his wallet was missing. His hand jerked toward his mouth as he thought of the Polish woman and wanted to go back, but remained fixed to the spot. He was still undecided when – ten more seconds had passed – four shots rang out from the Hayat Restaurant that was no more than one hundred meters away. The reverberation of the shots cut through him like a knife. The first bullet pierced the chest of Hüseyin Çerçi, his cards dropping from his hands. His eyes in convulsions, he at first stood up, but then fell to the floor where the others were cowering in fear. The second shot caught him in the left hand, the third in the head, while the fourth entered the tabletop. The four shots that flared up were like four bolts of lightning or X-rays that completely erased the thoughts of money in Zander's head. There was a scream, a bellowing in a foreign language and Hüseyin Çerçi said to his nephew in the Hayat : "Korku."

The boy answered in German: "No, don't worry, I'm with you. Hüseyin! Do you hear me?" But the only reply was "Korku," the rest of the answer lost in fear and drowned in a torrent of blood that poured from the dying man's mouth. Someone called out for an ambulance while several of the windows in neighboring houses were cautiously being opened. Weapon in hand, the culprit in front of the Hayat's windows began to flee in the direction of Zander who squeezed his body into the shadows of the entry hall and held his breath.

The jury had been called for eight o'clock in the morning. He didn't know the nature of the crime that had been committed, but had merely been given the time of the hearing.

He hadn't gotten up at six thirty since he finished school and because he had arrived early at the court house, he decided to drink a cup of coffee in the canteen. He didn't want to attract attention for his obsessive punctuality. He didn't want to stand out in any way under any circumstances. So, as the clock struck eight, he entered the room last. Since everyone else had already assembled and they all were waiting for him there, he came into the crossfire of their glares all the more despite his precautions, maybe even because of them. It was here that the the discussion before the trial was to be held.

The foreman administered an oath to the jury. First, however, he inquired whether anyone belonged to a religious denomination – the Jewish faith, for example – that required another wording. As he said this, his gaze lit upon the tall, gangling student Morgenthau who was the last to arrive. Morgenthau was silent as he massaged his upper arm where an irritation had flared up, a swollen, scaly rash that he treated with salves of all kinds and sometimes wrapped in a bandage. Judge Heinrich Waller didn't want to make any mistakes. He especially wanted to appear sensitive toward Morgenthau, even gave him a wink, because the case itself seemed taxing enough. "One of those Turkish affairs," he huffed, his corpulence hidden beneath his robes. He rolled his eyes and made a plea for agreement with a nod of his head. "The murder in the Hayat Restaurant – Like I said, one of those Turkish affairs." He hastened to condemn any kind of prejudices. He had nothing against Turks, but the relationships and customs in Middle Eastern families – blood reprisals, feuds between clans, a husband's rights over his wife – these would remain a puzzle for a European.

Later, when the judge had turned to his colleagues, Morgenthau spoke to the foreman in a whisper about the oath and its wording. He avoided the foreman's eyes, looked obliquely to the corner of the room and rubbed the skin of his upper arm as if he were shivering. Dani Morgenthau didn't want to deny his faith, but even more than he believed in God, he believed that religion was the concern of the individual. The citizen Morgenthau wanted to be a Jew and follow the dictates of tradition separate from the state and its laws. It wasn't as if he considered his background merely a religious denomination. He saw it rather as an historical community, even a people that was not bound together by any allegiance, but which had been unified by persecution. Dani Morgenthau's parents came from Eastern Europe. His father had been instructed in the *Cheder* as a three-year-old and almost everyone in the family had been murdered. Gitta and Mosche Morgenthau had been born and raised as Jews, made to wear the yellow star, herded together, penned in, and starved. But God, his mother said, needn't concern her, since he had, after all, not looked after her. The Morgenthaus celebrated all the annual festivals and did not fail to observe the days of commemoration that had been established after the War and the founding of the state of Israel. But they had never accompanied Dani to the synagogue on the Sabbath and only entered the Temple on the High Holidays. Since he had moved out he had given up pork which he had still eaten at home. Dani Morgenthau had begun to adapt his life to those customs which no one else in his family still followed. It was the practices observed by those ancestors who had been killed. His mother remarked: "Exactly like Uncle Marek."

Since the time he was born Dani had appeared to them as the reincarnation of various relatives, as a recurrence in multiple forms, as compensation for those who had been destroyed and murdered. They secretly felt that Dani's existence repudiated all of the plans for extermination, every sentence about the inferiority of Jews and their lives, the mutilations, the sterilizations, the murders, the eradication – everything. It was not only Mr. and Mrs. Morgenthau who lived on in him, but all the family ancestors, no matter whether they had been shot, beaten to death, gassed, or had been ravaged to death by hunger. Dani Morgenthau was to be the resurrection of the Jews, their beliefs, their way of thinking and their dignity.

Judge Waller knew nothing about all of this. He merely wanted to demonstrate that the sum total of official tolerance as well as his personal devotion were appropriate to all denominations, especially that of Morgenthau. The brotherly love which he today employed in his adjudication of a Turkish affair was to serve as proof for everyone involved of his fairness. He undertook the swearing in of the student using the full bass tone of his vocal organs since he held that religion was the most public profession of belief in the fundamentals of the community. As a little extra, the judge closed with a Jewish joke of which he was especially fond. He called it a "Jew joke," which it truly became in Waller's recital. In Yiddish syncopated rhythms, he smirked, screwed his head tighter to his shoulders, wrung and rubbed his hands, and soaped up to a lather until everyone, except Dani Morgenthau, laughed.

The High Courtroom: Heinrich Waller sat behind a cross which had been screwed to the table since an incident a few years ago when a defendant had used the iron object to attack the judge. The prosecutor had tightened his robe securely while the defense attorney wore his casually thrown over his shoulders. Visible from underneath were his suit, his necktie with gold tie pin and the yellow handkerchief in his breast-pocket.

After the reading of the charges, the defense attorney spoke and declared his client innocent of all charges. He added, however, that the court should impartially consider the characteristics of the culture under whose influence the crime was committed. It should understand the customs to which the suspect was subject.

A man stepped up, gave his name and personal information when questioned. He said: "Yilmaz Akan." The judge interrupted and inquired whether an interpreter would be necessary. The accused said no. He spoke perfect German. Dani Morgenthau figured his age to be twenty four. He searched the face of the Turk. "Waiter and musician."

His eyes to the ground, Yilmaz Akan denied the charges. The accused mumbled that he had wanted to kill his boss Hüseyin Çerçi but had not committed the murder. Judge Waller wanted to know why he had admitted his guilt to the police and whether he had been beaten. Akan answered: "For me it was a matter of honor to confess. After visits by my friends, relatives, and my wife I took responsibility for the crime. Everybody, not only the police, thought it was me. No one believed me. Everyone had waited for it to happen and was proud of me when I admitted it – everyone, even the police." Suddenly Dani Morgenthau knew where he had seen Yilmaz before.

The foreman nodded: "Honor, of course." And he smiled at the jury members to remind them of the cultural group in which the crime had been committed. With a furtive note in his voice, he continued: "Why then are you recanting your confession now? Is honor a seasonal phenomenon for you?" Had his attorney not brought him round to a denial in order to escape punishment?

Suddenly Akan was no longer capable of a complete sentence. He stammered: it wasn't the attorney, but he . . . over the months . . . the fear of a conviction . . . even more the loneliness, the detention before his trial had affected him. He had thought it over . . . but at this point Akan stopped. Dani Morgenthau, the prickly rash on his skin inflamed, could scarcely believe what had become of the Yilmaz he had known. He had attracted Dani's attention a few years ago when Gülgün, a fellow student, had taken him along

– to his astonishment – to a concert by Akan's group.

The judge asked how he would explain the gunpowder on his hands which had been discovered by chemical examination after his arrest. Akan maintained that he had practiced shooting that morning. Exactly, the foreman broke in, he was planning to shoot Çerçi. Absolutely not, the accused insisted. The neighborhood and all the relatives were expecting him to take revenge because Çerçi had mocked and insulted him. He had boasted of dishonoring his wife. A colleague, another waiter, had gotten hold of the weapon for him.

There had never been a discussion about killing Hüseyin in his restaurant or even in this city. "It was supposed to happen in Turkey. The family was pressuring me. A murder here? Never! Some thought I should have raped his wife in Anatolia and confronted him during one of his business trips. At home it would be a fight between two men. I took the weapon and practiced aiming, but believe me, I didn't want to do anything against him here. Everybody advised me against that. It was clear from the beginning: You can get away with killing him in Anatolia. They'll only initiate a half-hearted search there and let you escape across the border."

"You didn't get the revolver in order to shoot Çerçi?"

"No," replied Akan and the jury members murmured. The defense attorney whispered something to the prosecutor who burst out laughing. Akan continued: "I just had to have it with me. I was afraid of Hüseyin." But the foreman, looking at the jury, his words drenched with scorn: "Why did you throw the weapon away after you heard about the crime? If we had it we could determine if it was the murder weapon. Why did you want to get rid of the pistol?" As Yilmaz spoke, he stressed every syllable as if he were hinting at a secret: "It was already old, very old."

The judges and attorneys exchanged amused glances while the jury members smiled. The prosecutor brought his hands together over his head, the defense attorney shrugged his shoulders and a journalist chortled as he let his pencil glide across his notepad. Even Akan's relatives bowed their heads and his father, Osman

Akan – a small, motionless, heavyset man with a mustache – let his
Tespih or prayer beads slip through his fingers.

Yilmaz Akan followed the circuit of laughter with his eyes,
looked around in confusion and couldn't understand why his words
had given rise to such amusement. Akan's puzzlement didn't
escape Dani Morgenthau. He even noticed the uncertainty in the
face of Osman Sarica, the second suspect, who was accused of
procuring the murder weapon. Upon hearing Akan's statement that
the weapon was old, very old, Sarica nodded thoughtfully and
slowly.

Only Dani Morgenthau was able to understand the sense of
Akan's statement as well as its comic effect. Yilmaz didn't dare
tell the real reason he had thrown the weapon away. The pistol, as
the saying goes, had become "hot," since it could have been used
to commit other crimes. The registration number had been effaced
long ago. The mere possession of this killing instrument could
have been dangerous for him, the suspect, since it could have
connected him to other crimes. Yilmaz simply said: "The weapon
was old, very old."

Dani Morgenthau was able to make out such secondary
intonations because he himself was made up of these dissonant
combinations. He lived in the dual tonality of various harmonies.
He knew the melodies which his parents still carried around in
their heads as well as the folk songs of this alpine country.
Morgenthau knew that Yilmaz too had lived in the reverberations
of foreign melodies. When he used to be questioned about blood
reprisals and feuds between clans, about the customs in the
mountain villages, he would emphasize with a smile that these
practices were out-dated.

Gülgün, on the other hand, had refused to answer: "Why are
you asking me that? Am I responsible for it? Why don't you read
Through the Wilderness of Kurdistan." And a whirring shudder
fluttered across Dani's arms. She came from Istanbul where she
had attended the German school. After graduating she had left the
city to study economics abroad, never to return to Turkey again.
Dani had seen her at a party where he had scarcely dared to glance

in her direction, yet had not been able to take his eyes off of her. He had tried to get close to her through the line of other men who nudged each other when she entered. The few words he risked he had chosen with care, but nevertheless blushed with each one. He believed he had been seen through as well as ignored. At night he had written her a love letter and the following morning had folded it into a boat and thrown it into the river.

Later at the library he spoke to her and asked whether she would like to come along to a concert of an acquaintance of his, Yilmaz. He had just stared at her, the dark skin, the beauty spot on her right cheek. Her boyfriend was Siegwald Hammberger. He was studying law.

Dani soon understood that Gülgün would never have met nor paid any attention to Yilmaz in Istanbul. She had fled from Turkey without being able to escape it. Now she was reminded of everything she had set out to forget, everything that had been alien to her in her country. Raised as a European on the Bosporus, she had tried to become a citizen of the world. She wanted to be cosmopolitan but to others she was merely stylish.

At the university and at friends' parties she was one among many, but at Greißler's she – who spoke the language fluently – was addressed in overly familiar terms and broken German: Where come you?

The laws and conditions which had made her enrollment at the university easier were changed and tightened up over time. She would not, however, have been forced to find her way into communities of local foreigners, into guest-worker districts. Yet, both here and in her native country, she resisted the arrangements of the community. She really had a choice between two social circles. It was not so much that she had been defeated by the processes of exclusion and separation, but rather by her own revulsion at everything that appeared closed and settled.

Although he became a close friend of Gülgün's, Dani didn't dare send her his letters, but instead sent them down the river as paper boats. Dani was the first to learn about her cheating on Siegwald Hammberger, about the night she had spent with Yilmaz.

He dreamed about having the last laugh and gloated when she left Siegwald. The budding lawyer was so badly hurt that he broke off his studies and, to the disapointment of his father – a government official – he ended up a detective.

A longing had taken hold of Gülgün over time, a desire for something from which she had fled in vain. Yilmaz introduced her into that exile which existed in the middle of the city: businesses with Turkish signs, Middle Eastern music playing behind apartment doors, children spread out in front of foreign-produced broadcasts of video films, series and instructional programs. The television set was the house altar.

When Dani had seen her the last time five years before the murder trial, she had already been married to Yilmaz. At that time she was living with his relatives, his parents, brothers, sisters, nephews and nieces. Her father had disowned her. Dani paid her a visit while Yilmaz was at work. As soon as he walked into the apartment a cousin of her husband pulled a scarf over her head, said a few words in Turkish and left the room with her small son. Gülgün – on the left side of her face a smile, on the right, the beauty spot – interrogated him about their mutual friends, smiled at his astonishment and uncertainty in this atmosphere. She was friendlier than ever. He promised to come again soon, but didn't return again, even though she, by chance, lived just a few blocks away.

Dani Morgenthau thought he knew what had happened. Gülgün's manner and clothing must have been a provocation for the victim Hüseyin Çerçi, and the waiter Yilmaz had aroused Çerçi's envy. As if he had been there, Dani believed he could visualize how the boss had stared at his employee's wife when she came into the men's presence in the bar, how Çerçi, the proprietor and small businessman, had followed her home, threatened in the stairwell that he would wake up the neighbors if she didn't let him into her apartment. Moreover, he threatened to lie to Yilmaz about her behavior and fire him. Later, he had likely slandered Gülgün in front of Yilmaz and the others and boasted while she was in the bar. The other men must have sat in a cloud of silence and listened to him. Yilmaz was among them. A trench ran through the bar that evening. A few stood by Hüseyin, while one man implored the drunken Çerçi to stop all the loose talk. Others rallied around the waiter, assuring him their support by the urgent looks in their eyes. Dani saw that Yilmaz had been driven to conflicting emotions. He could picture how the relatives had asked Yilmaz when he would finally carry out the revenge. He imagined how acquaintances had begun to talk behind Gülgün's back and to turn away from Akan's family. While Judge Waller asked his questions, Dani Morgenthau was reflecting on how Yilmaz had been coerced into revenge by family members, yet had neither been able to withstand nor fulfill their demands.

In the courtroom the jury member Dani Morgenthau asked to speak. He then asked Akan if his wife had told him that the victim had molested her. Yilmaz replied: "She told me that he came into our apartment. He threatened her and tried . . . , but then my cousin knocked on the door. She was babysitting for us. . . " What had Yilmaz done when she told him that? "Nothing. We didn't want to cause a stir. We didn't want a feud or revenge. My wife Gülgün just avoided him from then on."

With a confused look in his eyes, the judge's head swung back and forth between Akan and Morgenthau. Morgenthau sat with his arms folded, each hand resting on the other arm.

It was natural, Dani Morgenthau thought, that Yilmaz had confessed. In this way the family's honor had been saved and Akan's father must have said to his son while he was in detention awaiting trial something like: "You don't need to tell us anything. You don't need to lie. We knew that we could count on you, my son."

The other defendant admitted that he procured the weapon, but asked for leniency since he had had no idea of the quarrel with Çerçi or of any homicidal intent. The judge asked: "Why do you think then that Akan needed the pistol?"

Osman Sarica replied: "For security. In his apartment."

The foreman looked at the jury members: "Oh, for home use then?"

After the crime Gülgün had been sent to Turkey, to her husband's relatives in Anatolia. It had been decided by her, Yilmaz, his brothers and his father that she and her child should wait there in the village for her husband. A female police officer who had interviewed Gülgün after the murder was called to the witness stand in her place. The officer, her long hair bleached peroxide blond, entered court in civilian clothes – a short miniskirt and green silk stockings. The defense attorney sat up, looked her up and down. According to the witness, the wife of the accused had testified that she had been pestered by Hüseyin Çerçi and had told her husband about it. There had been no difficulties in the talks between her and Gülgün Akan. "Discrepancies were completely absent in her testimony," the policewoman declared. Dani Morgenthau secretly felt a deep satisfaction in the absurdity and inconsistency of the sentence: "Discrepancies were completely absent in her testimony." The woman repeated these words several times without being corrected by the judges, and Dani was happy it was not Yilmaz who made the mistake but a native-born official. The witness said that Mrs. Akan had been clearly aware of what she was saying and that she had spoken High German. No, the officer responded to a question, the wife of the defendant most certainly knew nothing about her husband's murderous scheme. Such wives never knew anything about their husbands' affairs. With his eyes fixed on the members of the jury, the foreman added that the men defended the honor of Turkish women.

A detective took the stand and gave an account of Akan's hearing. Everything had gone smoothly. The accused hadn't caused any problems and, after the gunpowder had been discovered on his hand, he had soon confessed. Actually, the detective continued, he had admitted the murder right after his father, brothers, and wife had visited him in jail while he waited for the analysis of the tests.

Dani Morgenthau asked to speak again. He wanted to know whether other persons had also been tested for traces of gunpowder. No, the official replied, there had been no further suspects.

Dani spent the afternoon after the trial in a café. The next day he was to help decide whether the accused should be sentenced. As far as he understood it, all the evidence spoke against Yilmaz Akan. In the conference room after adjournment, the judge had asked the jury members who else could have committed the murder? "It must have been someone."

His father Mosche Morgenthau had tried to persuade Dani to refuse jury duty. "Why do you need to get mixed up in such problems. You think you could stand in judgment over someone? If I know you, you'll claim responsibility for the murder in order to free him? You were already feeling guilty yesterday when I asked you how late it was?"

Dani had, in fact, replied to the question about the time: "It's quarter to five. I know, we were supposed to meet at four thirty. It's my fault." Dani's problem wasn't, however, hyperaccuracy or an obsequious politeness. Dani Morgenthau was constantly asking to be pardoned, but very few people took notice. In a certain way he thought he had to justify his whole existence.

His parents never said that they had survived just for him, yet he heard their sighs and saw in his father's eyes that his son could be the excuse for their existence if the dead should one day ask why they both had not been killed along with the others. At night – Dani Morgenthau knew it to be so – the dead appeared in his parents' dreams and interrogated them. He absorbed all of their feelings of guilt. Other children might possibly have answered by rebelling and denying their origins. Some would have defiantly thrown off any self-reproach, become quick-witted, taken courses in hand-to-hand combat and actively taken out their resentment or emigrated to Israel. Dani hid all thoughts about revolt and liberation. Every rebellion that existed in him roused his conscience and seemed to be a threat of extermination against the survivors, against the victims, against his parents. His failure made him into a perpetrator, into an accomplice of all individuals who still today are filled with hatred. His flaws appeared to confirm all prejudice and all contempt.

He became more and more caught up in these feelings as his father grew older and his mother sicker. Who knows, if he had lived in another country, he might have escaped this short-circuit, but he lived in this country. No one here had called back those who had been driven away. No political party had fought for compensation for those who had been robbed. No government had put up a fight to convict the murderers. He reflected the past simply by his mere presence.

He had developed this alarming phenomenon over the course of the years, an inexplicable sickness about which no doctor had ever yet read a single word. If he heard about a criminal, he then felt the desire to put himself in the perpetrator's place and to give himself up to the police. Even as a child he had confessed to pranks that other children had committed. Just the threat of punishment exhilarated Dani and filled him with a longing charged with mystery. It was just because of these attacks that his father advised him against jury duty. "In the end you'll say that you're guilty?"

But Dani wanted to be a jury member in order to prove the opposite: that is, that he could render a judgment just like any other citizen. He would conquer his sickness, his leprosy. He surmised that someone else was the murderer, yet everything indicated that Yilmaz Akan had shot Hüseyin Çerçi.

Throughout the morning Dani had not found any arguments for Akan nor had he felt the pressing urge to succumb to an attack of self-accusation. Yet it was precisely this sense of composure that troubled him. Why wasn't anything driving him to put himself in Yilmaz's place? There were only two possible answers. Either he had finally overcome his illness or Yilmaz was unable to set off any reaction in him because he was not the perpetrator. Dani could think of no other possibilities.

If Akan was the murderer, then Dani had to be cured.

Otherwise, the rash on Dani's arms would have flared up during the trial when Akan was being examined. The irritant would not have let up until he had cried out: "I'm guilty. It was me. I did it." As soon as a guilty party denied his crime in Dani Morgenthau's presence, the itching began to spread out over Dani's body and he could relieve it only with his confession. The pustules, cracks and breaks subsided only when he confessed, when he uttered the right words whether they were a curse or self accusation. The important thing was that he confessed to something that someone else had done.

All of a sudden, however, Dani Morgenthau thought of Gülgün, her laugh, her mockery, her eyes. He recalled the spot on her cheek and drafted a letter of admission. Dani scribbled on the paper: "Akan is innocent. It was me. I did it." He put the letter in his pocket because he wanted to send it the next day to Gülgün, the judge or the police.

The next morning as he was going over the bridge on his way to court, however, he took the sheet out of his coat, folded it into a small boat and let it sail down the river. He watched it as it made its way on the waves in the direction of the Black Sea.

The defense lawyer who, to all appearances, had scarcely followed the court proceedings, seemed to come alive only during his summation. It was as if he wanted to demonstrate that he could win such a case without being fully involved. "Do we know what happened that night? Did anyone see the murder? Do we have knowledge of the murder weapon? No! It has not been proven that my client committed the crime. If there is any doubt, ladies and gentlemen, then you are obliged to vote not guilty." The lawyer maintained that Yilmaz Akan's guilt might be implied on the basis of the evidence and motive and – a smile curling around his lips – maybe he was denying his guilt merely to save his family from retribution by the victim's relatives. In the case that the jury members should come to the conclusion that the Turk had committed the crime – which to Dani's amazement, the lawyer said was at least suggested by the evidence – then they should not opt for murder: "You have to empathize with the customs of these people." The crime was manslaughter committed from cultural motivations, not a cold-blooded murder since this kind of revenge was customary in Akan's country. Actually, it was demanded of the person who had been dishonored.

Dani and the seven others agreed unanimously on a verdict of murder.

On that night around one thirty-one the pimp Franzi Kranz threw Herbert Zander's empty wallet in front of the arcade while Zander stood in the shadows of the entrance to his house, not one hundred meters away from the Hayat. Out of breath, he pressed his body into the darkness as the murderer, weapon in hand, fled the scene of the crime along the sidewalk, coming to a sudden stop in front of Zander. Standing in the light of the street lamps, head turned away, the culprit looked back at the bar. The light lit up the face in its reflection, brightening the dark complexion and casting a neon glow on the black head scarf. And so it was that Zander saw the young woman, the beauty spot on her right cheek and so it was that she stuck in his mind when she had hurried on past him. Zander was a witness.

Hastily he fished for his key, opened the door, and hobbled upstairs to his spouse who was already asleep. He intended to remain anonymous, not to offer testimony, and not even to report his stolen wallet the next day. Zander, in early retirement since his accident three years ago, didn't want to appear racist, but in the final analysis it wouldn't do that something which had happened in the Hayat ought to concern him. In the final analysis this was a Turkish affair.

Jakob

A cup near the coffeepot, marble-topped tables, customers talking, the waiter in black crossing the room. And the person representing me, sitting in the café. A clock over the entrance, its hands moving in circles. Inaudible conversations of the other people. Men in the grayish tones of their suits, women in skirts, underneath hats and behind eyeglasses.

A gong sounds over the loudspeaker and a voice announces: "Telephone for Mr. Peter Stamm." An individual stands up, goes to the waiter who motions toward the telephone booth. A few moments later the man comes out, presses a stack of money into the waiter's hand and leaves the place.

Soon, that person who's supposed to be me, hears another announcement which requests another customer to come to the phone. Once more someone else hurries off and is directed to a booth. He enters into it and afterward gives the waiter a bundle of bills and runs to the exit.

This is repeated at intervals and, despite the repetition – if not just because of it – remains a puzzle to me, the stranger, that I can't solve. The staff is not serving any food. The ringing phone interrupts the waiting that permeates everything, everything in me, until the signal and the person's name emanate from the amplifiers.

Once the announcement is made: "Doctor Kreuzer, Doctor Hans Kreuzer, please come to the telephone." At that point two men stand up, exchange glances, hesitate, and the one who stood up last, takes his seat again. The other one, however, follows the pattern: into the booth, money to the waiter and then through the exit.

The person who is supposed to be me has decided to answer first at the next gong. He will respond with such certainty to the call as if it could be no one else. Ringing, the stroke of the bell, and the voice says: "Would Mr. Andres Scheine please come to the phone." The person supposed to be me has already gotten up. No other name is called out, no one moves even a finger nor raises a head. I go to the waiter. He points to a booth.

I pick up the phone and the voice says: "Your name is Andres Scheine. You'll find your résumé and the documents in the slit behind the coin device. You owe the waiter eight thousand five hundred. Leave this place immediately." I hang up, pull out the papers from behind the apparatus, stumble out of the booth, and take out my wallet in front of the waiter. I notice that the amount is all the money I have. I hand over the bills to him and see – as I pass by – that I'm being observed by a man in the café at the exit. On the street, as my lungs rattle for air, I want to turn around and demand the small fortune back, but I don't dare go inside the coffee house again. The man in my role screams: "I paid too much" and wakes up. Jakob Scheinowiz woke up with the words on his lips: "I'm Jakob Scheinowiz. Do you hear me? Doctor Jakob Scheinowiz!"

He saw himself in a hospital room. The bed to his right was empty, but made up and used, while the bed to the left seemed to be unoccupied. Across from him near the door, a patient was staring at the ceiling, his face frozen over with a grin. The nurse, a Filipina, greeted Scheinowiz. When he tried to answer, he swallowed his phlegm and coughed to clear his throat.

How had he gotten into the hospital? He tried to recollect what had happened, but only recalled that he had searched his memory for information at the request of the doctor even before he fell asleep. He was doing better, the nurse commented cheerfully. "What hospital am I in," he wanted to know. Delighted that he seemed responsive, she said the name and told him about his nervous breakdown and how he had been picked up, unconscious, a day ago.

When she went out of the room, he got up, took his wallet, walked quietly down the hall, stumbled down the stairs and called his wife from the telephone booth. She had scarcely heard his coughing when she said: "Jankel! Where in the world are you? What happened? I've notified the police. Do you want to kill me, Jankel?" He calmed her down and asked her to forgive him for not calling sooner. He explained that he had suffered a fainting spell, nothing serious, and that she should pick him up. All of a sudden his memory returned as he thought about Arieh and then about his mother.

As he leaned against the wall in the corner, patients and their families walked by and avoided looking at him. Tears trickled into his sleeves. He finished smoking one cigarette and lit up a second one.

But he didn't want to appear tear-stained in front of Ruth. His wife – he knew as much – would want to comfort him without understanding him. She would succumb to his pain. He immediately picked up the phone, dialed various business partners and hung up before the phone started ringing. This continued until he looked up the name of a friend whom he had not called on in twenty years. From time to time, the friend had written him but he had never written back.

When Fischer picked up the phone, Scheinowiz whispered: "Leon, it's me, Jankel." The other man hesitated and asked: "What's the matter with you? Where are you calling from?"

At first, Leon Fischer had contacted him by telephone and invited him to his daughters' weddings as well as his grand-children's *Brith Milah* and *Bar Mizvah*, but Jakob Scheinowiz had always declined – always very politely, of course. For some time now he had completely vanished from his friend's life. Fischer had lost sight of him when his letters failed to reach him and he could no longer find out Scheinowiz's address.

Scheinowiz shuffled into his room where the worried nurse scolded him. He fled underneath the blanket and pretended to sleep when he saw the doctor hurry in. Now he recalled the young doctor who stood in front of his bed as well as his admission.

The intern Walter Stoß looked at his patient, switched gears from what he had intended to say, and paused with his thoughts in neutral. His notes were in his left hand, his right hand in his coat pocket, his feet in tennis socks and wooden clogs. Dressed all in white, his hair like a copper helmet, an outsized body, a golden boy under neon light, his knees buckled and he laid his papers on the blanket and scrutinized the old man.

An announcement disrupted him: "Doctor Stoß to forty-four, please." A nurse stormed into the room and cried out: "Doctor, Doctor, heart failure in forty-four." He hurried away, his steps pounding like blows against a wooden wall or shed, sounding like the clattering of brake pads in train traffic. The person I'm supposed to be, hears screams, dogs barking, runs for his life, is unable to find any escape in the crowd, loses his breath and struggles for air. Then someone whispers: "Jankel," and Scheino-wiz woke up with a start from his dozing.

Ruth and Leon stood at his bedside. His wife, twenty-five years younger, was stroking his brow. She had a pageboy cut and, although her face had been creased by time, her skin was without wrinkles. She had a delicately taut figure and her youth was still evident in her silhouette. She was dressed in the latest fashion. She had brought along pajamas and fresh underwear for him as well as newspapers and a book by a Russian novelist. Scheinowiz sat up, embraced her with a kiss and calmed her down.

He had difficulties recognizing Leon Fischer again. His friend had shrunken into an old man. In his youth Fischer had resembled an athlete, a boxer with dangling arms and swaggering hips. Only later did his stomach and his face puff up. Now he had decreased in height, but not in girth and he seemed deflated like bagpipes which had lost their air. Fischer was holding three bags but put two of them down and limped up to the bed – over the years one of his knees had stiffened up. Then he began to empty the contents onto the bedside table, opening its drawer and checking to see if there was room there. He rocked his head back and forth doubtfully and mumbled: "Oh!" He had bought incredible amounts of food, enough for a holiday feast.

He began to stuff the drawers of the adjacent cabinet until Scheinowiz called him to order: "Leon, what *reboine shel oilem* are you doing here? Stop it. Do you think that I haven't eaten anything in the last twenty years? I'm sick, not hungry."

"Sick? What's the matter with you?" Ruth stammered.

But Leon replied with total composure: "Do you know if they have a refrigerator here? The milk and the cheese have to be kept cool and the ice cream has to go into the freezer. Do you want a melon? Or an apple? I'll wash it for you."

"It's nothing, Ruth. – Leon, stop buttering that roll! No, I don't want any grapes. – Just sit down Ruthy. – How are Rita and the kids, Leon? – By the way, my dear, I've got to tell you about Arieh before I forget . . ."

At that she interrupted him: "I know everything, Jakov. I found his letter. And the letter from the community concerning your mother."

With his eyes wide open, Leon Fischer looked at her for explanations. She continued: "Our son left us yesterday to go to a kibbutz in Israel."

"That's good," Fischer said with a smile and: "*Be esrat ha shem.*"

But she replied: "Good? He didn't tell us anything about it, didn't say good-bye, and just left a note behind. It's no wonder that Jakov can't cope with it. He wants to kill his own father."

"Don't talk such nonsense, Ruth! Arieh is grown up and can go wherever he wants. The letter is his good-bye. Besides that, he hasn't disappeared from the face of the earth. Sit down, Ruth, please, you're making me . . ." but his words trailed off into a coughing fit. "Just a chill. And smoking doesn't help it any," he assured Fischer who was watching him with concern.

Moving a clipboard on the bed so she could sit down, Ruth handed it to Scheinowiz and smoothed the blanket. He held on to the medical chart without looking at it until she sat down and he gave it back to her. She took the notes and, at first, didn't know what she should do with them. When she did glance at them, she grew numb, brought her hand to her mouth, let out a cry and showed them to Fischer. He bent over and studied the spot above Ruth's finger. In the meantime, however, Scheinowiz had noticed that something had horrified both of them and tore the papers out of her hand. Holding them firmly, he raced through their contents until his eyes came to rest on the same paragraph that had caught the attention of the other two.

"Bronchial carcinoma?" Scheinowiz whispered incredulously and turned pale as if he were under a neon light. He reached for his cigarettes and wanted to light up, but was trembling so much that he threw the pack away.

Fischer said: "You don't look sick at all. Don't panic. It might simply be a mistake, a mix-up," but his words were lost in his friend's coughing fit.

Scheinowiz had become silent while Ruth cried and Fischer

lamented: "Even if you're sick, Jakob, doesn't mean that you're going to die. You can't give up. You have to fight this."

"Absolutely, Leon. Certainly."

After a few minutes of anxious silence Scheinowiz said: "Calm down, Ruth, please don't bawl. I can't stand that. Maybe it can be cured. Besides, I'm old and have outlived all my relatives . . . You'll be taken care of, sweetheart."

But Fischer stamped his foot and tears flowed down his cheeks. "I haven't seen you for twenty years and now I find you again on this miserable little deathbed. I can't believe it. It's unfair."

"That's a huge exaggeration, Mr. Chairman." Scheinowiz tried to console him: "The bed is not miserable and I will most certainly be moved to a single room." But Fischer sobbed even louder and the patient screamed at him: "You even said yourself that there might be an error in the diagnosis, so control yourself Lew Fischer. Otherwise, lung cancer or not, I'm going to throw you out of the hospital with my own two hands." Ruth dried her eyes and Fisher blew his nose with a snort while Scheinowiz gave his attention to the medical chart and searched through the results for inconsistencies.

All of a sudden he put his hand to his forehead and exclaimed: "Ruth! Do you want to drive me crazy? This is not even my name – it's somebody else! Can't you read? It's somebody else's chart."

Shaky and in tears again, she bent with trembling lips and open mouth over her husband and the papers, read the first lines she had not noticed before and whooped with joy. Fischer moved closer, but before he had a chance to examine the report again, Scheinowiz snatched it away: "Don't rummage around in other people's documents, you gangsters!"

Ruth embraced and kissed him as her laugh came out a sob. She hugged Fischer as well who had taken her hand and who said: "Unbelievable! What a piece of luck! Let me see."

But Scheinowiz retorted: "We can't do that. That's enough. Don't gloat over other people's misfortune, Leon." And he added in a quieter tone: "Our survival was always a mix-up. Didn't you know that? I don't want to hear any more about it. – Ruth, take the things home that my insatiable friend Leon brought. We'll be able to live for weeks off them. My fainting spell paid off. Go home now. I'll come either tonight or tomorrow morning. I'd like some time with Leon. I call him after such a long time and he comes right away. That's my Leon."

"Well, am I supposed to wait another twenty years? A fainting spell is a one-time opportunity."

"I should hope! – Leon, my cigarettes," Scheinowiz asked when Ruth has left.

Fischer replied, however: "You've hardly survived lung cancer and you have to smoke again so soon?"

Scheinowiz threatened: "Leon, one nervous breakdown in a week is enough. The cigarettes or I'm going to fall into a twenty-year coma."

Fischer handed him the pack as well as a lighter, but asked: "Is it even allowed here?"

"Most certainly," Scheinowiz explained, "but only by prescription and along with group therapy for anonymous cancer patients." He slumped into the thick smoke: "How are you Leon?"

Fischer described his own family and success, but didn't forget to congratulate Scheinowiz on his wife, son and business.

"In the final analysis I'm a failure, Leon. Everything about me is an illusion." When his friend tried to contradict him, Jakob went on in Polish: "You've always overestimated me. You still see my two doctorates and admire the professor of German that I once was in Cracow and the man who worked for social services in the ghetto. Just look at what's left of me. – Do you know why you didn't hear from me for so long? – Let me finish, Leon! – Twenty years ago I changed my name and then I married Ruth: I was not Jakov Scheinowiz any longer, but Jakob Fandler. That's the reason you couldn't find me after I moved."

Fischer repeated: "Fandler . . . Wasn't that your assumed name when you went underground in the War?"

"Exactly. Do you understand, Leon? Scheinowiz doesn't exist anymore. I let him die. My whole survival was a mistake. I married a young Jew, but I broke off every connection to the community and denied the ties to my history. There mustn't be any mention of what used to be. I've never told my son about myself. And now, without me, he's searching for Scheinowiz and I'll never find him or see him again."

"It's not too late, Jankel. Go visit Arieh in Israel. Take him to Cracow and show him the camps," Fischer interjected.

Jakob Scheinowiz smiled: "It's finished, Leon. I've failed as a father for twenty years. That can't be made up. I tried to explain things to Arieh a few weeks ago. I told him where he comes from, who I am and who I was, but now he's gone. I promised to try to find out, to learn who was killed where and how, and I wrote letters and made inquiries. I got a letter from the community yesterday . . ."

Fischer nodded: "Yesterday? Oh now I . . . When I was given the confirmation of where my parents had been shot, I asked myself why I was crying and was ashamed of my tears in front of the archive's officials. Hadn't I known for decades that the Nazis had killed them?"

Jakob Scheinowiz buried his head in his hands. "But my mother was not killed. She survived, Leon. Do you understand? Survived. – And she lived here. Here! Lea Scheinowiz came to this city in the sixties, right after I had changed my name. Up to a few years ago she went to commemorative services in the synagogue here without being able to find me and I never looked for her. I had withdrawn from the community as well as from the Scheinowiz family. I missed her. It's finished, Leon. I would have been able to introduce Arieh to his grandmother. It's too late."

They remained silent. After a while, Fischer said: "Jankel, you thought she was dead. It's not your fault. Quit tormenting yourself. You're my model, you know. You've made it. Don't interrupt me, Jakov Scheinowiz. You're my proof that it's possible. What do you know about me? I'm in treatment. Depression . . . I haven't been able to work for years. When I go into a room full of people, I'm afraid I'm going to suffocate and my grandchildren laugh at a grandpa who is frightened of crowds in trains or of going to a movie; who always drags along large amounts of food as if he thought they could starve. You didn't purposely hide from your mother, didn't disavow your identity to any one. It's no crime to change your name. That's no sin."

"Isn't it?" Scheinowiz asked. "Have I survived because of it while others were murdered? – Do you think I didn't intentionally disavow my identity? You're wrong. – Was it at *Pessach* or *Rasch Haschanna*? At some point I got to know a woman at your house at a banquet. You and Rita tried to set me up. I really despised you for doing that. It was Tonja Kruzki who, with her daughter, left her husband before the War. Adam Kruzki, a printer, was supposedly killed. I didn't know him. Probably had never met him. That evening though, I, Jakob Scheinowiz, whose wife Hannah and daughter left him before the invasion, posed as Adam Kruzki to Tonja. Do you understand? I let her believe that I was Adam Kruzki. It hadn't been planned but just happened. She thought she had found her former husband again in me. Something about me must be reminiscent of him, and I didn't contradict her but led her on instead. I don't know why. All of a sudden I discovered, however, that any return was impossible, even if she had been Hannah or I had been Adam. We could never again come together. I left without revealing to her that I wasn't Adam Kruzki. A short time later I broke off contact with you, married Ruth and changed my name. – Wasn't that a sin? A crime? Tonja Kruzki must still think that Adam survived and scorned her. – I've been thinking about it for years and had the desire to call you. Could you tell her that I wasn't Adam?"

Fischer said: "That's been tormenting you for all these years? You needn't worry about it any longer. Tonja Kruzki asked about you that very evening. You couldn't fool her even for a day. I explained to her who you really are."

"Who I really am?" Scheinowiz echoed.

"She found out about it just after you had left. You don't owe her a thing if we disregard the fact that you behaved improperly."

Fischer basked his face in the neon light of the ceiling lamp before he asked: "Why did you lie to her, Jakob?" And then: "You see that you don't owe Tonja Kruzki a thing."

"That's not the whole story, Leon," Scheinowiz replied and started to cough when Fischer looked at him. "Something about me must have been reminiscent of Adam Kruzki. I remembered only in the weeks after that holiday: It was in the ghetto – one of the first operations; they tracked us down with dogs, harassed us with informers and rounded up those they found. – Why am I telling you that? You know . . . But then I too was discovered and chased onto the square and stood there in the crowd. Then an SS officer came up to me and said: 'You're the printer. We still need you.' He separated me out of the group. For the first time in my life – who knows why – I was taken for the printer Adam Kruzki. Something about me must have resembled Adam Kruzki. I was spared and saved in his place. Do you understand, Leon? My survival depended on a mix-up."

They were silent. Then Leon Fischer spoke: "Adam Kruzki. I knew him. You're right, something about you has always resembled him. Adam was a printer. Right before the Germans invaded, he sold his print shop in order to be able to finance his escape. They arrived shortly afterward and every way out was blocked." He sighed: "The print shop – he probably never should have sold it. Without his workshop he seemed lost already."

Before Fischer left, he promised his friend to come again soon and asked if Jakob needed something. When he was leaving he said: "Is it right, Jankel, when they say we're dead men on vacation? At times it seems to me, as if liberation was a dream, as if we were waking up again one morning in the barracks. – Don't worry about Arieh. I'll tell him about Jakob Scheinowiz. Don't be afraid, I'll help you. As far as your relatives are concerned, I'll ask Lebensart."

"But he chases Nazis, not the dead victims."

"He knows his way around. Lebensart will know how to go from here for sure."

After Fischer had gone, Jakob Scheinowiz tried to go to sleep, but he was lying there awake, rolling around, and incapable of closing his eyes when Doctor Walter Stoß came through the door. The doctor said: "Mr. Kruzki, I have to talk to you."

"First of all, Doctor, " Scheinowiz interrupted him, "you should know that my name is not Adam Kruzki. I am Jakob Scheinowiz."

"Scheinowiz?"

"Yes, but my insurance is under the name Jakob Fandler."

"Fandler?"

"Call me Scheinowiz. Another thing," Scheinowiz added as he held out the papers to him, "you should never leave the chart lying near the patient. That's not right."

The younger man stood there embarrassed, slightly stooped, his voice cracking and asked: "Have you already read it?"

"I've been able to read since I was three."

There was a silence and then the physician said: "Why are you here under a false name?"

"Please Doctor," Scheinowiz retorted, "Did I have a nervous breakdown or you? Are you meshuga or am I?" and then: "How much time do I have?"

"Probably two months. Maybe three. But I can't say with certainty. You have to fight for your life yourself," the doctor whispered. He had lost his professional protection but was trying to win back his authority. "Those cigarettes will certainly not help you. Smoking, by the way, is not permitted in patients' rooms."

The discussion then touched on the further course of treatment, the effects of the medication, the sequence of the illness, but brushed aside one question, avoiding the ultimate issue of death. "You don't need to tell my wife anything about this, Doctor," Scheinowiz recommended.

But he replied: "But at some point we'll have to confess it to her, Mr. . . . . Scheinowiz."

"Confess?"

"It can't be kept a secret."

"What?"

"Your condition. The results of the examination."

He would now let him rest, he said, so that Scheinowiz could be alone. But he would be there as soon as he called, or at least, the nurse would be there to assist him. Before he left, the internist decided that Scheinowiz would be moved to a single room the next day.

It was only hours later after the doctor had gone, that Jakob Scheinowiz – who had lain there, petrified, his face furrowed by its wrinkles – could fall asleep. He dove down under the blanket, his eyes half open.

Mullemann

Short, short and long – and long, long and short – short and Mullemann is tapping. Do you hear it? Mullemann is drumming on his wounds. His fingers touch on his pain. Mullemann is tapping for help. Do you hear it? Be still now. Listen carefully. Can't you hear it yet? All around you: the hustle and bustle in the hallways, the whispering in the alcoves, the stammering behind the walls and the groaning – that's right, the groaning – but also those skillfully voiceless, those abruptly silent and those quietly cunning ones. All around you. Do you hear them? Don't listen to them.

The ticking of time, the humming of the air conditioning, or the gurgling of the radiators. You can make out automobiles and trams in the distance. Don't listen to them, just pay attention to my tapping on hollow objects. Against the water or heating pipes or the bed frame. Short, short, long.

Sometimes I hear their voices, I hear their voices all around me. I can see nothing. Mullemann lies motionless, fettered to his bed. Gauze bandages lashed up in several layers are wound around his body. He can move neither of his legs, none of his limbs nor any of his joints. If I stick out my tongue, I lick and twist the already separated fibers and the pain spins itself into my lips and gradually stretches across my entire mouth as if – like when I was a child – I had eaten too much cotton candy, chewed too many of those sweet billowing strands. If I suck on the threads, I taste that substance I had never tasted before, I taste the ether, the medicine and the hospital. Mullemann: I'm lying here all alone. I live in my bandages.

At times I sense her proximity and feel her groping for me. I feel her clutching my body, listening intently for my heartbeat and breath. Mullemann sends his Morse code.

I know nothing about the beginnings of my suffering, nothing about the extent of my wounds and nothing about the circumstances of my injury. I can't recall any illness that suddenly descended on me.

I lie a prisoner in a network of bandages that are tautly stretched – even to the point of breaking – across my whole body, lacing up its festering, scarred surface.

Hours may have passed since Mullemann's last tapping signs, but he taps again. This is his diary. Drumming from the maze of his bandages. Someone in another bed, another room will hear me. His pen will lurch along in rhythm with my tapping. He will be the seismograph of my banging, my movements and tremors.

Mullemann is lying in a medical facility and doesn't know why. It's precisely this ignorance which makes me fear the worst. The people standing and walking around me, those people attending to Mullemann and me, they brought me here and bound me to this bed. They've wrapped me up in gauze – my eyes, my ears, my neck – bound me from head to toe with elastic bandages and left me a small opening for my nose. Even my jaw is bandaged tight. I can scarcely open my mouth.

When I suck on the bandages I taste the surgical wool as well as the complications and entanglements which Mullemann once let himself be caught up in and involved. I follow every trail of blood, sniff every trickle. I take up my own tracks.

The memory climbs up from under the roof of my mouth, the images become clear. I see myself in a car, driving down a mountain road. I think I'm on my way home. Twilight sets in and beneath me, the city lights flare up.

All of a sudden there is a blast under the ground as if a mine were exploding. I couldn't steer, the brake pedal went to the floor and I fell helplessly, yet fully conscious straight into the abyss. The car crashed against the rocks, turned over and someone screamed. It must have been me, can only have been me. The vehicle exploded in flight and I no longer hear the screaming, but see myself trapped in the burning automobile.

So it happened – it must have been that way. Do you hear me? Short, short and long, and listen. I was burning. I see myself, see myself burned to cinder, but Mullemann is tapping again, and I no longer know – can no longer explain to myself – how Mullemann survived and why I'm still alive, if, in fact, I am alive.

And who – and my tongue is grinding the connective tissues – who set the explosive device that tore apart the axle – I'm twisting the gauze into curls – who triggered the detonation? By radio signal. At the vortex of the curve.

Arthur Bein was lying there in fever. Pain shot through his stomach and he felt like throwing up. He had brought back the infection from a trip to Egypt. He had, the doctors had determined, poisoned himself with something that had spoiled. He had been rushed to the hospital and hooked up intravenously.

Dehydrated by vomiting for days, weakened by acute diarrhea, he sank into the mattress. He suffered silently. He scarcely moved his flabby, frail body and he thought he was seasick. Against his dark hair, his skin seemed even paler.

Under the top of Bein's skull there had been an agitated thumping. He had clearly heard it but couldn't explain the source of the noise that penetrated his fever.

His thoughts remained fuzzy, and only slowly did he again get to the question about the origin of the sounds. He struggled to comprehend what he had heard.

Finally, he understood: it was not an arbitrary rhythm that had reached his ear. He had vaguely recognized the signs. Someone was sending Morse code.

Or was it simply his feverish heartbeat that he heard? Nothing reminded Bein of a Mr. Mullemann, however. He had never had a bad accident, had never survived deadly misfortune. He knew why he was lying here and for how long, yet it was just this knowledge that didn't calm him down but rather made him fear the worst.

Bein tried to turn his head around, saw the heating pipes that touched the bars of the bed frame.

All of a sudden there was the tapping again, and he heard it quite clearly: short, short and long – long, long and short – Mullemann is tapping.

Mullemann is busy in his web and tries to become active, tries to move against all the pain. First, I opened my hand and doubled it into a fist. Hours later Mullemann rouses himself in his agony. He can raise my arm and bring my hand in front of my face and, with his fingers, is even able to loosen up the bandage over one eye and open up a slit to give me an unnoticed perspective.

Remembered images gather once again. Mullemann sees himself falling over a stair railing and feels that he has been pushed. He falls head first and tumbles onto the tiles on the ground floor, where he breaks his skull.

Then the knife, a stiletto, coming toward him, plunging into his breast and heart. And, from a safe distance, the shot in the woods. I fall down into the snow.

Sometimes when the nurse in her close-fitting uniform comes into the room, she unfolds sheets to make the beds up fresh and I breathe the scent of newly laundered linen. She turns the radio on, tightens up the sheets over the mattresses. I've scarcely begun to hear the classical music when I'm wrapped in new bandages. The new dressing is spooled out and then wound around me. The gauze which had twisted, worked itself loose and shifted, is again tied tightly.

On the other side of the wall in the room next door Arthur Bein was resting. He tried in vain to answer the tapping, but whoever it might be over there hitting the radiator could not hear Arthur Bein's signals. Mullemann was lying so that he could reach the heating pipe with his hand, but couldn't hear the knocking answering him. Arthur Bein gave up trying to contact Mullemann. He just listened.

Mullemann was remembering: No, I wasn't the one who was the victim of all the murders. I didn't burn up in the automobile or fall to my death in the stairwell nor was I stabbed to death or shot. Because I'm Mullemann and Mullemann is tapping.

Arthur Bein lay there motionless. He could not yet think about standing up and walking over there.

A suspicion dawned on him and fear stirred in him. He knew nothing about Mullemann, but he knew the murders which Mullemann was describing. He recognized them anew. He had worked on the cases himself.

Mullemann is sending Morse code because of all the murderous images flaring up in his mind. I was not the victim, it can't have been me. Perhaps Mullemann was the photographer who hurried from the editorial office to the scene of the crime, from the flash to the darkroom. Was I a forensic physician who sawed open the skulls of the corpses and broke their sterna with poultry shears? Still more likely, Mullemann could have been the police inspector on the track of the murderer. But what does a commissioner, a pathologist know of victims still clinging to life and their terror in the face of death?

Arthur Bein had dealt with these cases. He had been in charge of them and focused on the investigations – but, before and not after the murders had been committed. He had observed the victims, established their daily routines and recorded them neatly and tidily on a weekly planner. He had examined their garbage for confidential information and wormed his way into the confidence of their colleagues. He had followed them for days on the opposite side of the streets, had tapped telephones, bugged their auto-mobiles, offices and homes, had searched through their apartments, observed their private lives from buildings located across from their own, looked though his telescope into their bedrooms.

Disguised, dissembling and at times equipped with candy, he had approached their children and spoke to them in an avuncular tone. He had asked their wives friendly questions or even un-settling or trivial ones.

In the course of his intelligence work Arthur had been assigned to this reconnaisance. For the operations themselves, Arthur Bein, alias Alex, didn't seem suited. He lacked the determination to carry out a lethal strike, but his retiring nature and keen sense of hearing were the best qualifications for covert employment. He was always on guard, preferring a premature retreat to an unmasking. Although he was thoroughly trained in the martial arts, he avoided – he abhorred – violence. He didn't want to know anything about the moments when the murders took place, to hear any of the screams and moans of the dying or to see the expiring victims. Even more unpleasant for him were the shrieks of the bystanders, the grieving and crying of the family members. Arthur Bein didn't want to have anything to do with all those things.

On the other side of the wall, however, lay the other man, Mullemann, the killer who turned Bein's work into action. His murderous deeds resulted from his reports – the Morse code signals that had been transmitted to Mullemann. The latter exploited the weak points that Bein had discovered; Arthur could read about his final implementations later in the newspaper.

They didn't know each other. They were a murder conspiracy on tour, but never crossed each other's path because when the murderer arrived on the scene, Bein had already pulled back long before.

All of a sudden I know something which I've suspected for a long time. Do you hear me? Just listen. It was me. I'm Mullemann.

But why was I murdering and what am I suffering from?

Mullemann remembers. The skin rash had spread out over his entire body. I had wanted to cover it and protect the healing process, but one day I discovered that my skin had taken on the pattern of the gauze, that it suddenly seemed different. It became moist with a discharge, dried up and peeled off.

Mullemann soon no longer knew where his dressing ended and where his skin began. It seemed to him that he could take off his own upper cell layers by unrolling them with the gauze. He saw his body surface banded by lines, as if his skin grew in spirals and swerves, as if it were following the tracks of the fabric.

Mullemann is lying in the hospital, yet I no longer know who is underneath all those layers of material. I no longer know what name he once bore and why the man I once was killed other people or whether he hasn't already disintegrated – disappeared in this dressing. I don't know whether I have turned completely into gauze.

I'm incessantly working myself free. Gradually Mullemann can move his whole body. First he gained control of his hands. Later he learned to turn his head and then he found out how to bend his legs.

The bandages loosen with every new movement. They stretch out of shape and get tangled, but when the nurse turns on the classical radio station, the gauze again tightens the slings. The dressing adjusts its twistings to the freed movement that the joints have won. The structure ceases to be shackles and turns into more of a brace and directional aid for Mullemann. His limbs glide along in their bindings with support and guidance.

Last night I got up, tottered out of the room into the hallway, stole the cane of a sleeping patient, slipped on a coat and put on a cap. I was even able to slip my swollen body past the watchman. Mullemann was already on the street when a slight drizzle began.

I quickly realized that I had to turn around immediately before Mullemann's bindings were soaked with water. The material began to get heavy, swell up with moisture and to molt with every step. I again fled to the hospital and reached my bed.

I'm here again: Mullemann is sending Morse code.

When the nurse steps into Mullemann's room she comes toward me in her white underwear and, all at once, no longer needs the music to revive my bandages.

I hardly need to look at her and Mullemann's gauze begins to itch and the desire for the nurse gnaws at him.

Mullemann longs to be wrapped by her anew and then, suddenly, the material glides into fresh paths and flattens out.

If the nurse should actually try to wrap Mullemann, I can see how she would get tangled up in his loops. Mullemann – I'm certain – would be compelled to tie her up and wouldn't be able to let her go. He would choke her down, devour and digest her.

Behind the wall, Arthur Bein was following the tapping and forgot his worries, his sickness and was just listening to the Morse code signals. Fear intensified in Bein.

Someone over there was hitting on the heating pipe and could clearly be heard. Mullemann was audible, and if he could hear him then others could. Police or the other side – the enemy.

Mullemann lay in his bandages and gave up all his secrets. Apparently he could already get up. Mullemann was a walking time bomb. Arthur Bein couldn't wait any longer. He knew that something had to give.

Perhaps it wasn't his associate lying on the other side of the wall. Maybe it was an enemy who was trying to drive Arthur Bein crazy. It might be an adversary who wanted to lure him into a trap and force him into a definitive confession.

It's possible that his killer, the man who now called himself Mullemann, had made himself independent. Maybe it was because he had turned against the machinery that had employed him as a murderer or maybe simply because he had just plain gone crazy carrying out his assignments so that he wanted to be done with everything and everyone he had been associated with.

In the case that Mullemann had become a renegade, had discovered Arthur's identity and wanted to kill him, Bein could only do one thing: beat his killer to the punch and kill him. Arthur Bein was at Mullemann's mercy, however. He was still tied to his bed and could scarcely move. Mullemann, however, had gotten up.

Mullemann is lying under his bandages, but who is Mullemann? Maybe I'm not – i.e., Mullemann isn't – a flesh and blood human being. Maybe I'm nothing more than bandages and compresses, totally consumed by them. It seems to me at times that Mullemann is a clump of pains made of numerous deaths and nothing more than a commemorative bundle of various rolls of gauze accidentally woven together. At some points Mullemann thinks: Maybe there is no me.

"Wonderful," Bein murmured and grimaced, "Maybe he doesn't exist any more." The very man whose existence was made secure by destroying other lives, had doubts about his own.

Maybe Bein was trying to calm himself down and maybe the tapping was, in actuality, only the echo of his feverish imaginings. Mullemann: maybe there wasn't any such person and he was merely the phantom of his guilt. He was lying in bed, languishing, and now, those things had the power to obtain a hearing that faded in the noise of everyday events.

In spite all pacifying thoughts, Arthur had to contend with the fact that someone was lying behind the wall and sending Morse code.

It was not out of the question that Arthur Bein was being tested by his own people. Such checks did sometimes take place in order to gauge agents' reliability. Afterward, they became a general warning and were reviewed and discussed in continuation courses as illustrative examples of possible extreme situations. A total failure could mean a demotion, an unfavorable transfer or even a discharge in disgrace. Arthur Bein couldn't allow himself to make a mistake.

Something had to be done. Arthur Bein wanted to act quickly but didn't know how.

Should he call in his contact to tell him about a man called Mullemann whose bandages were freshly wrapped to classical music? Should he maybe explain to him that the agent Alex believed he was hearing Morse code in the radiator or that he believed something was ticking in the back of his head? He couldn't permit himself any error: Arthur Bein had to be certain.

Mullemann had to be certain and find out whether he existed under all that gauze. He had been lying in doubt for days. Today I have to find out.

As Mullemann picked and punctured, I screamed out from under the muzzle of the dressing, but no one heard him. The needle was centimeters deep in my arm. A pale pinkish color suddenly appeared near the puncture hole in the material, gradually replaced by an emerging red spot that finally exulted in its crimson boldness.

Arthur Bein was a little better that morning. The fever, the pain and the sick feeling had passed.

And all the questions that had tormented him in the past few days were finally answered. No, the tapping behind the wall was neither a subterfuge nor a deception.

The thoughts of this Mullemann were too abstruse. They could not have been thought up to drive him crazy. The person lying there had turned his blood lust against himself and his family.

Although this insight was no reason for cheerful consolation, Arthur Bein had finally located and made out the danger. Mullemann could only be liquidated if he existed and were not a ghost in Bein's conscience. Bein also believed that he was ready to get up and able to face the threat.

Arthur was smiling when the morning round of visitations had reached his bed. The primary physician said: "Ah yes, the travel infection. We're doing much better already. I think you should be able to go home in two or three days." Then came the orders for the nursing staff, a discussion directed at the young doctors, and a few words to Bein about his diet.

The medical procession had scarcely left the room when Arthur heard the signals.

Mullemann sees them coming. They go from one bed to the next. They stop in one corner. The doctor speaks and Mullemann taps: "Nurse, the first-aid course is over. Put the dummies away. The mummy too – we don't need it any more. Take out the needles and roll up the gauze."

The nurse remains alone with Mullemann. She walks toward him. And she rolls me up.

Bein raised himself up. Everything was spinning. He strained to get out of bed. He was dizzy. He wanted to get to the other room as quickly as possible, but he arrived there only after ten minutes of panting and sweating.

Under one bed there was a nurse's shoe; on the sheet were gauze bandages. Bein shuffled nearer, took a bandage in his hand, then another one and poked around. The pieces of tape knotted together and he tried to separate them. He let a roll slide through his fingers like a filmstrip, studied it as if he could read it, and wound its loose end around his left arm. He took hold of the next one, wound it around his right arm and picked up a third one.

He bent over the material as if he were trying to decipher its pattern, as if he were lost in it. He rocked, lost in thought, up and down, swung back and forth.

The he saw his reflection in the mirror: Arthur Bein, his arms and forehead swathed in white. He stood there and said the *Kaddisch* for Mullemann.

The day he was released a nurse came and packed his things. He sat on the edge of the bed and inspected his appointment calendar. The workaday world had him again. He looked at the young woman who was turned away from him and stood in front of a window. She wore a white uniform, her black hair tightly swept up. With her slender, powerful hands she straightened up a pair of pajamas, folded a pair of pants and a shirt and put them all in his bag.

She let out an abrupt scream and let his alarm clock fall to the floor. Arthur stooped down, picked it up, and, not without eyeing her legs, handed it to her and said: "That's all right." The nurse was staring motionless out of the window. He got up and looked in the direction where her eyes were fixed. Six floors below them he saw a man, entirely wrapped up, standing at the crossing on the opposite side of the street. Even his face was encased. Holding a cane in one hand, he let it dance – noiselessly from this side of the glass – on the asphalt. Bein read quietly along: long, long and short; and short, short and long. And Mullemann is tapping.

Keysser

The spring light spread out in the room and brightened up one part of the carpet, but didn't reach to the chaise longue near the wall. The psychoanalyst Caro Sandner sat behind the walnut table in front of the window and sank down into the upholstery of a wing chair. Her face was lying in the shadows.

She looked at the patient who sat across from her. Agitated, the latter returned her gaze, his eyes in motion, his mouth open wide, wheezing through the gap.

Caro Sandner, clicking her fingernails, shuffled through the reports looking for information and organization. The patient followed the woman's snapping while rocking his knees back and forth with his legs wrapped around the chair. His eyes darted this way and that. He was taking short breaths. He began to clear his throat. Caro Sandner started, letting the sheets of paper fall from her hands she had picked up. She asked quietly: "You are . . . ?"

"Pardon me?"

"Your name, please."

"Peuntner."

She attempted to write it down: "Bointha like Bertha?"

"No, like Paul; Gerd Peuntner."

"Why Gerd?"

Caro Sandner went through all the possibilities of turning the sound of the name into letters. She included all the most unusual spellings and didn't notice the dismay and distrust mounting in Peuntner.

"Oi like de-void?"

"What?"

"Like Mobil Oi-l?" The patient had come into the office because he thought he was being followed. The therapist was now driving him to despair: "With an umlaut? An '*äu* ' like in '*oi* - st*∂*r'?"

"Oyster? What do you mean?"

"Well, like in '*oint* -m*∂*nt'? With a 'Y' then."

"How do you mean that?" Crossing his arms, Peuntner stared off to the side and srceamed: "What do you want from me?"

She replied: "Are you afraid of my questions?"

"My name is Peuntner," the patient whispered with tears in his eyes. Looking at the floor he then went on, his voice darkening a shade toward dissonance: "Like in German Eu-sebia . . . Eu-ter . . . or Eu-ropäische Union . . . like German Eu-reka!"

Caro Sandner winced and suddenly noticed that Peuntner was still sitting at an angle toward her and was now refusing any more communication. His lower jaw jutted forward and fear no longer allowed him to say anything about his inhibitions. Caro Sandner, from the very beginning excited and intimidated by her first session with Peuntner, gave up as well. She dared not make any further approach after her initial pushiness.

The therapist didn't lack sensitivity, but at times she wasn't able to activate her understanding, to set it in motion and act it out. When she discussed cases with colleagues in a supervisory capacity, cases whose files she had studied, or when she illuminated the inner life of a person who had just left a session, she amazed everyone. In a patient's presence, however, in the isolation of a therapy session, Caro Sandner was often a failure.

At the end of the hour she dismissed Peuntner. Ten minutes later she stumbled sullenly down the stairs, seething with defiance. She knew she had failed. She was capable of attaching her own thoughts to those of another human being and of aligning her feelings with the other's emotional world, but as soon as that person sat in front of her, she tripped and fell over her own feet. She stood in the way of her own capabilities. If she was trying to get close to someone, she couldn't find the distance to her own inner world that was necessary for objective judgment.

She stalked out of the building's main entry. Her step was firm and quick. Turning toward the right, she went past a passageway and a man who immediately looked up. He stepped out from under the arch and stared after her, letting his eyes glide over her silk stockings, her miniskirt and her back. Caro pulled her patent leather jacket more tightly around her. She wore her black hair in a pageboy with impertinent bangs framing her face, a cat's face behind glass. Without being noticed, the stranger started out after her.

She climbed into a bus and took a seat in the last row. Pulling off a leather rucksack that she wore for reasons of fashion rather than function, she fished out a book, leafed through it until she found an essay by a Dutch analyst and expert on post-traumatic depression.

The stranger really didn't know what attracted him to this

woman nor why he should follow her or if he should approach her. It was a day he had taken off work and his spouse would not have a clue – how could she? – about his secrets and the passions that overpowered him at times. She would never suspect that he was hunting, foraging for desire. Because he had grown estranged from her. And from himself. But he was also a stranger to Caro Sandner, who had no idea that she was being pursued but was thinking about her teaching analyst Hans Wiegenfeldt who had said: "You're constantly in front of, even faster than the patient you want to follow. You see a goal and it blinds you." If only she were not always so apprehensive, Caro Sandner thought, she could discard her inhibitions. She got out of the bus and the stranger followed her.

Women like her seemed perfect and unattainable to the man following on her heels with his gaze fixed on her frailty. The stranger tried not to attract attention and brought his staring under control. He looked around to see if he had aroused anyone's notice and saw that she had gone into a bus stop shelter. He let some time pass and waited until the bus drove up. Then he moved toward her. He had reached her with just a few steps and was taking his hand from his pocket when the telephone in his coat rang. Frightened, she looked around. They stood across from one another, a breath's distance away. The phone chirped as he unfolded it and did not say: "Hello," nor "Keysser," but simply: "Hello. Who's this?"

"Helmuth?" asked the voice at the other end. Keysser stopped short, turned his head and asked: "Yes. What's up?" With that Caro Sandner hastily disappeared.

"Can you pick up Petra from ballet," Hilde Keysser wanted to know.

He answered: "Sure."

"Helmuth, is something wrong?"

"What? No. Everything's fine, my dear."

"Did I disturb you? . . . It's for Petra . . ."

"You never disturb me, Hilde," he said and tried to drown out the irritation which he had allowed to slip out as if he had just waked up – as if she had torn him away from a nightmare, a brief slumber.

He stood there after she had hung up with the phone in his hand and slowly put it away. He looked for the woman he had been following, but she was gone. He wouldn't see Caro Sandner again.

He felt like he had been discovered. He felt ashamed as if the phone call had been a confrontation instigated by the police of the one Keysser – stalking a total stranger – with the other one, the family head and father.

He took the bus back to his car. There he spotted another woman. She was wearing an army jacket and a peaked cap covering her closely cropped, red hair. Crossing the train tracks, Keysser chased after her.

As soon as they're alone, he cuts off her path of escape. He looks into the woman's frightened eyes and assures her he has no evil intentions. Then he grabs her at the neck. She screams and yells at him, digs her fingernails into his arm, but he pulls her toward him and wraps his hands around her throat. He watches her eyes grow large and breathlessly orders her to be quiet and stay calm. All the while, a rattle in her throat and tears in her eyes, she gasps for air. Unable to let her go, he finds his physical being, his pleasure when he presses her body to his. He crushes her throat, shuts it off until the cartilage breaks and her eyes glaze over. Draping himself over her, he penetrates her with violent convulsions.

Afterward, with loathing rising in his throat, he hurried away and raced to the bus. Once in the car he noticed the scratches on his forearm and wiped the blood away, but he had to stop, get out of the car and throw up.

At home Hilde asked about Petra. Raising her hand to her brow, her face went pale in fear as she suddenly understood: he had forgotten the child. He was crying during their drive to the ballet school. The little girl who had waited for her father in the dark didn't say a word.

The next morning he read about the murder in the newspaper. Nothing pointed to him – there were no clues as to the person responsible, so the report was almost calming. All of a sudden everything seemed distant. No one would learn who had strangled the woman and assaulted her. As a sales representative, his working hours couldn't be checked. None of this should ever come to the surface again. He never again would follow his lusts and track down a stranger.

Was he a butcher of women just because he had killed one time? Had he murdered this woman with criminal intent? No, to him everything seemed a chance event, an accident.

His colleagues respected Helmuth Keysser – a man who worked in the field for an insurance company – without being able to get close to him. He performed his job quietly and didn't cause any stir. He was invited to Christmas parties, but by the office flyer. His name had been incorrectly spelled on the envelope: "Helmuth Kaisser," but he was used to that. His pay slips were addressed to "Keiser," his electric bills to "Keyser," and his rental notices arrived at the address of the "Kesser" family. For some reason no one was able to spell his name. His attempts to correct the mistakes and all his comments were simply answered with further mistakes.

His wife said: "Don't get upset. When a bill comes due, you can imagine they mean someone else when you're making the payment. And when they transfer money to you it will get into your account anyway."

He replied: "That's the way it is. Names are just empty words."

Keysser had the reputation of a loving father. He and his wife didn't quarrel and Hilde felt that she was lucky to have found such a person. She believed she was living without passion with this man, yet in security and harmony. He fulfilled his duties toward his daughter without appearing exaggerated in his tenderness. All of his caring for her and the child led Hilde Keysser to believe that he loved her secretly but all the more honestly. Helmuth Keysser allowed her to retain this feeling since he knew nothing of his own. Why should he burden her with doubts?

He lived alienated from himself and was not at any greater distance to her than to his own self. They had come together through a misunderstanding that was later never clarified. She had fallen in love, and he had not wanted to raise any objections. Hilde seemed pleasant and brought out the best in him by altering goals of his which, in his mind, had always been dubious. He respected her but without that desire that sometimes struck him when he looked at other women. He married her because he didn't know what else to do and stayed with her because he was comfortable.

The tranquillity with his wife, the closeness to his daughter provided fulfillment with time, but was like the satisfaction of desires and needs by surrogate means. As soon as he was together with his family, the turmoil he experienced in solitude was appeased. It was when he was alone that he felt hollow and weak.

He placed the blame for the emptiness he felt in his marriage and life in general squarely on his own shoulders. It was his fault from the very beginning. Had he gone stalking in order to discover himself? Was that the reason he had begun to follow women?

Only his daughter was able to touch him. He devoted his leisure time to Petra, laughed and went everywhere with her – to the zoo or the circus, the puppet theater or to the movies for cartoons. In the summer they hiked as a pair through the woods and in the winter they went ice skating on the city ponds. She turned pirouettes while he carried the rucksack with food and school materials.

The day after the murder he swore to himself that he would never pursue these passions again. The terror set in only the following morning. A letter claiming responsibility had appeared in one of the tabloids. Someone else had assumed the guilt for the crime. The unknown person used a pseudonym. The newspaper printed a facsimile of the letter and, in a commentary, sneered at the language – according to the editor-in-chief – of an obvious psychopath. This stranger didn't merely claim to have killed the woman, but was also able to describe the crime just as Keysser had experienced it:

"The person writing this signs with the name 'Mullemann' because that's not my name. The person confessing to the crime will remain unknown."

Keysser read the letter and shivered with fear since he could not explain the knowledge of the details that the writer had in his possession. Keysser's family, his habit of lingering at his wife's side, his affection for his daughter were mentioned as well as his furtiveness, his life spent in preparation for the chase after other women.

The text went on: "Mullemann accompanies me like a stranger, but at the moment I was committing the murder, I was completely at one with myself."

As much as Keysser had wanted to forget his crime – also part of this Mullemann's confession – he could no longer find any peace after reading this article. How did this stranger know about the stirrings in Keysser's soul? Had he drawn up the confession himself without knowing it? In another state of consciousness? Was he splitting? He rejected the idea after he had searched through his desk and wastebaskets, his study, office and automobile. There was no sign that suggested such a possibility.

Was someone able to summon up so much empathy that he could steal into Keysser's soul?

It might be that the person who had written the text was able to sense Keysser's murderous desires by simply reporting about the crime, committing it only in his imagination and freeing himself from it by putting it in words. Was his self accusation, the confession of his guilt enough for this man to attain gratification?

Had he been observed? Was there a witness to the crime? Had someone near to him suspected him for a long time and followed him? The media interest flared up. The case was being discussed everywhere. Colleagues and customers wanted to talk about Mullemann in the office, on his sales rounds and during negotiations. Psychologists discussed the letter on television and a weekly magazine attacked the tabloid press for publishing it. Cultural programs on television – without any reference to the actual event – presented the newest films on violence against women.

The public clamor strengthened Keysser's resolve never again to succumb to his murderous desires, yet at the same time he could think of nothing else. A feverish wave seemed to sweep over the country engulfing him along with everyone else in a seasonal virus, an influenza infection. He set out in search of the person who had confessed to the crime, looked for someone at work who was spying on him. In the morning when he left the house, he looked around to see if anyone were following him. At the tobacco shop where he bought his newspaper he peered through the display window. The clerk asked: "On your rounds again, Mr. Keysser?" Recoiling, he looked up in terror into the face of the young man with greasy leather jacket and oily hair and paid without answering. "Thanks and have a nice day, Mr. Keysser," he called out after him. Keysser could only muster: "Good-bye."

When he became aware of a woman who excited his desires, he looked around for someone following him. He scarcely noticed a woman who reminded him of his victim and he felt himself ensnared. He wanted to suppress what welled up inside of him since he believed the whole world was taking notice, listening carefully to him and expecting his eyes to fix intently on the exquisite figure and for his breath to quicken. There was someone suspicious of him, Keysser sensed, standing behind him and watching his desires come to the surface.

After several weeks during which he had not given in to his longings, it seemed he had completely overcome them. At that point at the end of November, a second letter from Mullemann appeared. He wrote about his distress, about his unquenchable needs. It was during this time that Keysser began to lose his self-control. He read Mullemann's remarks as a call to a further transgression, as a summons for the next crime. He found it impossible to carry out his tasks at work and he fell behind in his orders. The letter claiming responsibility was being discussed everywhere. A rival tabloid called for a campaign against its publication. It called the murderer an animal and said the other newspaper printing Mullemann's words was acting irresponsibly. For the sake of sales, it had turned into the criminal's accomplice, sharing the appetite for perversion and sensation that fester around the violent murder of a female. A psychologist on a television news program warned that the perpetrator would be spurred on by the general attention. He sought it out to use as the backdrop for his blood ritual – as the expert expressed it.

In the weekly where the first argument against the reproduction of the first letter had been printed, an analyst, Doctor Paul Deutsch-Liebenthal, now wrote: Mullemann should not be demonized, he explained. On the contrary, the texts were cries for help from someone in despair, from a sick man who would be forced to kill again in the case he did not find a way out. Deutsch-Liebenthal closed with an appeal to Mullemann to turn to him – the Doctor – for his own good.

During the early twilight of a December day, a woman plods through the snow of the city's outer edges to get from her apartment house to the street where her boyfriend Herbert was to pick her up in his car. She speeds up her footsteps when she hears a crunching in the snow and spots the stranger pursuing her who, just in case, reaches into his pocket and turns off his cell phone. She knows that she is safe because Herbert is supposed to be parked around the corner and waiting for her. What she doesn't know is that he has been delayed today because his boss has held him up to make out the duty roster for Christmas day. She has blue eyes, is five feet five inches tall and weighs one hundred twenty pounds. Her identity card reads Petra Sommer. She was twenty-five years old.

Reports of the crime appeared on the following day. When Keysser read the name of the victim he thought of his own child. Was Petra startled when he came into the room? Soon afterward another letter from Mullemann appeared. Why did the clerk smile at him the past few times he had gone into the tobacco shop? Was his grin mockery? Was his occasional wink evidence of some secret knowledge?

"Good day, Mr. Keysser," the employee said. "What about this Mullemann? Another one of his letters appeared today. It's interesting, isn't it?" Keysser paid without a word.

His wife had never satisfied that hunger he felt when he set eyes on those women on the streets. He was consumed by his desire for them. Afterward he experienced an emptiness but not a release.

While his wife had never particularly aroused him before, he now avoided all physical contact. One night when she aggressively threw herself toward him he closed his eyes and suddenly thought of how it was with other women. He laid his body on top of hers, pressed her to the bed with his hands on her throat, and had her under his control.

In the morning she sang softly as she woke him with a kiss and murmured in his ear. During breakfast she sent him adoring glances – she behaved as she never had before. And he had never before been so nauseated by her. He looked at her and was overcome with shame. He looked down at himself and was filled with guilt and fear.

That very day he stormed into the office, headed for the secretary's desk, slammed down the invitation to the Christmas party in front of her and screamed: "Keysser! Do you hear me? That's the way you spell it! With a 'y' and a double 's'!"

That night his wife tried to calm him down: "Names are just empty words, darling."

"Yours maybe."

"But we have the same one, Helmuth!"

All his hopes that the first murder was just a chance occurrence, an aberration, now melted away. The urge inside him was too powerful for him to be able to dismiss or deny it. He began the days when he committed a crime with careful preparations. He put on sturdy shoes and picked out gray clothes. One morning he bought a knife to bend the victims to his will and break their resistance. It was not intended as a murder weapon since he needed his hands for this.

Although he now knew his passion, he had no more of a taste for it than before. He obeyed it like a curse and was in constant fear of being caught. He scoured the newspapers for the reports. He read Mullemann's letters which terrified him, but which he saved and constantly read through again. Someone – but who? – was on his tracks, someone who either was anticipating or following him. Keysser was afraid of the man's letters and his predictions of further murders because they seemed like curses that drove him to the next slaying.

It was his fifth murder, a violinist. She had hurled her violin case at his head, but Keysser had thrown himself with all his weight on top of her, put the blade to her throat and grasped her neck with his left hand. He stealthily made his way back to his car that he had parked at a distance. As he was coming around the corner he crossed the path of a man and reacted with alarm when he recognized the clerk in the tobacco shop. The young man greeted him with a grin, a wink and: "Good day, Mr. Keysser." Helmuth Keysser nodded in reply, mumbled an answer that didn't take the form of words and ran to his automobile. He sped away and, without noticing it, drove though a crosswalk against a red light. He didn't hit the brakes until he realized in a moment of panic that a radar camera had flashed.

Helmuth Keysser believed he had found Mullemann in the employee from the shop where he had bought newspapers, parking permits and stamps for years. He lacked, however, any concrete proof. How could he be sure? He knew of only one way of refuting his suspicion. If he were to kill the man, he could no longer write letters claiming responsibility.

The thought of such a test made his blood run cold with fear. He sat in front of his apartment in his car and told himself: "I can't do that! I'm not a murderer!"

He had never killed according to a plan. He considered himself merely an amateur criminal who killed out of passion, a devotee of the dark side of life. He drew close to his prize like a collector approaches a butterfly. Strangling women meant that he exchanged his self-control for control over his victims. As soon as life had gone from the corpses beneath him and he had ejected his semen into them, his intoxication quickly tapered off. He could no longer torment lifeless bodies – they had escaped his power.

At this point he could not lose control in an encounter with his opponent. Keysser wanted to eliminate the tobacco shop clerk not merely to discover whether he was Mullemann or not, nor out of fear of what he knew. More precisely, he was conscious of a hatred directed toward the clerk's smile as well as toward the person who confessed to his, Keysser's, crimes. He despised the man who boasted about the atrocities that he – his name either forgotten or misspelled by everyone – had committed.

He had no difficulty in finding an axe. The next evening he waited for the man on his way home. He stood unobserved on a lonely corner and watched the tobacco shop clerk Gunther Seefried approach. There were only the two of them. Shaking, he stood in the shadows behind a wall, lifted the axe as he heard Seefried's steps, closed his eyes and struck at his head. The point of the axe split open his skull and Seefried buckled at the knees as he let out a scream. He began to turn around but the frightened Keysser yanked the metal out of the bone and attacked Seefried's head broadside. While Seefried fell to the ground he smashed his head to pieces until the brain came gushing forth.

Keysser staggered off, threw up in a nearby garbage can, and in the car, wiped off the splattered blood and vomit from his clothes. He then drove to the riverbank and threw the axe into the water. It was several hours before he was able to calm himself down and return to his family. That night Helmuth Keysser went to the bar in his home and drank whiskey until his agitation waned and he fell asleep.

The next morning a letter from Mullemann appeared in the newspapers in which he predicted the murder. The confessional letter preceded the reports about the case of Gunther Seefried by twenty-four hours. This caused even greater intensity in the public outcry as well as in Keysser's despair.

Had he killed the wrong man or had Seefried anticipated his own murder? Keysser no longer knew what to do. From one moment to the next, he thought he saw the one way out. In the case that Seefried had written Mullemann's confessions before his death, he would at least be unable to send off any more letters. The only confirmation that Mullemann had expired – Keysser exulted in this thought – would be to strangle one more woman.

Keysser hoped that with this last crime he could attain clarity about the fate of his adversary.

Helmuth Keysser intended to return to that point where his activities had begun. He waited for the woman at the same time and on the same day as before and in the corridor where she had passed by. He recognized her immediately. She had a steady gait, wore silk stockings, a patent leather jacket and carried a rucksack – everything was as it should be, even her black hair. He followed her bus in his car and saw her cat's face with glasses at the window.

As he stepped in front of her he brandished the knife in her face. When she raised her head, she remained silent while recalling who he was and looked him straight into the eyes with complete composure. He warned: "Just stay calm! Be quiet and don't scream! Shouting would be useless. No one is going to hear you, understand? You're better off not irritating me, get it?" But she had not uttered a sound as she looked silently into his round face. She observed the full cheeks, the flabbiness of his features and asked coolly: "So you're Mullemann?"

"No", he roared and raised his weapon while coming ever closer to the woman while she despairingly tried to think of something to distract him. He remarked emphatically: "I am not Mullemann! My name is Keysser! Do you hear me? Keysser, Helmuth Keysser!"

"With a 'y'?" she now asked as if she needed to fill out a form.

"Yes," he answered hesitantly.

Taking advantage of the pause, she added: "Keysser like Konrad, then 'e' and 'y' . . . . "

"Right!"

"With double 'ss', right?"

"Sure. It's very simple: Keysser." Confused, he lowered the arm with the knife.

She said: "That's clear. Keysser. Nice to meet you. My name is Caro Sandner." His train of thought had been broken. Since that urge had not emerged during the conversation that usually swept him away, he no longer felt the desire to murder this woman.

He said: "This whole Mullemann affair is a fake. It's a brazen plot, pure nonsense!"

Keeping her eyes fixed on the knife, she agreed with him: "It's an insult." He now also looked at the blade in his hand and suddenly knew that he could no longer muster the courage to use it. He threw it away and ran off.

Helmuth Keysser was picked up later that night. The next day the newpapers published accounts of the arrest and spelled his name in numerous variations, all of which had only one thing in common – they were all wrong. No one had any information about Mullemann and his whereabouts. Nor was there anything to find out.

Jael

The train lurched gently through the Italian summer. He was standing alone in a first-class compartment looking out the window at the blue ocean underneath a cloudless sky. He had opened the door and he went out into the corridor from time to time, peering through the window at the other side. The man searched the countryside not knowing what he was looking for, even though he had no doubt that he would find the place where he was supposed to carry out his instructions.

When the conductor looked in, the stranger bought a ticket and indicated a destination at a considerable distance. The rail official was to have no hint that he was leaving the train at one of the next stations.

There were never any clues when he began a new project. He had neither names nor pictures nor did he know the facial features or particular characteristics of the people he was tracking down, but he had never gone wrong.

Mishaps had occasionally occurred to others in the department, and their failings could result in a catastrophe. Every mistake endangered the lives of one's own people, could condemn an innocent human being to death, and startled the opposing side into action. It was a defeat in the face of the enemy as well as a disgrace for the domestic government and the other arms of the Israeli state.

Arthur was thinking of Tel-Aviv and his summons to the present job. He recalled Teddy's phone call and what he said: "We can't do without you any longer."

Then, in spite of Arthur's excuses: "I'm not over it yet," and despite his questions: "Why now? Why me?" the old man wouldn't back off his request for a meeting within two hours. It was a request, Arthur knew, that was tantamount to an order.

"If not me, then who and if not now, when?" Arthur muttered as he saw from the train the sandy Italian beach, the hotels and a church with a bell tower become visible behind a pine forest. The train went past the harbor and some old houses with tiled roofs as it pulled into the station. Feeling the urge to drop out of sight here, it took him only seconds to take in the seclusion of the place and the beauty of its landscape. He picked up his briefcase and hurried past the train cars to the exit.

At the hotel the agent registered under a false name, although if he had been asked for his real name he wouldn't have known how to answer. Even his father before him had denied the name Scheinowiz and hidden behind the pseudonym Fandler. The boy had been prudently called Arieh Arthur so that he would not be an outcast among either Jews or Christians and would have a choice between these worlds. Jakov Scheinowiz had been dead for a long time but his legacy lived on. His son changed his name much more often than his father ever had. When he was abroad the agent called himself Arthur and while in Israel he was called Arieh by those closest to him. When he was on assignment he treated himself to still other *noms de guerre*. In order to escape the confusion his father had caused, he had shed both family names Scheinowiz and Fandler and assumed that of his wife Navah. Now his name was Arieh Arthur Bein. He believed he had thereby overcome the farce, not noticing that this decision had actually put the crowning touch on his father's comedy of errors.

He signed his reports to the intelligence service with Alex. He could rattle off his various cover names in his sleep and could spell out his contrived identities for the clerk in this resort hotel without missing a beat. When he was pursuing leisure time activities like ordering theater tickets by telephone, however, he would hesitate because he would momentarily not know under which name he should make the reservations.

Bein moved into his room and looked out over the balcony toward the ocean. He took off his suit, shirt, tie and underwear and washed away the sweat and grime of the train ride in the shower. Just like every other time he had been in this country he mixed up the cold with the hot water. Later, he left the building in jeans and T-shirt. He was never supposed to stand out from other people because of his outer appearance.

He strolled along the promenade scouting the surroundings without being able to discover anything remarkable. There were children on rented bicycles, a pair of lovers on a tandem bicycle and a few families in pedal cars crossing here and there. Arthur took a seat in a café near the harbor and read a newspaper article about the tensions between Kuwait and Iraq. When he noticed that he was on the verge of becoming part of the background in a photograph – a woman was posing for her companion a few meters in front of Arthur's table – he turned his head to the side.

The first thing the next morning he looked into the mirror and searched his face and body for any kind of changes which might have descended on him overnight. He thought he could make out a darkening of his complexion and a shading under his eyes. His beard seemed to be thicker than normal. He noticed that his posture had straightened and that the curves in the small of his back and on his rounded shoulders had been ironed out. Anyone else would have believed that the sunlight at the spa was responsible for the transformation of his skin and the growth of his beard, while they might give credit for his new trim carriage to the relaxed atmosphere that excited all the village guests. But Bein read something else in the metamorphoses which he had undergone: they were the enemy's tracks. That was the way it was when he went hunting. He believed that he took on the appearance of the man he was following and, by this method, discovered the path to his goal or prey.

"You're a marvel, Arieh, a medium . . . We need you." Teddy

had said to him a week ago in Tel-Aviv: "Six months of sick leave because of an infection has got to be enough."

But Arieh's colleague Nimrod had chimed in: "Nobody is irreplaceable. If Arieh would rather relax, there are others who will take on the risk." To Arieh: "You'll have to decide."

Bein merely repeated: "Right, others?"

At this, Teddy's eyes became steely and he said in a whisper: "Enough of that! I had you called because it's time. We know the crime but not the guilty person. We have nothing – neither name, picture, or description. This project was made for you, and Arieh . . . there's no way around it, there's no alternative. We need you!"

Arieh's was a singular talent; he was an exception among his colleagues. There were others who sat in their offices and ordered their files, collected newspaper clippings or wrote their daily reports. Some very cautiously took up foreign contacts, cultivated these ties, won confidences, traded in secrets and bought up intelligence. Such operatives were civil servants or agents. No one possessed Arieh's remarkable talents, yet the entire organization was driven by the same motivation that had made a medium of him: the search for the mortal enemies of their existence.

"I'm not over it yet, Teddy."

"So it's just that more important to get your mind off it. We've looked into the whole thing. In the hospital you thought you had been contacted by a mysterious stranger named Mullemann who knew everything about you and your activities. There is no such person. Nobody made contact with you. You told us that Mullemann was someone who murdered the people you were investigating and was now following you. Arieh, this was just a figure of your feverish imagination at the time. You were sick; it was simply unreal. Anyway, that was six months ago. And that's why I called you – because it's time. We need you!"

Arieh Bein stood in an Italian hotel room and looked into the mirror. He decided against shaving and combed the curls out of his hair until it seemed smoother than ever before. In the city he bought some swimming gear and summer clothing.

On the beach, where armchairs and umbrellas were standing in neat order, a woman with a little girl caught his eye. The mother, a blonde, was the only one of her gender lounging without make-up in her beach chair. She obviously paid little attention to her looks and had no interest in the rivalry among the other female vacationers. The child, a mass of tousled black hair on her head and her skin a shimmering dark brown, resembled her mother only in her blue eyes.

His thoughts wandered to his own daughter Jael with her hand in his as they sauntered together the ten minutes from their apartment on the *Arloserov* to Tel-Aviv's oceanfront. He thought of her silky, dark brown hair and the sweet scent surrounding her, a mixture of vanilla and banana. He heard her rollicking laughter when she jumped up on him as soon as he returned home from an assignment abroad and when she hopped into bed with Navah and him. Such moments had been rare ones, however, since Arieh Arthur Bein had spent most of the first years of his marriage traveling. Whenever he came home his daughter snuggled up and stayed close to him. On the few days of the month when he did see his family, Navah was visibly restless putting her efforts into chores connected to his return. She invited relatives and friends to their house as well as traveling with him and Jael to her parents in the kibbutz. As much as he wanted to be alone with her, there was never any time.

Navah had complained about his frequent absences at the beginning of their relationship, but later had become absorbed in her studies. She was writing historical articles about the Jewish community in Czernowitz in the previous century. Surrounded by dictionaries and standard texts, she sat in a blouse and trousers in front of the computer screen, her delicate form and flaxen hair set off by its faint glow. As soon as he was there and could watch the child in her place, she retreated into her study. For six months he had refused any further assignments and had first applied for sick leave and then for vacation time. He had not left Navah's side, prudently avoiding the impression, however, that he wanted to get in her way.

Actually, he had allowed himself the several months of

vacation for others reasons as well. Arieh Arthur Bein had run into a figure by the name of Mullemann and carrying on further with his work seemed impossible. This character followed him, *haunted* him with descriptions of all the murders that had been committed with the help of Arieh's investigations and reports. Even though Teddy didn't believe his stories for a minute and took Mullemann to be a figment of his imagination, Arieh had heard Mullemann's Morse code quite clearly while lying in his hospital bed.

Arieh's claims to have met a phantom seemed like delusions, and Teddy didn't trust them even though the old man otherwise needed no explanations for his agent's mysterious abilities but just exploited his telepathic and parapsychological skills. To his superiors, Bein was regarded as an intuitive phenomenon, as a medium whose powers were used without searching for a source or drafting any crude theories. Teddy made use of all the talents that could be exploited.

Teddy called Arieh's report "a feverish hospital dream, a sailor's yarn made out of surgical dressing."

Nimrod amplified: "This Mullemann – a vision of German melancholy. That's what was in your gut. It wasn't an infection, just those unbearable emotions."

One evening, however, Navah – whom he had told nothing about his encounter – said: "Your exhaustion, Arieh, comes from your restlessness; your search for others is a way of avoiding yourself." He had never talked to her about his work and she had never complained or asked him about it. Silence had moved in with them and made itself at home. When he was called to an assignment she took an sharp breath and rolled her eyes.

Arieh Arthur Bein was sitting in his beach chair when he saw the blonde mother and her child get ready to leave. He also decided to return to the hotel. He wanted to go to lunch and was hoping for mussels and spaghetti. Later, when he went to the train station, he made sure that no one was following him. At the post office he went into a phone booth and called Navah. He had asked her to wait for him with Jael in a village on Lake Garda. It was the first time he had given in to this kind of impulse. When he had finished his job he went home. This time, however, he had reserved a room for them in the same country in which he was carrying out his mission. Afterward, he planned on spending his vacation here with Navah and Jael. Arieh said: "I really need you."

"When are you coming?"

"It will take a little longer than I thought . . . I really need you," he said and repeated it after she had not responded.

"We'll wait for you," Navah replied. "Come as soon as you're finished."

He stepped out of the booth. What in the world was the matter with him? Even though he was certain he was on the right track, he wasn't finding the enemy he was looking for. He had picked up his adversary's scent and sensed the change that was taking possession of his body. He could feel the small of his back being stretched by his gait and perceive the form of his beard and the outline of the hair on his head. It was always this way when he got closer to the person he had been set loose on, that person whose guilt was to be avenged and whose crime was to be redressed. For some reason, however, he had not met up with a possible suspect this time.

He left the train station building intending to walk back to the hotel when he heard a woman's voice call out: "Sayid!" He continued on until he heard running steps behind him and another "Sayid!" Arieh Arthur Bein turned around – "Sayid!" . . . – and looked into the blue eyes of the blonde woman he had seen on the beach. The girl held her hand.

When the mother looked at his face, she hesitated and seemed to search his features. Disappointed, she then said in a north German accent: "Oh, excuse me . . ."

"Can I help you?"

"No . . . A mistake . . ."

Bein responded: "That's too bad. Do I resemble someone?"

"No, actually not at all."

He smiled. "Maybe in the meantime you might make do with me? Would you like to have a cup of coffee?"

She declined politely and disappeared, telling the little girl: "Come along, Maria."

Arieh now thought he knew the object of his pursuit: that Sayid was in all probability his Palestinian enemy. Possibly he was a husband, maybe even a loving father, who loved and was loved. It would be Arieh's job to spy on him, to write a report about his life and habits, and to propose a method for his liquidation.

Arieh didn't believe that such actions could decide the war. No victory would bring about a definitive solution in the battle. Sayid was an agent on the other side, subject to the logic of power just like Arthur Arieh Bein.

It was not a matter of territorial gain for either one of the countries, but both had reasons for the murder and hatred. Arieh had become acquainted with the unfounded resentment, the sheer boundless passion directed against Jews in the land of his birth far removed from Israel. The conflict in the Middle East, however, had been shaped less by unconscious fantasies than by the reality of opposing interests.

Although Arieh held out hope for compromise – not for military solutions – by division of the territories as well as an end to the occupation and the terror, he obeyed the rules of the conflict. Arieh didn't vote for nationalistic parties that wanted to preserve the status quo and understood that politicians were already negotiating a settlement between mortal enemies. He considered this rapprochement to be a good thing and realized that the need for his talents would still be there even after a peace accord. His kind of work was in demand as long as assassinations were attempted.

The myth of the secret service spanned the entire world. People lowered their voices when its name was mentioned. The state had risen from the underground and originated during a time of persecution and opposition. The organization and its agents had enjoyed a good reputation in this pioneering era. At the time, it was said that they had waged a shrewd and courageous war against a superior force. After the many years of occupation of foreign territories, however, the image of the agency had changed. The reputation of the organization now was determined by the struggle against the revolt of a suppressed population, by the pursuit of terrorists, and by its embroilment in the bloody intrigues of the Middle East. It had become the brand name for harshness and intransigence. The earlier admiration for its style and goal had changed into a mistrust of its means. Even Arieh Arthur Bein had doubts about some of its actions since they appeared merely to worsen the possibility for agreement while the resolution of the conflict was becoming more and more concrete.

His colleague Nimrod Levy had it easier. There were no half measures for him and he considered any thought of a future reconciliation as treason. Nimrod Levy had entered the secret service at the same time as Arieh. They had completed their training together and repeatedly backed each other in emergencies. They were mutually indebted to one another, yet also bound by their rivalry which their superiors knew how to stir up and exploit.

For Nimrod, Arieh's illness after his mysterious encounter with Mullemann was a further reason for annoyance and jealousy. While Levy conducted operations in various countries, Bein was resting and relaxing at home with Navah and Jael.

On his way to his hotel Arieh went into a toy shop. In the store he had to smile at the unusual merchandise and he thought about Jael. He stopped in front of a basket of rubber balls, picked one up that was transparent and bounced it high above his head. He caught the ball, placed it in front of one eye and, keeping the other eye tightly shut, he looked through it at a rack with stuffed animals. The whole world was in a jumble, topsy-turvy, and distorted. All of a sudden he thought about four months ago when he had returned home from the hospital abroad.

It had been an April night in Tel Aviv. Arieh had called Navah from the airport without telling her that he had already arrived. He wanted to surprise her. He was startled when he entered a completely dark apartment. Nobody was there. As he wandered through the darkness, Navah's and Jael's absence puzzled him even more. He smiled to himself when he noticed that he had still not turned on the light – it was as if he were in someone else's rooms, as if he were on a job. He sat down in the pitch-black living room and thought about what might have happened.

Then he had an idea. He took out his cell phone and dialed his own apartment phone, the one which stood in front of him. He heard the ringing in the receiver he held but none in the room where he sat. Then he heard Navah's voice answer: "Hello."

He inquired: "How are you?" Neither one ever mentioned names during long-distance calls.

She replied: "Fine. I'm already in bed."

"I wish I could be there next to you. I really need you."

"Really?" she answered. He heard music in the background, Charley "Bird" Parker. It was turned down.

"Darling, would you do your husband a favor? Don't ask why. It's important. Put something on and take the cordless phone into the living room." He waited and then asked: "Are you there?"

"Yes."

"Open the balcony door and step outside." He carefully opened the sliding door and went outside as he had asked her to do. "Tell me, darling, isn't the view beautiful?"

"What?"

"I know that it's late and you're tired and alone. I can feel it. It's just the same with me. I'm lonely here too . . . "

"Listen . . . ," she began.

But he interrupted: "But in two hours, sweetheart, I'll be there with you."

"Really?"

"Surprised?"

"Very!"

"I didn't want to barge in on you – just raise your anticipation. I'm really looking forward to seeing you."

"You succeeded," she said and her laugh sounded desperate. He asked about Jael and she responded: "No, Jael is at my parents' house."

After their talk he left the apartment and went down to Jossis' bar. It had become clear that Navah had had the telephone company reroute their number to another place. Now she had two hours.

Arieh Arthur Bein was unsure of his feelings and didn't know what to do. Although he traveled from one country to another, incessantly lying to, deceiving, and cheating other human beings, he remained honest within two institutions: the secret service and his marriage. These were the fixed stars of his universe. He had never betrayed Navah and his colleagues nor been disloyal to them.

Shaking, he drank a barack, then a vodka and, as usual in an emergency, he called Nimrod. His friend answered and Arieh heard his "Hello" and music in the background. He listened to the syncopating saxophone – Charley "Bird" Parker – and again Nimrod's "Hello?"

Bein comunicated his return: "The goods have arrived. Everything is in top condition. I wanted to let you know, my friend."

"That's good to hear," Nimrod answered. "Praised be His Name. Great. Come to the office tomorrow."

Two hours later when he went back to the apartment, Navah ran into his arms. He neither let on nor did he reproach her in any way – neither that night nor any of the following nights. He believed there was only one way to win back his wife and her love. He had to fight for her – in secret. It would be a while before he would travel again and the next day, Arieh Arthur Bein reported that the agent Alex was sick.

The whole world was upside down. Arieh bought the rubber ball.

The girl was romping around on the veranda in the hotel. The woman was sitting in the hall. He walked up to the little girl and said, "Look" and bounced the ball. She looked up with her mouth wide open. "I'll show you something. Look with one eye through the ball. Shut the other one. Do you see? The whole world is standing on its head. Can you see it?" She nodded silently. "Do you like the ball? You do? What's your name?"

"Marie."

"What a beautiful name. Are you on vacation with your mother?" Bein asked where her father worked, if he was often in other countries, his name and what her mother called him.

The girl said, "Sayid" and: "Papa is coming this evening."

Arieh Arthur Bein smiled, rolled the ball to the little girl and whispered: "It's yours." Then he disappeared.

Weeks after he had called in sick, Navah had said to him: "You've made yourself into a mystery for your daughter. You hide what you think, what you do, who you were, what you are. You take pleasure in being someone unknown and inaccessible. You're a stranger to her. Don't you notice?"

"What are you talking about Navah?"

"Arieh, you're doing the same things to your child that your father did to you. Don't you understand? You're only a guest for us. She doesn't know who you are!"

He simply imitated her: "Who I am?"

During those months in Tel Aviv he spoke for the first time about his problems, his work, and even about Mullemann. Navah declared: "You can't find yourself in others, Arieh. When will you finally understand? Just like your father Jakov Scheinowiz, you act as if you were living underground and hiding from extermination – in eternal flight – under a pseudonym."

"I can't stop, Navah. They could close my file. If I break away, I'm dead for the organization, but my enemies won't forget me . . . Do you understand? . . . They'll hunt me down. Do you think there's a no man's land?"

"Haven't you covered up your part, wiped out your guilt yet?"

After this conversation Bein had to think about the tiny American traps for cockroaches. The tiny containers were called "Roach Motels" and the ad slogan ran: "They check in, but they never check out."

Nimrod had yelled at him: "There are others who will risk their lives for you."

Teddy had stayed calm: "There's no way out. How will you live? What else can you do? How do you imagine it's going to be? It's no picnic here! It's not a vacation spot! Who's looked after you up to now? We have! – Arieh, at least think about Navah and Jael and their security – even if you aren't thinking about state security. Arieh, we need you!"

Bein lay down on the beach in front of the hotel and watched the waves. After a few minutes he was asleep.

He dreamed he was sitting in a café. When one of the guests was called to the phone over the loudspeaker, a gentleman stood up and the waiter directed him to a phone booth. The man left the booth after a while, handed a packet of money to the waiter and disappeared from the café. Another one was called, hurried to the phone booth and afterward gave the waiter some bills and hurried out the exit. This was repeated at regular intervals. Once a name was called and two men stood up at the same time. They looked at each other and hesitated until the one who had stood up last, sat down. The other one went to the booth, gave the waiter money and exited. Then Arieh decided to be the first one to stand up at the next announcement as if only he could be the one who could be meant. The amplifier blared: "Mr. Peter Schwarz to the phone, please."

As he got up, he noticed that no one else had moved as much as a finger. He walked to the booth, picked up the phone and a voice said: "Your name is Peter Schwarz. You'll find your résumé and the documents in the slot behind the coin box. You owe the waiter eight thousand five hundred. Leave the café immediately." He hung up, pulled the papers out from behind the phone, stumbled out of the booth and opened his wallet in front of the waiter. He gave him the money and fled past a man in front of the exit who was watching him. Once on the street, Arieh understood: Peter Schwarz, the man who he now was and whose papers he had been given – this was the man he was supposed to kill.

Arieh Arthur Bein had awakened at the words: "I am not Pet . . . ," but the beach wind had diffused the sounds.

Bein looked at the ocean and at the women lying in the sand, ignoring the men next to them. Then he caught sight of Sayid: his hair was like a black bathing cap; he had a full beard and a muscular body. Arieh put on his sunglasses and began to rub sun screen into his skin. He dared not attract attention. He had bought Italian sun glasses and swimming trunks in the local fashion specifically for this purpose. Arieh now noticed that Sayid had bought similar styles.

Sayid romped around with the little girl Marie and smiled at his wife. He seemed to have forgotten all the caution that surrounded an agent like a discrete aroma. Arieh was immediately able to make out many adversaries by their attempts to disguise themselves into seeming older. But Sayid, Arieh thought, was not on duty and, for the moment, had left his work behind him. He was playing tag with the little girl at full volume and joking with the the bystanders who spoke to his daughter. Now Arieh's real work began. He had to find out Sayid's last name, where he lived and his habits. And he had to locate his weak points.

For such details he was able to use other people and occasionally he would do just that. A colleague would be smuggled into the hotel as a room waiter. Arieh left the beach, went to his room, showered and changed clothes. Then he set out for the lobby and engaged the porter in conversation. Earlier he might have broken into Sayid's room, but such an undertaking had seemed all too risky for the past few years. While Nimrod Levy had operated over time in an even more cold-blooded and unflagging manner, Arieh had gradually been intimidated by numerous fears. He proceeded with caution. For half an hour he chatted with an employee about the area, its history, the hotel, and the porter's wife who suffered from a female disorder. This topic created some intimacy between Arieh and the Italian since Bein fabricated the name of a medicine which he highly recommended as a cure. After that they began to gossip about the guests. Arieh soon found out that Sayid's last name was Taher.

That night Arieh headed for a bar. He saw his adversary sitting there on a stool. Arieh sat down next to Sayid and asked him if he could possibly have already seen him in the hotel where he was staying and if he were the father of that charming little girl. Mention of the little girl was the key that unlocked Sayid.

"What line of work do you pursue?" Bein asked.

Sayid smiled and ordered another whiskey: "You're right – I pursue it in the truest sense of the word."

"Let me guess. You're traveling on business."

"Nicely put. How do you know?"

"You represent a company?"

"You might say that."

"We share the same fate."

"Is that so?"

"That's right. The same profession. My name is Anton Maurer," Arieh said.

"Nice to meet you. Sayid Taher," Sayid answered. He spoke with a definite accent.

"Did you just take care of your business before you arrived?"

Sayid merely repeated: "Take care of business. . ."

"And are you satisfied," Arieh continued, "with the way things turned out? Did you get done what you had set out to do?"

Sayid fell silent. He cracked a smile and declared: "No," clicking his tongue and twitching his head upwards as is customary in the Middle East with a negative answer.

"Anton, neither am I satisfied nor have I taken care of anything." Taking a vigorous swig of whiskey, he continued: "The truth is, Anton, I didn't do my job. My work? What is it anyway? Traveling around? Taking care of things? No, I just wanted to get to my wife and daughter. *C'est ça.*" But then Sayid broke off, scrutinized Arieh, gulped down the rest of the whiskey and said with sudden gravity: "If you'll excuse me. My wife is waiting for me."

Later in his room Arieh rinsed out his hair, rubbed it dry with a hand towel and shaved his stubble. In the neon light his skin no longer seemed tanned in the mirror but paler than ever. His body was delicate and frail.

He decided to break off his job without finishing it. He would tell Teddy that he had not found Sayid and that his skills had disappeared. He took the first train in the morning and in a few hours reached the town where Navah and Jael were waiting for him. At the hotel he woke up his wife with a kiss. She smiled and pulled him down to her just like she had done when they had first fallen in love.

Later while he was still lying in bed she went into the bathroom. Jael stormed in and gleefully bounded onto the bed.

Suddenly he saw the rubber ball in her tiny hand, hesitated, and asked: "Where in the world did you get that?"

"A man gave it to me," she whispered.

Arieh mumbled: "That's nice. What did you talk about?"

"About you, Papa," and Jael held the ball in front of his eyes.

"Just look. You can see right through it. Just look, Papa. The whole world is on its head."

Sina

Ever since Kreuz had stepped out of the café into the blowing snow, that peculiar stranger with a cane and concealed face had been pursuing him. But hardly anyone was able to follow the old man unnoticed – too many had already tried it.

Kreuz ducked into a passageway around a corner and, in spite of his sore knee, he hurried behind the veranda of a building entrance in order either to shake off the stranger or to confront him. The younger man fell into his trap and stumbled past Kreuz, whose right hand closed around the nine millimeter caliber baretta in his coat pocket. From the darkness of his narrow hiding place, Rudi Kreuz cast out the question: "Can I help you with something, sir?"

The enshrouded man turned around without any sign of emotion. He had a Siberian air about him: tall, a down jacket, mittens, with his hood up and his wool scarf wrapped tightly around him – even his forehead seemed to be wrapped with rags or bandages. He murmured quietly into the frosty air: "It was me. I was the one. I did it."

Kreuz's eyes began to gleam: "You? You knocked him off?"

"I have murdered."

Kreuz smiled and said: "Terrific. You've already bumped him off."

"I killed . . . " the other man certified, but Kreuz continued:

"Bumped him off, that's what I said. That was quick service. Good for you! But why this stalking? We have a rendezvous. Were things getting too hot for you?"

"I've killed someone," the man beneath the disguise repeated.

The old man amplified his words: "That's right. For sure . . . Follow me and you'll get what's coming to you." When the stranger began to talk about culpability and liability, Kreuz, who in his old age had started to suffer from a hearing loss, assured him: "No doubt about it, debts have to be paid off. You'll get what's coming to you, Antonov."

But the man in disguise objected: "Call me Mullemann."

Kreuz laughed: "All right. You have already met the phantom of our city? Mullemann," he snorted, "has knocked off Waldser."

But when the stranger remained deadly serious, Kreuz cleared the joking from his voice, put up the collar of his cashmere coat, pulled down the brim of his green hat and said: "Follow me, but be inconspicuous."

In the office Kreuz handed the stranger a coat hanger, but he refused it and sat down in the chair in front of the desk. The older man sat down on the other side. "I have the money here," Kreuz said as he fiddled around with his silk scarf, fingered his gilded cuff links and smoothed out his blue pinstripe. For younger eyes the suit might be all too worn and extravagant – like threadbare and faded boasting.

The guest muttered: "I killed him in cold blood."

"Certainly. I don't doubt your professionalism. Our Slovakian friends recommended you to me just because of the coolness that marked your work already in frostier times. Besides, I'm acquainted with the Ice Age . . . You may come from the Cold War, but my roots are in the Tertiary – the Third Reich – you understand. Don't underestimate Rudi Kreuz. I'm a gray wolf from the Cretaceous period. But what do you know of that, my young friend."

"Nothing, except that I'm not your friend. Shall I tell you how it happened?"

"Antonov," Kreuz began, but the other man interrupted him:

"Please call me Mullemann. It was me. I was the one. I did it. Do you want to hear how he died?"

Kreuz was surprised at his guest's behavior, but remembered the words that his agents in Brno had used in recommending, even praising, this killer to him. He had been told that the murderer was an oddball, someone who planned his jobs perfectly and carried them out swiftly. But he also had the reputation of being an eccentric who only showed sympathy toward his cat and who got unpleasant when there was a breach of contract. If his customer didn't pay, he immediately had to fear for his own life. Rudi Kreuz studied his guest. Was the former agent of the Bulgarian secret service concerned about his fee? His remarks indicated otherwise. "Do you want to know how he died?" or: "It was me" – incomprehensible. The stranger probably wanted to intimidate him, to convince him of his dangerous unpredictability.

"If you want to and it's no trouble, you can tell me how Georg Waldser died. In case you don't want to, the money is in this briefcase – a half million. You can count it."

"I first want to talk about what happened . . . "

"As you like. I was and still am interested in your work. I've been a lifelong enemy of Waldser, and his death . . . ," but then Kreuz fell silent. Why should that young man from the Balkans who killed for money be concerned with the hatred between two old men. On the contrary, one of his kind must certainly want to know nothing about the disputes and entanglements that led to the crime since the more the murderer learned about his victims, the easier it became for an emotional attachment to develop between him and them: an emotional jungle of sympathy, a thicket of remorse and conscience.

Rudi Kreuz realized that the Waldser affair had been a melodrama from the beginning. That's why he had envied his former comrade in arms, this archenemy, and had him hunted, abducted, charged, and indicted. But he had never escaped Waldser, this man of principles. Destiny had bound them together until Kreuz put out a contract for the murder of his antipode. How liberated he suddenly felt!

Rudi Kreuz had never subscribed to an ideology and had never

joined a party out of conviction, although he had taken member-
ship at times for his own advantage. During his youth in the early
thirties he had attempted to become a renegade, a Lothario, and
free spirit who inwardly disdained morality, but who knew how to
demand it from others.

Rudi Kreuz wanted to be able to afford everything for himself
except morals. He never felt better than when he was making a
mess of things. He *tried* to be obnoxious. He wallowed in his
attempts. Consequently, it was as a *parvenu*, adventurer, and con
man that he had penetrated certain select circles. He had, moreover, found entry into the company of artists and would-be
revolutionaries where he looked for adventures, pranks, recognition, and upward mobility. At that time when anything offensive
became a passion for him, he sought out the company of Jews,
especially Jewesses. To be reflected in the eyes of these young
women exaggerated his sense of power. All of the admiration and
envy that he felt for them were counteracted by their alien allure,
by his knowledge of the aversion and hostility to which they were
exposed. They seemed *different* to him and reminded him of his
own inner being. Even before he had been in their homes, he
sensed that he had been summoned into a jail cell or brothel. He
felt he had reverted to the arousal of his childhood when he had
rummaged through his parents' bedroom and his mother's
clothing.

When emigration became the only escape from persecution for
the Jews, when their businesses had been plundered, their homes
raided, when they had been hounded through the streets, beaten
and raped – at this point, Kreuz, with his connections to the
families, gained their trust. At the same time, however, due to his
acquaintance with rabble-rousers and hotheads, he also gained the
interest of the new rulers. The *flaneur* Kreuz, who in reality had
been a *parvenu*, now became a fellow-traveler and status-seeker,
an agent for those in power – an informer. Yet it was to save his
own skin that he sold others out, not out of sheer malice toward
them. At the same time that he supplied the secret police with
information, he offered his services as a mediator to those being

persecuted. And in a sense, that's what he was.

This was how he had become the putative trustee of the refugees and their property. And it was in this context that he had met Georg Waldser, a smiling great hulk of a man, the Trotskyite resistance fighter and non-Jew who, even among the intellectuals, was an outsider. Waldser had been persecuted by the Nazis, libeled by the Communists, abandoned by most of the functionaries of the former unions, but finally betrayed by Rudi Kreuz. "You can get rid of Waldser," Kreuz had told SS Sergeant Gerbing at the time.

It was only after the War that Kreuz's hatred of the Jews erupted into the open. In every one that returned he saw a debt collector, someone who had come to collect what Kreuz withheld from the victims. Yet the survivors had just as little chance to prosecute Kreuz as those murdered, since, just at the right moment, he had joined the small band of guerrillas in the western sector that had rushed to the aid of the Allies. Kreuz, who had in the meantime become an intelligence expert and an experienced hand in investigating radical circles, simply changed bosses. He became an informer for the Americans, who magnanimously overlooked his former transgressions as well as those secondary sources of income that were ongoing.

He soon moved back into the apartment into which the former owner, an exiled Jew, had been resettled. Kreuz drove out this former owner for the second time since it was determined, with the help of his good connections as well as new regulations and laws, that Kreuz had neither aryanized nor misappropriated the flat, but had acquired it legitimately.

At the outbreak of the Cold War the Nazi informant was transformed into a professional spy, an agent. He traded in speculation and information. His dealings extended simultaneously into the murkiness of the black-market economy and into the twilight of enemy reconnaisance. His superior turned out to be that great hulk of a man, Georg Waldser, whose smile, Kreuz thought, had grown restrained. Waldser had managed to escape capture by the Nazis by fleeing the country.

He had returned home with the American Army, gotten rid of

his uniform, and become a citizen of the newly founded Republic. He stayed associated with the liberators and worked for their secret service because Georg Waldser wanted to help expose the erstwhile murderers. That's why he accepted even joint efforts with the collaborator Kreuz. As a cover, Waldser and the detested Kreuz opened up a business. Waldser, however, was no longer pitted against his archenemies, but against the new adversaries and onetime Stalinist allies. For most of his countrymen, the former resistance fighter had committed high treason; for the Americans, on the other hand, he remained a leftist, a subversive; for the left, he was a capitalist businessman.

In the early sixties, understanding and detente were beginning to materialize between Khrushchev and Kennedy; Madame Nhu in Vietnam distrusted the young American president just because he seemed to be conciliatory toward the enemy. At the same time, old war criminals – long overlooked in the turbulence of new conflicts and changed alliances after the victory – began to emerge. They were abducted from Argentina, sought for in Paraguay, tracked down in alpine villages and ocean port cities. To Georg Waldser the time for retaliation finally seemed to have arrived. It was then that he presented his co-worker Rudi Kreuz with a tab that had been overdue for years. He demanded full cash payment and insisted on balancing all of the Nazi informant's delinquent accounts.

At that time it was not difficult to get rid of Waldser. Kreuz said slanderous things about him to his friends in the East as well as in the West. Shortly thereafter Waldser was apprehended and interrogated by the Czechoslovakian authorities during an official trip to Prague. They forced him to sign a preformulated statement and let him go. On the basis of Kreuz's pointed accusations – concerning the hostile machinations of the enemy – but finally also because of the statement forcibly extracted from him in Prague, he was suddenly considered a traitor by his own staff when he arrived home. That the resistance fighter Waldser had already broken with his country during the War was taken as an indicator of his unreliability and disloyality.

Waldser, however, was not charged with treason but rather with commercial crimes. Businesses which he had used merely as covers for his secret contacts in the East formed the background of the fabricated charges. The judges – who had earlier wanted to arrest Waldser for his resistance activities and whose jurisdiction he had then escaped – came to the same decision that they had pronounced decades before: guilty as charged.

It was not the persecution during the time of tyranny that had broken Georg Waldser. Nor was it the chaos of war nor the intrigue of the great powers after the victory over the German Reich. Nor was it the failure of the world revolution to appear nor the return of the onetime criminals to the reins of power that extinguished his smile. But after he had been labeled a traitor to freedom and democracy and denounced again by the Nazi informer Kreuz, Georg Waldser had been swamped by wine and tears, washing away his belief in a society marked neither by the humility nor the dictatorship of the proletariat, neither by the submissiveness nor the despotism of the masses. His hope had been drowned in alcohol.

Rudi Kreuz had always remained a winner. There had been just one time when someone had been able to blackmail him and snatch away one of his early pieces of booty. The Jew Scheinowiz had appeared one day in a café threatening the Nazi informer with disclosures about the art works that belonged to the parents of one of his young Jewish acquaintances. He demanded their return to her. Kreuz had tried covertly to intimidate Scheinowiz and said: "Doctor, how's business? They've nabbed Waldser, you know; watch out. We live in different times."

But Scheinowiz had simply countered: "Everything is on the block, even me. Nothing holds me here." And, in fact, Kreuz had been unable to take revenge on the Cracow Jew. A few weeks later, Scheinowiz had disappeared without a trace.

All of this had happened more than two decades ago. Kreuz would most certainly not have wasted another thought about Scheinowiz or the fears of any disclosures concerning his life as a Nazi informer if Georg Waldser had not suddenly resurfaced. The

Cold War had become history and while old animosities appeared to have died out, even older ones were revived because they could no longer be concealed by the alliances of the postwar era. In the East reforms were announced, rulers deposed, elections held and states divided up anew.

As the ice in Europe thawed out, corpses floated to the surface. Archives in Moscow opened their gates, and documents in Berlin and Prague could be examined. So much dust was stirred up, it was said, that it took away the scholars' breath. In Washington, onetime pacts with the devil no longer seemed necessary, and former criminals who had been protected were no longer spared. The Americans even denied entry to that state president who had hidden his service in the armed forces – in close proximity to the atrocities – from the eyes of the world. So it was that the recurrent boozer Georg Waldser thought that his time had finally come since his name had also shown up in the documents of Eastern bloc countries. He had flushed out formerly secret masses of material that demonstrated his own innocence and proved Rudi Kreuz's double game. This time in fact, Rudi Kreuz had known only one way to avoid being exposed by Waldser.

"Now I'll tell you how he died," the disguised figure said. "Since it was me. I'm guilty. I did it." Kreuz looked at the coat which hung over his great hulk. There in his pocket was a baretta, but he kept another weapon, a revolver, in the top drawer of the table. His hand slid slowly over the tabletop. "I stood hidden behind the entrance to his apartment, but he turned around just after he had stepped inside before I could do away with him. With tears in his eyes when he saw me and a wine bottle in his hand, he suddenly laughed and asked: 'Somebody sent you to finish me off?' I pulled out my stiletto, but he lurched away and slammed the door shut. When he tried to lock it, I broke it down. There he stood, a piece of broken green glass pointed at me . . . "

Rudi Kreuz sprang to his feet, took hold of the knob on the drawer with his right hand, his briefcase with his left hand and cried out: "You just listen to me, Antonov . . . "

"Call me Mullemann."

"What do you want? Here's the money, take it!" He forced the disguised stranger to take the case, pushed him to the door and gasped out the words: "Get out of here before there's a disaster . . ."

After his guest was outside, Kreuz struggled to catch his breath. He took his handkerchief from his pants' pocket and wiped the sweat off his forehead. Exhausted and relieved, he then moved unsteadily to his chair.

But the man in disguise hurried down the stairs, his briefcase in one hand and swinging his cane in the other. Below, he went across the broad stone steps toward the porter, who had taken up arms against the slush with his snow shovel. The stranger stumbled and fell into the porter – a stocky old man – who yelled out. At this the stranger declared: "It was me. I'm guilty. I did it." He got himself disentangled and pushed open the door to the street.

Outside, he trudged on through the crowd, grasping his cane at midpoint, until he reached the entrance to a supermarket. Here he was enticed by the warm air pouring out of the heating ducts and caught up in the swirl of the other pedestrians thronging into the store.

A nondescript mix of musical sounds and conversational scraps surrounded him. As he stood in the cosmetic department, the clerks sprayed him with scents. All of a sudden he saw a young woman with pert green eyes and chestnut hair – he felt compelled to follow her; he was unable to do otherwise.

He watched her comparing various articles and then saw how she looked around before switching packaging, concealing the more expensive merchandise in less expensive wrappings and tossing it into her shopping cart. Lipsticks disappeared into her coat. As she tried out various things, fluttering from counter to counter, her hands trembled, her eyes flashed go, but her cheeks stood at red.

He sensed how excited and happy she was as she went about her business, keeping a lookout with furtive sidelong glances. He stayed behind her at the cash register and waited until it was her turn. Then, after she had placed the items on the conveyor belt, put them in a sack and took out her purse, a man – the store detective – suddenly blocked her path: "Just a moment, please. If you'd empty your bag and your coat."

Next came her protest, the grumbling of the crowd and the clerk's first shot: "Let's see what you've got." At this point the man in disguise stepped up and declared: : "It was me. I'm guilty. I did it. I stole the cosmetics. Arrest me."

A older retired woman cried out: "What were you thinking? The rest of us have to pay. It goes on our bill." But a pregnant lady countered: "Such prices are already a scandal." At that, a teenager asserted that the theft of something immediately consumed wasn't punishable anyway. The clerk shot back that if facial creme was something he'd like to consume, then he could kindly stuff his impertinent mouth with it. And, she went on, the stranger should open his briefcase. The detective abruptly asked if anyone had seen the thief and added that he knew the gentleman was completely innocent. In the meantime the culprit had disappeared into the confusion. Without waiting for an answer, he stormed out onto the street while those waiting their turn in line pushed their way toward the cash register. Shoving him out of the way, they paid no further attention to the eccentric in the down jacket and mittens who – hidden behind a scarf and bandages – continued to mutter: "I'm guilty."

Rudi Kreuz sat in an armchair in his office and had been staring straight ahead for about an hour. He was unable to do anything other than think about his archenemy Georg Waldser. There was a crack in the record he had put on – a Schubert trio, allegro, opus one hundred – wedged between two notes and a scratch. The old man nudged the player with his foot. The needle scraped over the vinyl grooves, the loudspeakers hissed and the piece started again from the beginning.

There was an abrupt knock at the door. Kreuz straightened up and hobbled over to open it. A man was waiting outside who wore a black coat and a hat with a narrow brim. "I'm here to get paid," the stranger said.

"Excuse me?" Kreuz asked, his mouth wide open.

"To get paid," the stranger repeated.

Kreuz barked out: "What do you mean? Get paid for what?"

The other man stepped past the old man into the office and whispered: "I delivered on time. We have an appointment."

But Kreuz squawked: "What are you talking about? That's impossible . . . Who's been delivered?"

The younger man glanced at the corridor to see if anyone was listening and Kreuz noticed a black kitten peeking out from under the stranger's coat. He said: "Listen to me Kreuz. It's me, Antonov. Waldser has been taken care of. Things are getting hot for me and I'm here for my payment." Antonov went into the room and sat down in the chair in front of the desk while Kreuz staggered around.

The old man lurched from side to side, slapped his forehead with his hand and groaned: "That won't do Antonov. You can't collect twice, once in disguise and now again . . . "

"What are you talking about Kreuz? You know that I've never been here before. I just want to get out of here. I've already checked out of my hotel. My suitcase is already in a locker at the train station. I have to carry around my cat; the train to Sofia leaves in two hours. Just pay up and I'll disappear again."

Kreuz paused and thought about the visitor who had been there. Then he said flatly: "But I gave away the money already to somebody else. Mullemann has it now. I don't have anything with me . . . Antonov?"

In the meantime, the Bulgarian had stood up. His cat leaped up onto the desk, crept over the calendar, jumped down to the carpet and brushed past the radiators in front of the window. Antonov's face reflected his contempt and anger, yet he spoke calmly: "Mullemann? Well, then, we were fortunate that it wasn't a Himalayan yeti since the money in that case would be long gone . . . Kreuz, our agreement was crystal-clear. I have more than my wages to lose. Think of my reputation! That's something I have to be very careful about – my very bad reputation . . . You will have heard about that and I can't let someone ruin it for me. Don't tell

me any shit about this city ghost, this guilt phantom that has the
whole city in a fever, or . . . "

"Antonov, I'm telling you: Mullemann was here – just an hour
ago. I thought it was you and I gave him all of the money – half a
million. That's not a trifle. There's no more here, and I can't get
any more at a moment's notice. You have to understand! Mullemann has all of the money. He's roaming the city collecting debts.
Eveything that's been denied . . . "

As he was talking, the old man tried to get his hand into the
desk drawer with the revolver, but the Bulgarian sensed what was
happening and recognized the danger. A stiletto shot out of his
jacket and between the ribs of the old man with the motion of a
professional killer. Before Kreuz knew what had happened, who
had paid whom or how much, he found himself on the floor again.
He noted that he, Rudi Kreuz, had been lying there for a long time
and that a record had gotten stuck again. He saw the blood
hemorrhaging from his body, heard the two notes and the scratch,
heard them getting softer and weaker, in the rhythm of his pulse
beat . . .

Antonov hurried down the stone steps of the staircase at the
same time that Rudi Kreuz's secretary was just getting into the
elevator on the ground floor. Carrying a bucket of sand and a
shovel, the porter was just stumbling in from the outside. On the
bottom steps that were slick today because of the snowy weather,
Antonov slipped and lurched toward the porter. He fell into the old
man's arms, knocking him to the ground on the marble stoop
outside in front of the oak door of the building's main entry.

The porter howled: "Can't you be more careful? Do you want
to kill me? That's the second time today. Has this turned into a
popular sport – has the St. Vitus's dance come into fashion? First
it was that walking mummy, those Pharaoh remnants, that
bandaged owl that dislocated my shoulder just an hour ago and
now you!"

"I'm very sorry," Antonov replied. He helped the porter up and
tried to be discreetly polite since he didn't want to leave any kind
of impression behind. With his kitten hidden underneath, he

wrapped his coat tighter around him. Rudi Kreuz's murder hadn't been planned but was an improvisation – otherwise he would never have taken Todor, the cat, along. For a moment the Bulgarian considered killing the custodian because he was a witness, but then he heard a door being unlocked and saw a fat woman in a hairnet – probably the custodian's wife – peeking out of her apartment door to see where the noise was coming from.

The custodian grew friendlier: "I wouldn't have gotten so excited if that lout hadn't knocked me down just an hour ago without an apology. You should have seen him. He looked like he stepped out of a horror film. He was completely bandaged up – really spooky. He threw himself with his heavy briefcase against my shoulder."

Antonov said goodbye and went on his way down the street. After his collison with the porter he now knew that there had indeed been someone all bandaged up roaming around the building and that he had passed himself off to Rudi Kreuz as Antonov. He had taken his money and, with this weighing in his briefcase, tumbled down the stairs. Antonov now decided to stay in the city for a few days to try to track down Mullemann. He had to find him – it was a matter of his reputation.

Antonov didn't notice the young woman with pert green eyes and chestnut hair. It was Sina Mohn, the art theoretician – a real beauty – who crossed his path. They walked past each other without noting the other's presence. Both were searching for the same man. She had been fascinated by this mysterious stranger who had wanted to take responsibility for her theft. She had been overwhelmed by the calmness and naturalness with which he had stood by her as if he couldn't do anything else. She wanted to see him again, her cavalier and the accomplice of her secret passion.

"The body was found by the secretary around one o'clock. She must have set foot on the scene of the crime a few moments after the murder," Siegwald Hammberger explained to his chief Karl Siebert who had just sneezed. The assistant Hammberger went on: "*Gesundheit*! Moreover, she's standing outside, chief, and we can question her. And apparently the porter is here too."

Karl Siebert was the foremost authority in the homicide division. He was a giant with his shirt stretched tautly over his paunch, his waist and belt pushed down to his groin, and his face swollen by red wine. Siebert asked the secretary to come in. She had not seen anybody suspicious and, like every Wednesday, she had only come to work in the afternoon. Siegwald Hammberger, his thin, blond hair parted neatly to one side, his pullover constricting his gaunt torso, white shirt and necktie, was in the meantime rummaging through the office files: "Chief, if you ask me, this Kreuz must have been a black marketeer."

"I most certainly won't ask you, Hammberger. Don't mix up the papers; just bring the porter to me. Right away!" the superior shouted at him. Siebert sneezed again, pulled a handkerchief out of his baggy pants' pocket and blew his nose. Feared by his colleagues because of his moodiness, the cop Karl Siebert was, however, repected for his shrewdness and his native feel for things. It was said that he had a nose for anything unscrupulous. Siebert hated his profession, his colleagues, dealing with body parts and murder weapons, yet he couldn't quit, couldn't stop the search for culprits before they had been found. His mood had gotten gloomier in the past few months, and at every opportunity he barked at his subordinate and his shadow, Siegwald Hammberger. Nobody understood why Siebert had been so ill-humored for several weeks, but the rumor was that the change in him had something do with that phenomenon that was in all the newspapers – that figure which announced its presence through anonymous letters and phone calls and seemed to know everything about every crime; that is, it had to do with Mullemann, whom everyone was talking about. That nonsense about a man of gauze bandages who had become the darling of news reporters and outstripped the master detective Siebert.

Siebert looked at the corpse. It had been stabbed to death with a stiletto just like Georg Waldser, whom they had found dead that morning. Waldser's murderer was unquestionably also the same one who killed Rudi Kreuz. There was no question that a professional killer had struck.

The custodian walked in. "Are you Mr. Franz Engel? Did anything suspicious happen today, Mr. Engel? Was anyone unknown to you in the building?" the commissioner asked.

The sturdy old man answered: "So there was, inspector . . . Excuse me, I meant to say commissioner. A stranger. Today at about noon – around eleven thirty – I had to go out to shovel snow. Someone completely disguised came tumbling head over heels down the stairs, fell on me and buried me in the snow. You've never seen anything like it! He banged into my shoulder with his briefcase. I thought it was dislocated. – I might not have thought about it anymore, but then an hour later someone else knocked me over again. Really though, I don't want to make a fuss about it since the man helped me up and apologized. But that first one you should have seen, commissioner. Like a figure at a masquerade – dressed up like a mummy – what am I saying, a masked man! He didn't even try to excuse himself or ask how I was after the fall. He just said: 'It was me. I did it,' and he was gone . . . "

"Really," Karl Siebert interrupted him and wanted to follow up.

But Siegwald Hammberger called out excitedly from the other room: "There's another room, chief! The light won't go on. There's another handle on the wall in the dark, chief." And in the next moment, the scream. Hammberger had turned the handle.

"Then I realized that the handle was a water faucet and I was in the shower, chief," Hammberger said, when he had found his way, completely drenched, out of the bathroom. Karl Siebert looked at his assistant. He hated this goblin Siegwald Hammberger, this eternal child of an official in the Department of Justice, Elmar Hammberger, who was just about to retire. Hammberger senior believed in the superiority of his whole family and despised commissioner Siebert because of his origins. Siebert, on the other hand, had rebelled in his youth during the late fifties and early sixties with American music and Italian pomade against senseless repetitive drilling and had tried to escape the oppressive atmosphere of suburbia on a motorcycle. He looked down on the quagmire of the high ministerial bureaucracy to which the

Hammmbergers belonged and felt disgust toward the mischief-making and bigotry of this elite class. It was an alliance consisting of conceit and arrogance whose fortune had required no competence.

"Quiet, Hammberger," the commissioner growled. He walked up to the window, sneezed, blew his nose in his handkerchief again and asked: "The man was all wrapped up? In gauze bandages? He said: 'It was me. I did it.' Do you remember if he also said that he was guilty?"

"Right," the porter agreed: "'It was me. I did it. I'm guilty.' It sounded like a confession."

The commissioner rubbed his hands and said: "Take this down, Hammberger. Notify all police units in the area and the media of a search for a masked figure wearing a down jacket, his face in bandages. He constantly repeats the words: 'It was me. I did it. I'm guilty.' He calls himself Mullemann!"

Everybody in the room looked at each other with consternation. "You're putting out a search bulletin for Mullemann, chief? For the phantom? Do you think that Mullemann was the killer?" Siegwald Hammberger asked. He obviously was asking less about his superior's suspicion than about his mental condition.

"Of course not, you nitwit," Siebert barked at him, "but this Mullemann has been at every crime scene. This man can be of help to us. Was that shower enough, Hammberger, or does your head need another one? The culprit is of course the other one!"

"The other one?" his assistant asked.

With total trust in his inspiration, the commissioner, his nose stuffed, replied: "Yes, the other one . . . Let the good custodian Engel give us a description of the second stranger, the apologetic one who knocked him over an hour and a half after the first collision – and so we get to the time of the crime, Hammberger! The one in bandages left the building much too early and was long gone. Besides – make a note, Hammberger – the most dangerous criminals have the best manners! We need an image for the search to send to all of the media. By the way, the killer most probably had a cat." Before the commissioner – who had suffered from allergies and the sniffles for decades and who had difficulty breathing when cats were around – was able to get his last word out, he fell into a fit of violent sneezing.

Four hours later, the double killing was already being reported in the radio news and the search for Mullemann was underway. Georgi Antonov hadn't heard the report. He retrieved his baggage from the train station, moved into a new pension, left his cat Todor there, bought himself some new clothes and prowled around again in the area in spite of the danger. He knew that the custodian would recognize him again and that he ought to have disappeared and that he was tightening a noose around his own neck. Yet for all his misgivings and reflections, and despite all caution, he was inexplicably still unable to give up his hunt for the man in the mask and his money. Georgi Antonov saw the police patrol nearby, and made out those police in civilian clothes with their collars turned up, the listening device in their ears and the wire down their necks.

The cultural theoretician and and artistic manager Sina Mohn had hardly heard about the search for the man in bandages on the radio, when she understood that it had been Mullemann who had sprung to her aid in the department store. Her dealings with this country's painters and sculptors, her preference for the avant-garde literati and theoreticians had awakened in her an understanding for and sensitivity toward those who were the objects of witchhunts. For it was those artists whose works she loved, who had once been slandered in this country and, who for the most part, had been driven out if not murdered. She didn't know the man whose eyes she had seen gleaming behind the bandages, but she believed that he couldn't be any more guilty than she was and that they were in harmony. This stranger had admitted in her stead: "It was me. I did it." It was a confession that echoed her guilt. She wanted to find her mysterious cavalier in the streets between the supermarket and her home before the police nabbed him.

Other people heard about the search for Mullemann on this evening. Mothers warned their children about men on the prowl walking around in disguise. Fathers muttered about the "bandage creature" living off the crimes of others and showing up everywhere in the country. He planted his traps and entangled everyone in his plans. It was not merely a matter of a phantom criminal, but of the web of politics, the entanglements of high finance, the embroilment of parliament that had steered and restrained the people for decades. All these had to be drastically trimmed with one ruthless stroke. Listening to their sons from their rocking chairs while watching the evening news, however, a few grandfathers warned that if all that should be brought into the open there would be terrible consequences. If these things began to unwind, the very bindings holding the community together would dissolve. And in the event that this "bandage man" really did exist and if he could reveal and expose the guilt of others, then his apprehension would mean the undoing of everyone who ran up against him, whether it be a policeman, guard, judge or jury member. Who – numerous grandfathers asked with quavering index finger – in this city and this country was free of guilt? How many crimes, squabbles, and animosities had been painstakingly swept under the carpet and how many bodies buried under ground? Should all the efforts of their generation have been in vain? Hadn't they covered over all the tracks during reconstruction, blotted out all the memories with their determined silence? Who knows, the old men wondered, which ghosts from the past were lurking beneath the layers of material covering this man? Who knows what secrets might slip out from this larva, this caterpillar that excreted confessions instead of a crimson fluid. We really ought to deport this Mullemann, drive him out, if not shoot him, the grandfathers murmured, waving their canes. But at this point, the children – worried about their fathers' hearts – handed the old men their sleeping pills, and they sank exhausted into their dream of earlier times.

Among those people who heard about Georg Waldser's and Rudi Kreuz's murder that evening and about the search for Mullemann was Israeli secret agent Arieh Arthur Bein. Bein was visiting the city where he had been born and had taken up quarters at the home of Leon Fischer, a friend of his deceased father who had himself become infirm in his old age. Bein pricked up his ears at the news of the man in disguise. It was just because of this Mullemann that he had come. Since he had run across the existence of this mysterious being – something he was unable to fathom – he couldn't carry out his job and, for the time being, had taken leave from his work in the Israeli security services in order to confront this figure. Almost six months before, he had returned home into the diaspora from Zion, home to that place of reverie and obliteration where generations of Jews had lived in doubt and uncertainty, dependence and servility. He had driven to the area where he spent his childhood in order to find the tracks of that *Dibbuk*, that specter covered with linen which pursued Bein even into his sleep and tore him from his Israeli dreams of the kibbutz and pioneering, of heroes and spies. It was true that Bein could justify his deeds and actions in that life-and-death struggle to which his country was exposed, but Mullemann had struck a nerve. During a puzzling encounter, this wrapped figure had clarified for him how those deadly enemies – that he, agent Arieh Arthur Bein, had found and exposed in his reports – had been murdered by special commandos. Mullemann could confess and divulge these secrets to anyone. He was someone who was informed about Bein, who could give witness to all his atrocities – he was someone Bein had to find.

"Have you heard about what happened to Rudi Kreuz?" Bein called out to the partially deaf Leon Fischer. Fischer, wearing a grayish-blue flannel suit with a beige vest, was just then shuffling through the door. He held a cane in his right hand and grasped the back of the chair with his with his left. Groaning, he slowly and carefully took a seat in the chair.

"Kreuz? Kreuz is an informer. Don't fool around with him! . . . Do you want something to eat?"

"You know him?" Arieh asked with surprise, but Fischer wagged his finger:

"Your father always said that Kreuz . . . "

"My father? How's that?" Bein interrupted him and assumed

that Leon Fischer was beginning to mix up people and names. His memory had been gradually strewn with shadows and splotches like his thinly worn skin.

"Listen carefully, Arieh: Rudi Kreuz was a Nazi informer and favored aryanization. He has countless victims on his conscience. After the War he simply rearranged his life and changed his life story. No one could prove anything against him. At the time, Georg Waldser, a former member of the resistance and Kreuz's business colleague – a decent man in spite of that – became the object of Kreuz's slander and court testimony. . . don't ask. . . he's an informer, a smuggler, a black marketeer. – Are you hungry? Shall I fix you a steak?"

"You knew Waldser too?"

"Waldser was innocent. At the time we didn't even understand what he was being accused of. Both had known about the matters charged against Waldser. Kreuz had participated in them and the government seemed to be interested, but they locked up Waldser for them. I plead with you: don't do any business with Kreuz! Incidentally, in case you don't want a steak, I could make you a salad. . . "

"Kreuz is dead. He was killed today. Waldser too, by the way, Leon. The police are looking for his murderer," Bein explained. Fischer expressed his sympathy only for Waldser.

After a long silence, Fischer continued: "The only one who saw through Kreuz was your father. He knew how to handle Rudi Kreuz."

"What is it you're saying about my father, Leon? What did he have to do with Rudi Kreuz?"

Leon Fischer twisted his mouth into a narrow smile. "One day your father got to know a young Jewish woman whose family had entrusted all of its art treasures to Rudi Kreuz, that traitor and *Ganev*, before escaping. As in so many cases, Kreuz claimed afterwards that all of this property had gotten lost in the chaos of the War. Your father put pressure on Kreuz and obtained this woman's property back for her."

"And who was this young woman?" Bein wanted to know.

"Well, who else? Your mother. They fell in love soon after they met. Jakov married her a few weeks later, moved and changed his name." While Arieh Arthur Bein reflected on his father, he clutched a vodka in his right hand and pressed the nail of his left thumb into the tip of his ring finger. Arieh scarcely knew anything about his father Jakob Fandler whose real name had been Scheinowiz.

"I could tell you a few things, Arieh, that you'd never ask me about. I've been saying for years that you should go with me to Cracow. Then I'd show you where your father and I come from. Maybe after that you'd know who you are," Leon Fischer said.

"Who I am," Arieh repeated in a flat voice and he said the sentence once more as a question: "Who am I?"

Leon Fischer answered: "That you must find out for yourself," and went on: "Should I make some chicken soup for you? You look so pale, my boy."

All at once Bein believed that his father's old friend had to be versed in every possible secret. In the course of his survival, nothing had remained hidden to him. The frail Fischer, whom Bein had gotten to know only after his father's death, made the impression of being invincible. The agent said: "They're looking for someone named Mullemann in connection with this murder. You must have heard of him. His name shows up regularly in the newspapers, his letters of confession have been broadcast on the radio and there have been programs about him on television. Do you know this Mullemann?"

Leon Fischer brushed the remark aside and giggled: "Just because I know something about Rudi Kreuz, I should now be able to tell you about Mullemann? At first you thought I was senile because I talked about Waldser, Kreuz, and your father. Now you think I also ought to know this *meshugana*. No, I don't know anything about Mullemann, but he's surely not the one who murdered Waldser and Kreuz. Who knows who Mullemann is? He doesn't know himself. What is he? A human being who chases after other people's crimes? A feather duster gathering up guilt by dusting off everything that's been denied? A rag picker who trades in sins? Whoever he is, the others will make a Jew out of him. Don't forget, the guilty party is always the Jew. First, he'll be crucified and then worshiped. That's always been their custom . . . Either the Jew Süß or the pure Jew, the devil or the saviour, Jesus or Judas; because when he's not a saint, the Jew is a Shylock, a demon . . . Just one thing is clear, Arieh: Mullemann is not unlike you . . . Don't interrupt me. I know nothing about your work or what you've achieved – in fact, I don't want to hear anything about it – but just like this Mullemann, you think you can find yourself in others. You're looking for yourself in others' crimes. You consider your destiny to be in the fight against enemies, traitors and terrorists . . . This Mullemann also reminds me of Tonja's grandson. Tonja Kruzki – that was a woman! In any case this Dani Morgenthau – maybe you knew him before you emigrated – Dani ran around as a child and delighted us with his confessions. He claimed to be guilty of everything. We thought he was kind of a cute little rascal, a clown, until we understood one day that the boy didn't appear capable of any feelings of his own or of any other expression. Later, he suffered from a rash, something that saddened his parents half to death."

"Dani?" This caught Bein's attention. "Sure I knew him. This might be useful for my search. Do you know where I can find him?"

Fischer shrugged his shoulders. "Not a clue. It's as if the earth swallowed the boy whole; he has to have left the city. His parents have spent many a sleepless night because of him. Don't ask . . . That's how you children are. All those murdered are supposed to find their resurrection in you – let me finish! – we wanted to survive in you. We wanted to buy our freedom from our guilt feelings toward the victims and transfer all the debts to your accounts, to those *Jungellachs* like Dani and you. Like it says in Jeremiah: 'The fathers have eaten sour grapes and the children's teeth have become tarnished.' – I don't know what became of Dani Morgenthau. But there's one thing I do know, Arieh. It may be that you've been forced to live with the legacy of our burden of guilt, but if you want to set yourselves free from it, you have to look into history's register. The only way out of the past into your own future goes through memory. Come with me to Cracow – otherwise, you'll get like this Mullemann. You'll turn into someone who has given up, like those figures in the camp we called *Muslims*, those doomed who waited for the end in rags and had given up all hope."

Bein had listened without saying a word, and Leon Fischer continued: "Do you remember the old saying: 'If you are you because you are you and I am I because I am I, then you are you and I am I. But, if you are you because I am I and I am I because you are you, then you are not you and I am not I.' – Shall I fix you a herring, my boy?" Arieh Bein sipped from his vodka and both were silent for a while.

All at once, however, as if he were dealing with a scientific problem, the Israeli agent spoke: "First, I have something else to take care of, Leon. Right now, I can't go with you to Cracow. But maybe, if I disguised myself, you know, and walked through the streets with bandages covering me, maybe then people who know Mullemann would take me for him and speak to me. That way I could maybe find people who know where he's staying. I have to get hold of him, so . . . Leon?" But Leon Fischer had fallen asleep at these last words, maybe from boredom, more probably, however, because of the exertion caused by the fantasies in which the son of his dead friend Jakov Scheinowiz had become entangled. All of the attempts to shift Arieh's thinking in new directions were extremely taxing.

Bein looked at the old man and smiled. He got up, taking care not to make any noise, and took the wool blanket off the sofa. Then he extricated the cane from the old man's shriveled hand, buttoned up his collar, put the blanket over him and turned off the light in the room.

Sina Mohn walked up and down the streets and alleys of the area where she lived looking for Mullemann. She tried to put herself in his place. Where would she have hidden? The movie theater next to the supermarket near her apartment occurred to her.

She waited in front of the exit for the next film to end; then she saw the man in bandages emerge with his cane and briefcase. He had spent the last few hours there, in the dark and out of sight. She hurried toward him but noticed a man on the other sidewalk across the street also heading toward the shrouded figure. He, however, slowed down his stride when Sina came to a stop in front of Mullemann. Georgi Antonov paused and turned away in order not to be obvious. Suddenly, he saw two policemen scouring the area coming toward him and, cursing his luck in Bulgarian, he jumped into the streetcar that had just pulled up at the bus stop.

Sina Mohn stood right up close to Mullemann and whispered to him: "I think, we know each other." He did not turn a hair, but Sina thought she saw a distant smile flickering in his eyes.

He then nodded and whispered: "It was me. I'm guilty. I did it."

Sina Mohn smiled and said: "Just as I thought." When she took his hand, he was startled, but she went on: "If you'd like to grab a bite to eat, you can come to my place. I stocked up today as you know. There's enough for two." As he still hesitated, she was aware that they might become obvious and added emphatically: "Come along. You can't stay here."

While Georgi Antonov rolled off in the streetcar, policemen in uniform and detectives investigated, while the radio repeated the news of the search on the hour, and while Arieh Arthur Bein looked for bandages in Leon Fischer's apartment – Sina Mohn put up her umbrella as if fending off the sleet. She held it in front of the disguised man's face and dragged him after her. Several people watched the woman in the leather jacket closely, but no one recognized the man.

When they got to her place she wrestled him out of his down jacket and extricated him from his pullover. With his head bowed, he tried to counter her efforts by moving away. Sina smiled and said: "Don't be a child. Somebody has to take care of your bandages." She removed several layers of clothes and rolled up considerable amounts of gauze before he balked, doubled up with pain and drew in a breath between clenched teeth. She observed the inflammation and rash; she applied ointment to the cracked skin, lubricated the blisters, smoothed out the mesh of material and skin and changed parts of the bandages. After she had given him a towel and a fresh change of underclothing, she left him alone in the bath and prepared a soup.

While he was eating, he began with his admissions and confessions, which, as she immediately recognized, dealt with her most secret dreams. They were about that hobby which she pursued after working hours: her nimble-fingered plundering expeditions through the gigantic department stores, her pillage of exquisite items in markets and boutiques. He described the bustle of the customers in the stores, the gong that sounded before announcements, the music in the background, and the clerks' patient gestures. As he began softly depicting the excitement that took hold of Sina every time she shoplifted, she suddenly felt her temperature rising. As Mullemann began speaking about her most concealed passions, her breathing began to be labored and her cheeks became bright red. All of this started to overwhelm her, to arouse her anxiety, because there was nothing the art theoretician Sina Mohn feared more than losing the solid ground under her feet. So she decided to be done with this phantom, to throw him out that very night.

She interrupted him harshly, smoothed back her hair, folded her napkin and asked what he had in his briefcase. He handed it over to her with the words: "I'm guilty." When she opened it and saw the numerous bills, she jumped up in alarm and screamed. But then, after a short silent pause during which he stared anxiously at her, she let her fingers slide over the money and burst out laughing. Now Mullemann, for the first time, also began to roar. She threw the money packets into the air, their individual excitement joined into a single exuberance, and they wallowed in the shower of bills. When Sina finally saw him happy and looked into his radiant eyes, her fear of this city phantom – his mysteries and rashes – melted. She knew that she could no longer send him out onto the street into the arms of his pursuers.

He spent the next few weeks at her place while the entire city searched for him. When she came home from work, he was waiting for her. Then she would apply the ointments, massage him, and change the gauze. Gradually, his rash seemed to let up at the same time that her hands soothed his injuries and her fingers eased his agony. He no longer wore many bandages since the sores, although not fully healed, were receding. Over time Sina neglected her adventures, forgetting and finally losing the urge that had driven her kleptomania. Mullemann's disclosures were just too exciting. She hurried home from the museum where she worked to hang on his lips and listen to his declarations of guilt, her passions aroused by his confessions. While she removed his clothes, groping at his bandages in order to straighten the gauze, her face burned with shame and desire and they became entangled. Coiled up together in a ball, they rolled onto the floor, gasping, panting and frolicking among the wrappings. During those nights Sina's neighbors could hear her through the frosted glass in the stairwell calling out: "Yes, yes, I'm coming . . . I'm coming!"

Right after that they heard the cock crowing, the cock-a-doodle-doo from her mystery lover: "No, No! It's me . . . I did it! . . . I'm the guilty one!"

Navah

Otto Toot stood in the cold of his unheated studio. He had been walking around in front of his painting for hours, swaying back and forth, taking measurements, and stretching his thumb out in front of his eyes. He mixed the paint and applied his brush – an experiment. As the paint mass dried, he mixed the shading, then applied the oils very liberally since Toot's paintings were like low lying mountain chains surging up in relief.

Because he painted in thick, dense layers, the entire room was pervaded by the smell of soft resin, of linseed oil and binder. Toot couldn't get enough of these odors; he was addicted to them. At the same time, he couldn't describe the material's scent. It was like bread – a unique and distinct smell. He believed he could recognize the works of various artists with his eyes closed merely by their aroma. It depended on the colors the painter used, how thinly he diluted them with turpentine or how thickly he spread them on the canvas, as well as on the charity in his heart or the level of precision in his mind as he went to work.

It was the same with his own portraits which he could make out just by sniffing them. The picture of his former lover, for example – "Helga's Emergency Likeness" – always stank like dog piss when it was raining. Toot had long been bewildered about his success in capturing in the painting the memory of her miniature fox-terrier, Puschkin, a creature driven by jealousy and a biting instinct. His bewilderment lasted until the day he stumbled over a stack of art books.

He fell and landed right in front of Helga's image. Only then did he notice the hairy channel of dried-up substance, the grimy remainder of the urine stream that had trickled into the cracks of the frame. Pushkin himself had made that contribution. Without it, the portrait would have been incomplete in Toot's eyes and nose. With it, the work now seemed a total work of art.

The art student Otto Toot worked on nothing but the depiction of human beings, the reproduction of acquaintances and self portraits. But it wasn't individual characteristics, hair color or eyes that interested him. On the contrary, Otto Toot, who had chosen his alias carefully, made his figures unrecognizable. He first sketched and then disguised them. He sealed all of them up, painted bandages on them, embellished the gauze with needles and clasps, put limbs in support braces, or shortened one leg to a stump with blood dripping into a puddle underneath. Sometimes he pressed elastic ligatures, a cotton wad or a pair of scissors into the paint layer and ripped open the canvas, finally dyeing the seams and ragged edges red and patching them up with sutures. Toot transformed wallpaper patterns in the background into welts, mocking the flesh. If he painted a light bulb, it appeared in the form of an abscess and suggested a running sore.

When Otto Toot saw surgical dressing, he couldn't turn his eyes away; they simply got caught up in the bolts of white material. A pedestrian wearing a cast on his leg disconcerted and flustered him. When he bought his art supplies at a pharmacy, his voice became hoarse and he began to stutter: corn plasters and toe cushions; triangular cloths and adhesive plasters; compresses and splints. When he uttered these words, Toot lowered his voice and his eyes dropped in embarrassment to the floor.

He stuttered out his order and was ashamed to buy supplies he didn't feel authorized to use. The young female pharmacist often misunderstood this shyly spluttering and guilt-ridden man. "One compress," Toot whispered.

The pharmacist: "Condom?"

"No, com-press . . . press," he muttered.

The painter was enthusiastic about clinical instruments in general and used every possible occasion to employ his mania in the assignments given him by professors. While his devotion to his passion was first scoffed at as a whim, the situation changed in the course of the few weeks after Mullemann made his appearance.

The figure of Mullemann, not dissimilar to all those images in Toot's creations, haunted the country. Every newspaper and magazine featured reports about him. He was a favorite topic in the feuilleton. This phantom had appeared first in anonymous confessional letters. He had admitted to various crimes and, over time, to more than he possibly could have committed. The reports about Mullemann threw the real culprits into a panic, the police into an uproar, and politics into a state of commotion. Inspectors and commissioners undertook searches for this apparently omniscient fugitive. All of society had fantasies about this individual who roamed the city in gauze bandages. Everyone speculated about which offenses and about how many crimes he would still confess.

If there was one person this didn't concern, it was Otto Toot. Still, the general interest in Mullemann did worry him, since he was afraid that the public might now believe that his paintings were a reply to this public ghost. He certainly didn't want to have any success based on this kind of misunderstanding.

Art in this country was often perceived merely as scandal and therefore in the reverse formulation as well: scandal as art. Under these circumstances Toot had come under the scrutinizing eye of the scene. A small market niche had opened up. During a private viewing at a bank branch that evening, one of Otto Toot's pictures was exhibited.

Otto Toot was still standing, his legs spread apart, in front of the easel and canvas in the studio that he shared with a few other colleagues. His eyes were calm and bright; his curls hung down over his forehead in front and far down his neck in back; even his brows and lashes were flaxen blond. He had thick lips, a broad nose and a bovine face on a bull's neck. His small but stocky body was nimble and powerful. His guileless expression contrasted with the tension in his muscles, the strength and ardor in his fingers. He still held his painting tool in his right hand. Toot looked at the clock on the wall and noticed that it was time to wash out his brushes, get ready and change clothes so he could be at the bank on time.

The art theoretician Sina Mohn – a slim woman with chestnut hair that had been cut in a bob a few weeks earlier – also left her museum office a little early today so that she could stop for a while at the bank's talent show.

She was an expert in and manager of the avant-garde and lectured on the subject at the academy. If she wanted, Sina Mohn could help an artist whom she liked or, as was sometimes said, discover him.

In contrast to Toot, Sina Mohn had no fear of the market conventions and its usual duplicities. She took these externalities for granted, even allowed for them but counted on quality alone to triumph in the long run over packaging, price tag, and the artist's name. She counted on quality to decide the value of an art work.

What enticed her in the first place, however, was what she had heard about Toot's pictures, about his paintings of disguised figures, those bandaged-up forms wrapped in gauze and racked with pain. Sina Mohn knew of various, particularly local avant-garde traditions which emphasized the painting-over of portraits, the depiction of pain, injuries, scars, blood orgies as well as bandages and masks. She could talk about her associations and the roots of these bloody subjects. She was familiar with Catholic depictions of Christian saints pierced with arrows, impaled on stakes, nailed to crosses, roasted on fires, and battered by stones. These were bodies in extreme pain that found their way to redemption through martyrdom.

She got to the bank after the official opening. As a result she escaped the board director's speech and was able to sneak in without creating a stir. With her eyes to the floor, she got by with a nod to the right, a quick handshake to the left and wasn't forced to greet anyone else. She hurried past the few people who had come despite of the winter cold and now were pressing toward the buffet in the foyer. Hardly anyone paid any attention to the works. Only a few individuals – a lady in a fur coat, a female student, her dyed blond hair in a crew cut, with a companion dressed entirely in black – roamed through the back rooms where the least known artists were exhibited. They moved from one painting to the next. With the exception of Sina Mohn, however, no one dared go into the third room, an officelike space that seemed off limits.

Unbuttoning her coat, Sina strolled through the exhibit without stopping. She came to a halt, however, in front of the last and only picture on the long side of the room, and with her mouth agape, stared at it in complete abandon. Her eyes scoured the painting's surface, feasting on the portrait. She stood there without moving.

Otto Toot had recognized Dr. Mohn as soon as she had entered the building. And, at a proper distance, he had followed her, peering around the corner where the art expert stood hidden from view. He knew a few of her essays and had heard some of her lectures. He respected her views even if they didn't always reflect his tastes. Craning forward, he looked at the shaved neck underneath her red hair. Here above the cervical vertabrae, a rhomboid-shaped spot began to flare up. It was a tiny blood speck that always began to glow when she got excited. Sina Mohn had forgotten about this fiery mark, this skylight into her innermost being, since up until a few weeks ago, the nape of her neck had been covered by a mane of hair. Otherwise she would have used great caution and circumspection in hiding the window of her soul under make-up.

Sina tried to keep her composure, but she had never before

seen anything similar. The oil painting bore the title "Ahasuerus." It was constantly changing and aroused in Sina a series of diverse impressions. She continuously discovered something new in it. The character of "Ahasuerus" shimmered in the succession of changes within her, her thinking, her look – it reacted to her point of view. The depiction flowed into several vanishing points and, with every new position of the observer, the portrait was transformed. Ahasuerus turned his masked face in Sina's direction, and she returned his gaze. As she began the slightest bow, Ahasuerus rose up. His figure grew into a threat, an accusation. The representation reminded her of portraits of absolute monarchs in which the rulers' eyes seemed to rest on their subjects, seemed to follow their every step and turn. It was a painterly trick that in some mysterious way Toot had accomplished, amplified, even perfected in his "Ahasuerus." It was not only because the sense of Ahasuerus's face had been narrowed to a slit – the masked figure looked down at her through a darkened crevice – and not only because the visual sensibility behind the crack as well as the entire figure moved with Sina, but rather because his attitude and impact changed with each new perspective. All of this would have been nothing more than technical gadgetry, the performance of a magic trick – less a work of art than a gimmick – yet Ahasuerus's essence was not solely dependent on the beholder's position. Sina noticed that the effect of the painting went deeper, aiming at her most hidden emotions. The truly unique thing about "Ahasuerus" was that it returned her gaze. At first, when she had been searching for something that stood out from the less successful works, Sina had merely been surprised by it. Now, unpleasant, even painful thoughts forced themselves upon her, as if "Ahasuerus" were behind them. She now felt like her thoughts were being shadowed and exposed. She had set out to discover him, but in the meantime it was she who had been discovered. The figure forced her into an inexplicably sad state of mind and her vision became blurred. It dawned on her that Otto Toot's "Ahasuerus" was a kind of mirror that, instead of the observer's exterior, reflected an inner light and blind spot: one's own conscience.

Navah Bein entered the bank but hesitated before continuing on when she saw the people at the buffet. She probed further into the back rooms, past the drawings, installations as well as past Otto Toot who followed her with his eyes. In the last room she went toward Sina Mohn, smiled pleasantly and asked: "Excuse me, where can I change money here?" Her German sounded more guttural, darker and more cutting then usual.

Sina Mohn woke up from her reveries, hesitated and then replied: "You can't change your money here any longer."

"Why not?" Navah wanted to know,

But Sina continued: "Nowhere . . . It's too late. The branch is closed. All the banks in the city are closed by now. This is an opening, an exhibit."

Navah Bein nodded and said: "Yes, so I thought . . . So, it is too late." At that point her eye lit on Toot's portrait. Startled, her hand jerked to her mouth. Behind her hand, a slight gasp and something held back.

"Right," Sina Mohn whispered, agreeing with her hidden outcry. "Exactly! It's unbelievable, isn't it? The painting is called "Ahasuerus" and the artist goes by the name Otto Toot . . . it's a pseudonym . . . Otto Toot . . . an anagram . . . he's still completely unknown, yet . . . do you see? . . . no one has ever painted like that. Just look. Do you see it? It moves and changes. The figure Ahasver has us in his sights. He's in motion, following us, probes our innermost being, takes root in us. You see, that's your self-portrait! No, listen, what I mean is that you're looking at the image of your soul."

The Israeli citizen Navah Bein grew rigid and stared suspiciously and with astonishment at Sina Mohn. She wondered if Sina had recognized her Jewish background from her accent and was making an allusion to it. She tried, however, to keep her suspicion in check that she had hit upon an anti-Semite. "Why my self-portrait? Do you think that there's a resemblance between me and Ahasuerus, the eternal Jew?" She added with a grin: "You probably mean a kind of kinship, right?"

"That's it, a spiritual affinity," Sina Mohn continued excitedly,

unaware of the undertone. "The painting touches on our own conscience, on all the guilt and shame that we have to bear and face.
It speaks to everything we've denied, concealed, and falsified.

These last words had a certain calming effect on Navah Bein.
Since this local woman was baring her soul to the picture of
Ahasuerus, she opened herself up to it as well, became absorbed in
it, yet a part of her rebelled. There she stood, Navah Bein, a
historian from Tel-Aviv who for years had researched the history
of the Jewish community in Czernowitz and its annihilation. She
had by chance entered a bank in this country – the native land of
Lueger and Schönerer, Hitler and Eichmann – in order to change
some money and, in the process, stumbled across the depiction of
this gauzelike figure, an Ahasuerus, an eternal Jew, a ghetto figure.
The artist had obviously not intended a pernicious caricature and,
possibly, just the opposite. From some level in her, however, the
thought surfaced: "That's the way they've wanted to see us in the
past and still want to see us: In rags and wreathed in our wounds,
crushed, bound up and injured. The eternal Jew has always been
worth an exhibit to them. The fathers condemned him as
subhuman, the sons make him a saint. No one here is interested in
what's going on in Tel-Aviv, in Jewish survival, Jewish self-
awareness, the *Jischuw*, the pioneers, the *Chaluzim* from Petach
Tikvah or the kibbutzniks from Degania."

Maybe, Navah thought, she was just defending herself against
the expressive power of the painting. Maybe she was unable to
bear the representation of suffering, the persecution, and victimi-
zation that she saw there. At the middle school in Jerusalem that
she had once attended, there had been history lessons about the
Palmach – the unterground battle against the English – and the
battles against the Arabs. Their history teacher, a native of Russia,
could scarcely talk to the children about the ghettos, camps and
killings. She began stuttering severely as if it were a personal
disgrace and embarrassment. Navah looked at the masked figure,
at the bandages, and she had to think about her husband, Arieh,
who weeks ago had traveled back to this city where he was born
and back into that past that she saw reflected in the portrait. Why

had he returned to this country? Why was Arieh suddenly trying to be like such a bum, such a torn and tattered tramp. How could he possibly find himself in this degradation and humiliation?

Sina Mohn, the academy lecturer, sensed the foreigner's consternation and revealed to her: "I want to confess something to you that probably sounds unbelievable. This is not a fantasized picture. It's not an invention nourished by newspaper accounts. He looks exactly like that. I know it for a fact. This man is my lover! Just hear me out! I have no idea when the painter met him, but there's no question of an error. That's a portrait of my lover! You must think I'm crazy . . . Maybe, but I had to tell somebody and since you're apparently a foreigner, I'm taking the risk of letting you know my secret . . . you, of course, don't believe me . . . but I had to confide in you . . . another human being, a woman, a total stranger . . . I see him every evening . . . Forgive me if I'm boring you . . . "

Astonished, Navah Bein looked at the depiction of the masked figure and could no longer suppress her suspicion: "You meet him in the evenings? He looks like the character in the painting?"

Sina merely nodded, her eyes still locked on the picture and a smile on her lips: "That's right. That's it . . . You must think, I'm a high-strung romantic who goes into raptures like a teenage girl. The whole thing seems ridiculous. You have to understand that it's secret! Nobody can know about him . . . or our love."

"How long have you known him, did you say? For five weeks?" Navah tried to ask casually.

Sina thought about it: "I don't think that I said. But yes, for about five weeks."

"And the painter did him justice?" Navah asked.

"More than that. The painting reproduces his secret skills."

"His skills?"

"He can see others' guilt. He finds it. That's his idiosyncrasy, his distinguishing characteristic." But Sina Mohn stopped here, because she sensed that she had said too much and exposed herself to a stranger. "Sorry, I have to go now . . . excuse me . . . "

She tried to turn away, but Navah who now felt her jealousy

confirmed, blocked her path. "My name is Navah. I come from Tel-Aviv in Israel and am new to this city. You said we should confront what we have disavowed? That we couldn't run away from it, right?"

Sina Mohn's preoccupation with this country's modern period and with those artists slandered and exiled because of their art had nourished in her a sensitivity and empathy for the persecuted, and for the Jews murdered by the Nazis as well. Sina Mohn felt that encounters with Jews put her to the test since the art theoretician remembered what prejudices her father, Horst Mohn, had suggested to her as a child. She was aware of her family background and although she had rebelled for years against her forebears, their past and the animosities passed on to her – if not just because of it – she distrusted her own unconscious, the depths of tradition. In conversations with Jews she chose every word with care, suppressing words or swallowing those on the tip of her tongue, always ready to retreat. Not only did she conceal what seemed questionable to her, but also what might be misunderstood. Such a meeting was a rendezvous on a minefield.

The spot on her neck glowing, Sina Mohn said: "Pleased to meet you. I'm Sina Mohn."

Navah pondered how she should frame the conversation with the art expert because even if her suspicion was substantiated, she had no reason to reproach Sina Mohn since she seemed so innocent. With great care she asked: "Why do you think the painter named the picture Ahasuerus?"

Sina repeated: "Ahasuerus . . . Maybe because he wanted to confront us with guilt – through this Jewish figure of atonement . . ."

At this point, however, Navah interrupted and, quite unintentionally, all the rancor that had built up inside her spilled out into the open. "What's that? Ahasuerus is hardly a Jewish figure of atonement! The story of the eternal Jew has to do with the curse of the itinerant journeyman who is in constant flight from his crime. The figure originated in Christ's Passion. If I'm not mistaken, it was a shoemaker who didn't allow Jesus to rest in front of his house on the way to Calvary and now . . . as the story goes . . . has to wander around until the Final Judgment. My dear Mrs. Mohn, Ahasuerus is not a Jewish figure, but rather a Christian invention that has been used against the Jews. An anti-Semitic myth, to be more exact!"

What Sina had wanted to prevent had now occurred. That first minefield explosive charge had gone off. "That I didn't know," she whispered.

Navah shot back: "Of course not. Nor did the artist know it. An entire country knew nothing, claims to have known nothing. The image of Ahasuerus is a part of tradition – it's accepted and then handed on. Is your lover a Jew?"

Sina intended to say: "I think you've misunderstood . . ."

But Navah interrupted: "This man tracks down guilty parties, you said. I know, he recognizes them by their crimes . . . The painting captures him perfectly. You're absolutely right, he looks exactly like that . . . I guess he didn't give you his real name, or did he?"

Sina suddenly realized that she was not in a quarrel about ideology or the past, but that it concerned her lover. "Why do you want to know what his name is?"

With a nod in the direction of the picture and with perfect composure Navah Bein answered: "Do I want to know what his name is? Did I ask you that? Not at all, my dear. It's not necessary. I simply said that you probably don't know his real name, since in all likelihood, he never said it – to you, at least." With these final scorn-drenched words – a phrase Navah Bein had not been able to suppress – an open feud had broken out.

Navah regretted it, but Sina was already exploding in response: "What do you mean by that? I've heard quite enough of your innuendos. You can't just show up and use that tone of voice. I won't stand for it! Do you think you can say anything you want?"

Her voice as cold as ice, Navah replied: "Oh yes, just show up and say anything I want, right? . . . Don't interrupt me! I know you didn't mean it that way and that you didn't know anything. In any case, I'll bet you don't even know your lover's name, not even his last name . . . Now you get quiet all of a sudden!" Navah hissed. "Now you get quiet! As a matter of fact, he never tells anyone his name – for professional reasons . . . Anymore than that I'm not allowed to say, even though I know his name. Actually, it's my name too. Yes, that's right, the man is my husband. Really! He's always on the move in various countries, and naturally we can't expect absolute loyalty from one another . . . but after a job has been taken care of, the affairs no longer have any meaning. It's sad but true. I should think he would have told you, Ms. Mohn. Don't you think so? I'm sorry, it really wasn't very nice of him . . . I hope, I haven't hurt you."

"I'm grateful for your solicitude, Mrs. . . . what was your name?" Sina said.

But Navah Bein only smirked: "Just call me Navah."

"Navah, okay, and what else?"

"Navah, that's my given name. It's Hebraic. Under other circumstances you haven't been so formal when it was a matter of the family names of your acquaintances or lover." The two women, locked in battle, stood facing one another in front of the picture of the masked man.

"You seem to be in greater distress than I am, Navah. Can I bring you a glass of water? There's only one of us here who's been deceived and it's not me."

"Sina, I should try to prevent any misunderstanding here! After all, I knew that there were others and you apparently didn't. Besides, affairs abroad are really unimportant, don't you think? I don't feel deceived at all."

Sina hesitated: "If affairs in your marriage are so common-place, I can't reproach him for not having said anything about you, since your relationship is apparently not particularly binding."

"Well, about that you really should ask our daughter before you draw any hasty conclusions," Navah answered and took her leave with: "I'm just afraid that we won't see you again."

Navah Bein left the room and Sina followed her with her eyes. All at once she noticed the face past which the Israeli had strutted, a blond man who was looking at her from around a corner.

Sina asked: "Have you been watching us? Do you want something from me? I don't believe I caught your name."

The man stepped up closer and said: "My name is Otto Toot. I painted this picture. Were you quarreling about my painting? What happened?"

Sina Mohn looked at him: "Who is this:Ahasuerus? Both the other woman and I thought we knew the man you've depicted here."

Otto Toot burst out laughing and exclaimed: "Jealousy because of Ahasuerus? Because of one of my masked figures? Are you trying to make fun of me? Is this a joke? Doctor Mohn, with all due respect, that portrait has been painted over! Gauze covers everything! How can you make out a person or identify someone? What are you getting at? That my works don't really depict anyone?"

At that point Sina recognized the absurdity of her confrontation with Navah, that scene in front of the shrouded character. But to be sure and dispell any doubt, she went on: "Does he have any kind of special capabilities?"

"Who?"

"Your model!!Ahasuerus!"

Toot looked at the painting and then at Sina Mohn. "But Doctor, that's me! Not in the sense of a self-portrayal, but just look at the body, the neck. It's me.Ahasuerus is Toot and Otto Toot is Ahasuerus."

Sina Mohn's eyes swung back and forth until she did, in fact, recognize the painter in his picture. And she suddenly was at a loss as to why she had seen Mullemann there, her lover. Characteristics now prominent, had not caught her attention before. Sina asked: "Why did you call it Ahasuerus?"

Otto Toot shrugged his shoulders. "Does there have to be a particular motive behind it?"

She nodded and said: "Nothing happens without a reason, whether it is profound or base. You know that Ahasuerus is the eternal Jew?"

"So what?" Otto Toot shot back. "Is this about political correctness? Do you want to deny my right to use that name?"

She shook her head: "I don't want to deny you any right. It seems to me quite the reverse, that you want to prevent me from asking my questions. Why Ahasuerus? Or maybe: if you wanted to be provocative, why didn't you call the painting 'The Eternal Jew'?"

Otto Toot felt that he had been cornered, since his strength didn't lie in such discussions. Besides, Sina Mohn was an authority in theory and ethics toward which he felt a certain trepidation. He became silent. She spoke as if she wanted to help him think: "Was it that by citing the suffering of the other you intended to reflect your own guilt? Maybe we were supposed to see the Jew in ourselves. But Mr. Toot, what is the Jew, the Jew *per se?*"

Defiantly, Toot blurted out: "Why should I feel guilty? Is there such a thing as collective guilt? Am I not allowed to draw any figure from Jewish tradition?"

Sina Mohn heard Navah Bein exulting, heard the echo of her words: "Of course not. Nor did the artist know it. An entire country knew nothing, claims to have known nothing. The image of Ahasuerus is a part of tradition – it's accepted and then handed on."

In reply to Toot, the art theoretician answered: "No one, at least no philosopher or academic has ever seriously talked about a collective guilt – except for those who constantly attack the idea in order to bring about a general innocence, a national absolution. Nor did I ever say that you should feel guilty, Toot."

"Why should I?" Toot barked back, wiping the perspiration from his brow and then wringing his hands while shifting his weight from one leg to the other. "I take it that you don't like 'Ahasuerus'?"

"Quite the contrary," Sina Mohn contradicted him. "You're a gifted artist. It's just your explanations I'm less excited about. If you want, I'll arrange an exhibition for you in the museum. We'll purchase 'Ahasuerus' – money won't be a problem. Here's my card. Call me tomorrow without fail! I want to look at all your works. All of them, do you hear me, Toot! Maybe I'll buy one for myself. And, by the way, would you like to paint me? Wrapped in gauze? In bandages? What do you think? That would be something, wouldn't it? The second number is my private number with an answering machine. I would have some time on the weekend. I predict you have a great future ahead of you, Toot! See you tomorrow!"

Arieh Arthur Bein was standing in the bathroom of the apartment where he had moved two weeks ago. After Navah had announced eighteen days ago that she and their daughter Jael were following him to his homeland, he had gone in search of an apartment. Arieh didn't want to bother his mother, so he left Leon Fischer – his dead father's best friend – who had housed him for a month and found a place for the whole family in the center of the city.

On this afternoon, he was alone. Jael was running through the amusement park with her grandmother Ruth Fandler. Navah was in the libraries and archives looking for material for her historical research.

Watching himself in the mirror over the sink, Arieh Arthur Bein wrapped a roll of gauze in even strips around his delicate face. He fastened the end of the material with a safety pin and reached for the next roll. Recently he had been outfitting himself this way every evening to try to discover why someone might go out dressed like this, to try to learn something about this Mullemann he was chasing. Arieh was reminded of Egyptian mummies. In the land of the Nile it was the task of the old priests to embalm the bodies of eminent leaders, since physicians were strictly forbidden to work on cadavers. By such means the past could be preserved. The body was a hieroglyph; it had rigidified into a fossil from antiquity. At the time surgeons were already using tweezers, scalpels, and bone scrapers in operations. For the first time, injuries were treated with medicinal substances and wounds were dressed. His thoughts wandered to the secrets of the pyramids, to their puzzling arrangement according to wind directions and the stars. Modern research assumes that the laws of terrestial magnetism, of electrostatics, of astronomy, chemistry and medicine must have been known to scholars during the era of the pharaohs and that they were then lost again. It was a body of knowledge that probably went up in flames together with the library in Alexandria. What great efforts and achievements, what toil and affliction, what blessings and crimes were forgotten and lost forever.

Moses, brought up at the court of the Pharaoh, had once started out from this empire in order to lead the Israelites though the desert and teach them monotheism. This is the only tribe, Arieh's people, whose memories and records reach back to those times.

Arieh's associations drifted further away as he disguised his face. He thought of the *Pessach* celebration in his father's house and suddenly saw Jakov Scheinowiz sitting at the table in his parents' apartment. He saw his mother Ruth bringing in the *gefillten Fisch* with *Kugel* and he saw himself as a child. *"Ma nischtanah ha lailah haseh mi kol ha leiloth,"* the boy sang. "How does this night differ from all other nights?" And following the *Haggadah*, his father narrated the exodus from Egypt, the trek through the Sinai desert as if he had experienced everything himself.

As he overlapped the last roll of gauze over his forehead under the hairline, he thought about the *Tefillin* or leather prayer straps that the orthodox bound around their head and left arm every morning in religious devotion and absorption. Arieh Arthur Bein had only put on those belts a few times, during the *Schiwa*, for example, that week of mourning for his dead father when, right after getting up from bed, Leon Fischer helped him lash the devices correctly. At the time, after the funeral, the bands had reminded him of early historical relics, relics of Egyptian antiquity. The bands seemed to be fetters that chained him to origins of the faith, to an archaic and atavistic practice. In the days following the burial of Jakov Scheinowiz, Arieh felt that his body had been marked or branded. Each of the *Tefillin* is decorated by a leather capsule into which parchment rolls have been sewn on which four verses from the book of Moses are inscribed. Arieh's body bore the scripture, and Leon Fischer had told him that the case on the left arm had to point to the heart.

The leather straps had been knotted to form the three letters that formed the Hebraic word for the Almighty and when he removed the belts, the strokes and lines stayed on his skin.

Arieh Arthur Bein stared into the mirror. As an Israeli agent Bein stood out from his colleagues by one characteristic and talent: he was deployed to find people, but now he was unable to locate Mullemann. He was able to track down a criminal because of his guilt. But how was he supposed to orient himself in his pursuit of Mullemann? This was someone who, as far as he knew, had committed no crime, yet who incessantly confessed to others' crimes. In other cases, Arieh Arthur Bein had a presentiment of the outward appearance of his prey when he heard about the crimes. In this case, he wanted to imitate Mullemann to understand him and identifying who was behind those bandages, why and, most of all, where.

Arieh was sure that Mullemann's various aspects all fit together in a whole: his confessions, his behavior, his masquerade. He looked in the mirror. The bandages seemed like fetters to the Israeli secret agent, even a straitjacket, yet like a support as well. They pointed to an injury, yet beyond that to its healing.

He heard the apartment door opening and closing with a bang, then Navah's footsteps. She stopped in front of the bathroom. He greeted her and smiled, but then was startled when he looked at her. "What's happened? Is something wrong?" he asked.

"That I would like to know from you."

He hesitated, then apprehensively: "What do you mean?"

Her lower lip protruding, she replied: "Is there something going on? Don't you have something to tell me about?"

Ignoring the antagonistic tone, he began to talk about his thoughts and what he was doing: "What I was thinking was that gauze bandages absorb a body's signature. They disclose all of its injuries, lay open its breakdowns and defects, but its recovery as well. The blood, the pus, the ointments – they're all memory traces. You should be able to identify anyone on the basis of this material and texture shouldn't you? You can hide and distinguish someone by bandages, or recognize him. You can mask and reveal him at the same time."

Navah cried out: "You don't know how right you are. You should tell these thoughts to your Sina Mohn sometime! Masked and exposed!"

"My who?" he asked.

"Are you going to dispute it and deny her? That won't help you. I know everything! I talked to her and she told me about you. I warn you Arieh. Stop telling me these lies! Nothing but lies! You go to her every night in this disguise. She's let it out. You're her lover."

"But Navah," he tried to explain, "be reasonable. The only point in all this is Mullemann."

She burst out laughing. "I don't want to know anything about the perversions behind this code name."

"Navah, I've already told you . . . I have to find him!"

"Oh stop, Arieh. Why are you still lying? Some people prefer leather, some rubber, while you and Sina want to be wrapped up tightly together. My husband, Jael's father, is Sina's Tarzan of the bandages. How did you imagine that: you'd be her rollmop and I'd be the jealous wife in tears? No, you miscalculated there, you bastard, you asshole!"

"Navah, I don't know any Sina Mohn!"

"Arieh, she told me about you."

She sat down in the kitchen and he, in his ridiculous outfit, tried to hug her. But she pushed him away and whimpered: "And everything seemed so good between us lately. Why? I don't understand it. I follow you here because you're pretending to struggle with Mullemann, and I want to look after you – this, despite the fact that you're neglecting your work, want to give it up and fly to this country, where you sit around with Leon Fischer and try to trace the past. Now I'm forced to recognize that you're simply having an affair and fabricating your inner problems and complications in order to have a good time as a gauze fetishist. If you don't leave her, I'll divorce you."

He shook his head and said: "Navah, I don't know any Sina Mohn. And I've never cheated on you. I was never able to. I had all the lies I could take, deceiving those people that we count among the enemies of the state. You have no right to accuse me. Not after what happened between you and my friend, my colleague Nimrod Levy!"

She flinched: "You know about Nimrod? How? Why did you keep quiet about it? Did you want to pay me back with Sina? That's over! That was along time ago!"

Arieh shrugged his shoulders. "Not really so long ago! It hasn't even been a year!"

Navah had just been sitting there motionless, when all of a sudden she began to tremble and gasp as if she couldn't get any air, as if her breathing function were failing. She was unable to sob, and her hands started to cramp up. Arieh took her in his arms, kissed her on the face and pressed her against himwith all his might. They squeezed each other and sank to the floor in a paroxysm of common tears.

Later he tried to explain: "I didn't want to lose you and Jael. That's why I kept quiet, so I could win you back . . . to shake off Nimrod. That's why I didn't accept any more assignments and devoted my time to looking for Mullemann . . . He exists, Navah. I have to find him."

Navah got up and went to the stove to boil some water for tea. Then she said: "Why can't we finally go back to Tel-Aviv? Are you trying to make yourself into a victim? Into your father's hostage?"

Arieh denied it. "You're wrong. I'm not a victim and I'll never be one. Even my father Jakov Scheinowiz was neither a broken nor a poor man. He was strong, successful, and had a sense of humor. People whisper: 'A survivor,' and mean: 'He was in a camp but still is such a nice guy with a zest for life.' Why shouldn't they have a zest for life or not be nice? In these people's eyes the survivors are less honorable than those killed. At least they seem to have become difficult or, in any case, they remain suspicious characters. If a person wasn't killed, then people ask how he made it through, whether he betrayed somebody, sold out, or was an informant. They think he just walked over corpses. If he denies all the accusations and still suffers like every normal person from such reproaches, he is pitied and declared a mental wreck. He's diagnosed as having feelings of survival guilt. The survival syndrome? That's a riot! If survival is a sickness, then I don't want to be healthy or normal."

Navah nodded. "You normal? We – our whole generation – were born with a blue number on our arm. All of us! It may be invisible, but it's tatooed into us under our skin. Why can't you do your work any more? What's haunting you? Why else did you come here? You can't fool me . . . "

Navah Bein poured tea into her cup and sipped it. Arieh took a mug from the kitchen cupboard. The frosty atmosphere between them warmed up only very slowly.

She answered his questions later.

"Sina Mohn and I were standing in front of a picture and she began to talk about her lover, a man who can recognize others' guilt and see right through them. His particular talent is finding this guilt. They've been meeting each other for five weeks and she doesn't even know his real name. And, she didn't mention a profession . . . It was as if she were describing you. I really could have sworn . . . Is it you, Arieh? I don't know anymore what I should believe."

Arieh Arthur Bein was still wrapped in gauze. But now, as if in a dream, he unclasped the safety pins, pulled off the rolls and coiled them up carefully. Then he stood up, went into the outer room and called out: "Did you say Mohn? Sina? And her lover is at her place in the evening?" And before Navah could say yes, he had picked up the phone book and was leafing through it. He left the phone book lying open, and Navah saw him getting dressed and throwing on his coat.

"Arieh," she burst out: "You're going to her place? Mullemann is nothing but a fabrication . . . I'm scared . . . What do you want with her? There's something eerie going on . . . Don't do it! . . .

Running off to an utterly strange woman at this time of night
without even phoning first . . . Or maybe you do know her. Arieh?
Don't go to see her! Arieh, if you leave now, don't bother to come
back! Ever again!" Navah Bein screamed after him. "Arieh . . ."

Otto Toot was standing in the bank with a drink in his right
hand and Sina Mohn's card in the left. The opening was over, the
hors d'oeuvres and desserts had been laid waste and the wine
glasses emptied. The organizers and most of the artists were sitting
together with friends in a popular bar. A bank employee was
clearing away the worst of the mess in the foyer while a colleague
in the back room of the bank was testing the lighting system. He
was trying to switch on the electricity for the door locks and the
steel window shutters as well as to set the alarm for the night. The
light from the chandeliers and lamps shifted and danced through
the rooms, glittering colorfully like the flickering of neon signs on
the roofs of buildings. Unnoticed by anyone, a man in a black coat
and hat with tapered brim stole into the second showroom. Otto
Toot was standing there lost in thought.

The artist was startled when he saw the stranger in the crossfire
of the light. "Are you the painter of that picture called
'Ahasuerus'? That painting of a disguised man? Listen carefully.
I'm not going to repeat myself. I'm in a hurry because things are
getting too hot for me around here. And believe me, the sooner I'm
gone from here, the better it'll be for you. I'm interested in this
figure, this Mullemann, you are supposed to have portrayed so
magnificently. Where can I find him? Who is it? Your answer is
extremely important to you . . . understand? . . . Maybe for me or
for him as well, but for you in any case . . . I'm waiting."

Otto Toot didn't know who was standing in front of him in the
flickering light. He didn't know that the stranger was Georgi
Antonov, a Bulgarian specialist who had once worked for Sofia's
secret service and who now killed for money. While Mullemann,
that figure shrouded in mystery, had passed himself off as the
murderer and confessed to his crimes, Antonov had been cheated
of his wages, his blood money.

Toot burst out laughing and waved his glass in front of the

stranger's face: "What do you want? You're making a fool of yourself."

But Antonov screamed: "I'm warning you! I don't have any time for jokes. My reputation is at stake! I have a very bad reputation . . . and I can't let it be ruined. The name! Who was this Ahasuerus? Or you're a dead man."

But Otto Toot giggled and raised his glass to Antonov: "To Toot," emptied his drink with one gulp and snorted. "Ahasuerus is Toot! Can't anyone understand that? Mirroring my own guilt by alluding to others' guilt . . . Just look, the body, the neck. That's me. Toot was Ahasuerus. . . or Mullemann . . . eternally, amen!"

"The money," Antonov said hoarsely and drew out his stiletto. "Enough jokes! Stop laughing! I want my half million!"

Staring at Antonov, Toot retreated, dropped his glass, and they stumbled into the last room. He whispered: "Don't be crazy, man."

But Antonov, brandishing his knife, bent over the artist: "The name! Or it's going to be lights out." He slid the knife along his cheek and threatened to slit it open. Just then the bank employee in the control room was clumsily trying to find the main lever that switched off the bank's lighting system. Instead, a lightning flash seemed suddenly to illuminate the room. Alarmed, Antonov looked up and saw the masked Ahasuerus in a crown of light thrown off by the lamps. He saw him reigning above and looking down on him. At that, the Bulgarian killer, once a farmer's son from Malko Kadiewo, cried out: "Isus Cristos." His mouth hung open, his knees buckled and the blade fell from his fingers into the painter's hand. In fear and anger Otto Toot grasped the handle like a brush or spatula and with thirty stab wounds, covered him completely in red.

Finally, the bank employee had found the right buttons. The rooms lay in darkness. Toot turned around and, without looking, plunged the knife up to its handle into the painting. He left the stiletto sticking in the canvas and drops of Antonov's blood ran off the knife out of the gash. Over "Ahasuerus."

Otto Toot never painted again. His name remained unknown. The next day Sina Mohn was unable to find him because he had disappeared that very night. He fled over the border to Hungary and had gotten all the way to Debrecen where, a few weeks later, he drunkenly staggered into the path of a truck and was instantly killed.

On the night of the murder, commissioner Karl Siebert found Sina Mohn's card under Ahasuerus's portrait. One hour later, the criminologist Siebert arrested a man in the apartment of the art expert, Sina Mohn. The man was wrapped up in bandages, and, when asked, called himself Mullemann. The Israeli agent Arieh Arthur Bein, who had just arrived in front of the house, saw the uniformed officers lead the man in bandages away.

Mosche

Commissioner Karl Siebert was sitting in front of a desk in the north wing of the old police station. He wasn't at all fond of the room, originally a foyer that had been allocated to him years ago. When Siebert wanted to get to his chair, he had to squeeze his body sidewards past the furniture and jam himself into the corner. Siebert had piled up on the gray linoleum those files that no longer fit into the filing cabinet. These then blocked the side door with the transom that led to his secretary, Hilde Schöttel. Whenever Schöttel wanted to get to her boss, she had to go around via the hallway.

Despite all these disadvantages, Siebert much preferred this isolated corner to the proximity of his colleagues. He didn't like the other detectives and they couldn't stand him either. Yet, while he simply despised most of them for their laziness and bigotry, they were forced to acknowledge his talents that were unsurpassed in the department. Siebert didn't trust their gushing. He could make out the echoes of envy and resentment. They were just waiting for a mistake.

Commissioner Siebert had been inundated with congratulations, his unerring instinct praised to the sky with compliments, when a few weeks earlier he had tracked down and arrested that mysterious figure calling himself Mullemann. But soon Siebert's success seemed forgotten. No one could understand why he had not already delivered his report.

It was said that the commissioner had had countless documents carted into his office and that he had been interrogating Mullemann for days on end – even during the nights – but that the investigation had gotten bogged down. Siebert knew about this talk. There was an abrupt knock on the door and a colleague, senior inspector Feldner, looked in and asked: "Are you finished, Siebert?"

The commissioner didn't move a muscle on his face and kept his eyes glued on the documents. "Do you want to take over? No? Well, shut the door. There's a draft."

A few minutes later the telephone rang and Siebert groaned loudly before he picked up the receiver. He guessed that it was his chief, Counselor Ludwig Gmeiner, calling again: "Siebert? Have you finally finished?"

"No, I haven't gotten that far," he answered.

But Gmeiner interrupted and pressed him for the final report. "Did you read today's newspapers, Siebert? They want to know why charges haven't been brought against Mullemann. Can you understand that? They're demanding a quick trial!" Siebert knew about these commentaries. After Mullemann's arrest, the chief of police had celebrated at a press conference and was now being pressured by journalists with a first cautious criticism. "Four editors inquired just this afternoon about when the case is finally going to be brought to a close. The Justice Minister has been questioned about the Mullemann affair in parliament. Siebert, if I don't hear from you soon, then you're going to hear from me!" Gmeiner hung up and the commissioner listened to the dial tone for a moment afterward. He didn't know what to do.

He suddenly heard a confusion of voices in front of his door. A slight man with black curly hair opened the door, but Siegwald Hammberger, Siebert's assistant, appeared behind the stranger and pulled him back out into the hall, bellowing: "What are you doing here anyway? Who in the world are you? That's not allowed! You can't just walk in . . . "

Siebert snorted: "Quiet, Hammberger!"

"If you ask me, chief, this person is trying to sneak in," Hammberger said.

"You, I certainly won't ask, Hammberger."

Siebert studied the stranger. He was a frail young man who held his head crooked, smiled and said: "My name is Arthur Arieh Bein."

"So? Do we know each other?" Siebert asked.

Bein replied: "We should get to know each other, commissioner. Two months ago I traveled from Israel to look for Mullemann. I can help you . . ."

"Do you think you're the only one who has come to me, Mr. Bein? Do you see these files? Only the most important ones are in this room. In the next room there are countless letters, hundreds of callers' addresses and interrogation records . . . good citizens who want to talk to us and who believe they know who Mullemann is. But all those tips that have been followed have, up to now, been nothing but garbage or slander. Most of the clues simply can't be checked out!" Commissioner Siebert shook his head, shrugged his shoulders and murmured: "And the most amazing thing, Mr. Bein . . . No one really wants to know who Mullemann really is or why he committed his crimes. These questions don't interest either my superiors or the Minister. And I won't even mention the journalists. All of them simply expect me finally to turn Mullemann, this constant confessor, over to the justice system. They want me to stop my investigation. This monster should be locked up and silenced . . . And you think, Mr. Bein, that we've just been waiting for you, right? You don't write, don't telephone . . . just walk in off the street, sneak into the station and break into my office."

"Your office?" Bein asked without being able to suppress his astonishment.

"That's right! Just look! This trash heap is my office."

Arieh Arthur Bein said: "Commissioner, listen to me, please! Give me only five minutes and not a second more. I can help you. Not only you, but I too want to know who Mullemann is."

Siebert looked up and thought. "You need five minutes? All right then. I can't give you any more time. Hammberger, close the door – from the other side!"

Arieh Arthur Bein sat down in front of the desk. "I know Mullemann. I met him more than half a year ago. While I was on a trip through this city I had to go to the hospital. We were lying in two different rooms separated by a wall. He sent me messages in Morse code . . . "

Siebert repeated: "In the hospital? Behind a wall?"

"Mullemann is not a criminal! I believe he's innocent. What would you think if I said we've come across someone who can see through us and has to report on what he sees? For him we're simply X-ray images, wandering skeletons exposing the shadings of our offenses and crimes." While Bein spoke, he continually pressed his thumb nails into the tips of his ring fingers.

Siebert took note, was silent, but then huffed derisively: "He sees a wandering skeleton? In me, Mr. Bein? Hardly!"

The visitor didn't respond. Siebert sat there motionless. He resembled a seal that had been packed into an old, gray woolen vest. Bein caught a whiff of the fat man's sweaty odor.

"Don't you want to use up your five minutes, Mr. Bein? Have you given up?" Siebert stood up with a groan, picked up a file off the floor, leafed through it and pointed with the back of his hand to a place that he showed to Bein. "Mullemann was, in fact, seen at the local hospital, Mr. Bein. The first time was more than half a year ago . . . then no more for months. A nurse reports that the disguised man hid himself somewhere inside, covered himself with elastic bandages, and made himself unrecognizable." Siebert sat down again and emphasized: "We're on his track."

While Arieh Arthur Bein studied the file, the commissioner's thoughts turned to Mullemann's first interrogation. Wrapped up in his disguise, the man had spoken in a monotone as if he were speaking to himself. From underneath the bandages he had squeezed out: "Mullemann lies underneath the bandages, but who is Mullemann? Maybe I'm not – maybe Mullemann's not – a flesh-and-blood human being. It seems to me, at times, as if Mullemann is nothing more than a packet of pains, a bundle of memories from different, accidentally interwoven rolls of gauze, injuries and wounds. At some points, Mullemann thinks: Maybe I don't exist."

Bein looked up from his reading. His words crossed Siebert's thoughts. "At the time in the hospital, he didn't know who he was and puzzled over his name . . . Maybe he's not a criminal, but someone who can't tell the difference between his own acts and those of others." Gradually a suspicion of agreement solidified between the two men.

Siebert said: "You should see him. I've never encountered anything like it. Always before I've chased suspects and convicted criminals and proven their guilt in the face of their denials. Now, I'm suddenly sitting across from a man who admits to all kinds of evils and makes unsolicited confessions. You know," murmured the commissioner, "most people detest the man behind the bandages. He calls himself Mullemann, but who's Mullemann?"

Karl Siebert jumped to his feet and straightened his chair. "That's it. Your five minutes are up, Mr. Bein. Come on, let's go."

Arieh Arthur Bein clicked his tongue and blurted out: "That's too generous of you. I'll find my own way out. Don't bother."

The commissioner smiled and said: "Are you going so soon? I thought you had come to see Mullemann. If you'll please come with me," and, when Bein in his amazement stayed seated, Siebert repeated: "Come along. Let's get going!"

Bein followed Siebert. They went past offices, then through a labyrinth of hallways and stairs until they descended into a section where they no longer met any officers and all the doors were made of steel and bolted shut. Siebert turned around and whispered: "You may be surprised why I've had Mullemann given quarters here. It's not because I wanted him locked up and confined. This isn't a prison. Mullemann has to be protected and watched over. He has to be shielded from my colleagues' curiosity, from public turmoil and exploitation. Many people are alarmed when they hear about the fraud, extortion, depravity, and murders that he has admitted to and afraid of even more disclosures. Yet everyone wants to silence him. Here, he'll be able to express himself without any hindrances. Come along, Mr. Bein! Let's go."

Finally they came to a door where an attendant was sitting.

Siebert walked into a small area with a window on one side that looked into another room. Siebert said: "Take a look, Mr. Bein. Nothing to worry about. He can't make us out. Do you see? That's Mullemann!"

Bein went up close to the glass. A man wrapped in a disguise was lying on the bed. Siebert spoke in an undertone: "These rooms are accessible from the street by a side entrance. So I can bring him food or other small items without having to pass by my colleagues and superiors. For the most part, he just asks for bandages . . . He's a puzzle to me, Mr. Bein. How, for instance, could an individual torment and kill so many others? The murders he has confessed to don't follow any system nor do they indicate any pathological tendency. He admits to everything indiscriminately. There has been conjecture in the news media that he's supported by powerful people and may be associated with a mafia. It's said that he has access to political connections. But I ask you, Mr. Bein, why hasn't someone caught him in the act of one of his numerous crimes?"

The visitor looked through the pane of glass: "He's not a criminal, commissioner. Possibly he's an individual who can detect all of our guilt."

"Our guilt? What are you thinking about, Mr. Bein?" Siebert asked and, without waiting for an answer, went on: "It may be that Mullemann confesses to others' crimes and even that he has a sympathetic understanding of criminals. But he doesn't enjoy his confessions, doesn't take any delight in the attention that the public pays him. He's not trying to deceive us and isn't a cynic. No, Mr. Bein. Mullemann isn't capable of doing anything differently. He truly believes in his guilt."

Bein turned away from the one-way window as if he wanted to leave. The commissioner asked: "What are we waiting for? Are you coming? Let's go inside," but all at once Karl Siebert noticed his visitor hesitating.

Bein asked: "Where to?"

Siebert looked up: "You wanted to visit Mullemann. Are you having second thoughts?"

"No, not at all. What do you mean?" Bein stammered and looked down. The commissioner took three steps back. What did he really know about this man? Hadn't it been imprudent to come alone with him down to this isolated room? Why had he thrown caution to the wind and brought him to Mullemann?

Siebert cried out: "Don't lie to me! You're afraid! What are you afraid of? You already met Mullemann in the hospital . . . some time ago. What coded message did he send you? What does he know about you? What do you know about him? – Don't move a muscle! – And don't interrupt me! Why did you want to find him? To silence him?"

Bein staggered backwards, raised his hands, shook his head and pleaded: "I'm unarmed, commissioner! I'm not out to get Mullemann. Believe me."

Siebert didn't let the intruder out of his sight. "I could alert the attendant outside in a second and ask for reinforcement. I could lock you up and interrogate you! You can't get away from here. – Just stay calm!" In one motion, Siebert pushed the other man, face forward, to the wall. He forced his arms and legs apart and pressed him against the wall with all his weight.

Bein didn't move. They both were quiet and puffing in harmony. Following a long pause, Siebert suggested: "Now you just listen to me, Bein. If you really don't have anything to hide, I'll let you come along with me to see Mullemann. Are you coming? We both want to know who's behind the bandages."

"Commissioner," Bein gasped, "he knows everything about me. Everything! It's horrifying. But not what you think. I'm not a criminal and not out to get Mullemann. But he knows every one of my secrets. Believe me. I have to know who Mullemann is."

Siebert let go of Bein. "You can turn around and relax. I have no idea about what you might be up to, Mr. Bein. And I really don't want to know. But, if you'd like to work together with me, then anything that comes out about either of us during the interrogation stays between you and me. Understand?"

That same day they began their joint investigation. They dragged out old police files from the archives, brought them on little hand carts, and Karl Siebert presented the exhibits to the man in bandages. Whether it was a case of murder, rape, or blackmail, the commissioner read aloud from the dusty files to Mullemann, one after the other. The man behind the disguise sat at the table, pricked up his ears, and began to fidget in his chair. His breathing became more rapid. He moaned and groaned until he had admitted all the evil deeds, one after the other. He exclaimed: "It was me. I'm the one. I did it," and in tears, Mullemann described how he had committed the crimes.

He confessed to everything, even a child murder and wailed: "I can't help it!" The crime had taken place in the thirties in Berlin – long before Mullemann had been born.

At times the man in disguise talked about an offense that wasn't in the files – the secret agent Arthur Arieh Bein got red and whispered: "It was me. He's talking about me."

Another time the officer Karl Siebert nodded and interrupted Mullemann: "That was me. That has nothing to do with you, nothing to do with Mullemann. That was my mistake, my failure." At such moments, the man whose guilt had not been brought up, looked to the floor as if he had heard nothing.

At the end of the questioning Mullemann demanded: "More bandaging material! More!" Siebert and Bein handed him new rolls, then left him for the observation room and watched him from there. Mullemann wound further layers of gauze around his body.

Although the man in the bandages couldn't hear them, Siebert whispered: "When I tracked him down and took him into custody, he was living covertly with a woman in her home. At the time he wasn't wearing many bandages at all. Here and there, you could even see a little spot of skin. During the interrogations, however, when I presented him with the murders, he complained about a mysterious rash breaking out on him and climbing up his legs. As soon as he admits to the crimes, Mullemann calms down, but the pustules spread further and further on his body."

Bein asked: "Who is this woman he was living with?"
"Her name is Sina Mohn. Even she doesn't know Mullemann's

real name. But she calls me every day, pushes her way into my office and demands to see him. You'll get to know her very soon. That's for sure."

The next morning the woman stood in the station, requested a meeting with the commissioner and demanded to see Mullemann. Arieh Arthur Bein asserted: "Let's let her see him and we'll observe what happens through the window."

Nothing happened. Mullemann didn't even greet the woman or seem to recognize her. Instead, he sat at the table, his upper body swaying back and forth, and read in the files about other crimes. He muttered confessions as if he were droning out prayers. Sina Mohn screamed at him, but he didn't seem to hear her. She ran out of the cell, slammed the door behind her and roared at Siebert: "You've destroyed him. With me his suffering was subsiding. He hardly had any more bandages on. Now, I no longer know him. Just look: what's the matter with him? What have you done to him? Allow him to leave . . . and come with me!"

Siebert shrugged his shoulders and said: "He can't be left alone with you any longer. When he walks out of here, he's a dead man, dear lady." As she looked at him with a blank stare, he added: "Mullemann may be innocent, but as long as he lives, there will be people who are afraid of him, people who can't tolerate an accessory . . . And there are many of these people."

Over the next few days Siebert and Bein continued to interrogate the man in bandages. They brought in prisoners awaiting trial who denied the charges against them. The commissioner asked, for example: "Did you kill your mother?" When someone guilty shook his head and denied everything, Mullemann said: "I'm guilty. It was me. I did it." He was silent when an innocent man sat there. Criminals, however, he exposed. He depicted their deeds until they conceded everything and their web of lies fell apart.

There was just one who seemed insensitive to Mullemann's statements. That was an old man, a former colleague of Siebert. One day his tanned face appeared at the door like a mask made of wax. His gaze was fixed, his smile unnatural. A dueling scar extended across his cheek. Commissioner Siebert had invited assistant secretary Anton Weilisch – before the War, his family name was still Welischek – to a meeting with Mullemann. Weilisch didn't know what to expect, but the pensioner was flattered that a former colleague from the station had asked for his help. Consequently, he responded immediately to the invitation. Karl Siebert had for years detested Weilisch's zealous obsequiousness toward superiors, his hearty vulgarity in his relationships with secretaries and his thoughtlessness towards petitioners. The civil servant Weilisch had enjoyed making life difficult for citizens who were less submissive and obsequious than he was.

The commissioner said: "Come right in, sir."

The old man had scarcely stepped into the room when Mullemann cried out: "They're all dead: women, girls, boys, and the old men. We obeyed without asking why."

At that, the old warrior only replied: "That's the way it was. We did our duty! An order was an order. War is war."

Mullemann, however, continued: ". . . Infants were grabbed by the feet, their skulls smacked against the rocks and then we threw their tiny bodies into the flames . . . "

Weilisch responded: "Yes, it was terrible," and then to Bein and Siebert: "You have to understand the man, gentlemen. Just look at him. Bandages over his whole body. What we went through together. . . It was a terrible time. You can't even imagine."

While Weilisch spoke, Mullemann talked further without stopping. He talked about piles of corpses, executions, about villages in the Ukraine and about violent rapes. . . The pensioner Anton Weilisch remained calm and asked for tolerance for this bandaged man who must have been a comrade in arms. Mullemann's descriptions were not at all distressing to the pensioner and had no effect on his conscience. Arieh Arthur Bein looked at Karl Siebert without saying a word. After some time, the commissioner responded to his stare and growled: "We don't need you any more, Weilisch. You may go."

Assistant secretary Anton Weilisch inquired: "Was that all?"

Siebert nodded: "More than enough."

With the icy smile on his lips, the scar on his right cheek and a waxen facial expression, the old man bowed and took his leave: "I wish you a pleasant day." He left the room, a resilient spring in his step.

Siebert and Bein worked for two weeks and the phone rang constantly. It was not only Counselor Ludwig Gmeiner who called. The moderator of a German television show "Nothing but the Truth" also made contact. "Tell me, could we maybe borrow this mass murderer, this Mullendorfer from your Alpine homeland? That would be a hit! But he'd have to appear in authentic costume! In gauze and safety pins." The talkshow host thought that the public had a real lust for the confessional frenzy and would be wild about his revelations. The audience hoped for the disclosure of secret passions and the description of new sexual perversions. "That would be a sensation. Five-minute confessions from behind the gauze!" Siebert hung up.

In spite of the experiments the commissioner and Arieh Arthur Bein were not able to discover who was concealed behind the bandages and what his real name was. The report couldn't be completed without his name, the charges officially brought.

Arieh Bein sensed Siebert's worries. And the foreigner from Israel who had accompanied and worked with the commissioner for the last two weeks smelled the perspiration under the grayish wool vest, smelled his fear of departmental intrigues and his anger about the stupidity of his superiors. Bein said: "Maybe we should concentrate more on the clues to Mullemann's identity that have come our way recently, Karl."

Siebert shook his head: "Where do we start, Arieh?" He pointed to the stacks lying at his feet, pulled out a list and read the names: "Shall we begin with Abel? Just look! There's no end to it ... Zerwanek, Feichter, Sailer, Gerner, Eichhorn, Morgenthau ... "

Bein suddenly interrupted him and exclaimed: "Did you say Morgenthau? Morgenthau! Is that right?"

Siebert repeated: "Right, Morgenthau. One name among many others."

But Bein slapped the table and roared: "Morgenthau! That's

where we have to begin. Listen to me, Karl! I knew a Morgenthau when I was a boy . . ."

"As far as I'm concerned, starting with your boyhood friend, you might come up with anything! . . . very nice, but what's that got to do with Mullemann?"

"As a child, Dani Morgenthau ran around delighting his parents with his confessions. He claimed that everything was his fault. I've heard that he suffered from a rash."

Siebert looked up, shrugged his shoulders, and tried to think of an objection. "This list doesn't have Dani on it, but rather Gitta and Mosche Morgenthau . . . an elderly married couple. Should I call them? I don't think there's anything there, but if you think so . . ."

Gitta Morgenthau refused to give out any information on the telephone. She said: "No! Please don't think I'm impolite, commissioner, but I don't want you coming to our apartment nor do we want to come to the station. Not for our first meeting! I'd prefer meeting in a restaurant. Would that be possible?" Siebert suggested a restaurant nearby where he regularly went for lunch.

The next day Bein and Siebert walked into the diner. "Same as always, commissioner?" the waiter inquired.

Siebert shrugged his shoulders and replied: "Are you threatening me? Let's say, bring me the same old thing, but better than ever . . . "

Arieh Arthur Bein ordered: "I'll have bacon dumplings and sauerkraut."

The diner smelled of hot cooking oils. A few customers were standing at the formica counter next to the tap and the espresso machine. The Morgenthaus were sitting at a table in the corner. The woman had dark, tightly bound hair, a severe look, yet a soft smile. The old man seemed rigid. Quite advanced in age, he had white hair and a hump on his back. Bein immediately went toward them and said: "My name is Arieh."

The woman asked: "You're a Jew?"

"And how! Ask my mother. Until the time I was four, I thought my first name was 'Eat a little bit' . . . "

She laughed. "We should introduce ourselves: Mosche and

Gitta Morgenthau."

"Nice to meet you. This is commissioner Karl Siebert," and Arieh stressed: "He's a friend."

Siebert glanced at Bein obliquely and didn't know whether he should be insulted or moved by this introduction. He bowed, reached out a hand to each and said: "My pleasure." He sat down. "If I understand correctly, Mr. Morgenthau, you wanted to tell us something about Mullemann."

Mosche Morgenthau blurted out: "I know Mullemann? I know who that is?"

"I didn't say that. But can you tell us something that might be of interest to us?"

The old man continued. "Something. You won't believe me! I'm a liar! I wasn't in a concentration camp."

His wife tried to interrupt and poked him: "Be quiet, Mosche! Let me talk . . ."

But the old man didn't let himself be drowned out and became even louder: "I'm not allowed to speak. I have to say it's raining when they're spitting on my head. But there weren't any gas chambers. There weren't any Jews murdered."

Gitta Morgenthau sighed, shook her head and looked out the window. What was the commissioner supposed to think of Mosche, of her, of all Jews? Scarcely had somebody in this country seemed candid, even sensitive and ready to help them as an ally, when another disagreement broke out. Arieh first looked curiously at her husband, then smiled kindly at Gitta.

Karl Siebert, however, was silent. He crumpled up a paper napkin in his hands and tore it into pieces. He was sweating. What did this old Jew mean by his frightful remarks? How could Morgenthau talk that way? Did he want to provoke or taunt Siebert? This was certainly their right. Jewish jokes found material in the crimes of his people, in the victims who had been murdered and their suffering. But heaven forbid that Siebert should laugh too. He could not move a muscle, but had to stay silent and utterly serious. Arieh, of course, had called him a friend, but now he again belonged to the others, to the guilty. Siebert felt pushed out. Was he being put to a test? Was Mosche Morgenthau trying to draw him out into some taboo area? Was the old man lying in ambush waiting for Siebert's agreement? Was there no way out for him and his countrymen, no way to escape the suspicion that they were all anti-Semites? Why him, of all people, Karl Siebert, who had hated his compatriots' narrow-mindedness and prejudices from the very beginning? There were others who deserved much more than he did to be sitting here. Siebert thought of certain of his colleagues and a neighbor.

At this very moment the waiter arrived at their table to take the order of the elderly couple. "And what would you like?"

The old man turned around and said: "You don't have veal cutlet!"

"Oh yes we do," the waiter replied, "would you like veal cutlet?"

"I want veal cutlet?"

"You don't want it?"

"I said I don't!"

Now confused, the waiter asked: "What would the gentleman like?"

Losing his patience, Mosche Morgenthau demanded: "Bring me a veal cutlet?"

"For me too," Gitta Morgenthau declared. The waiter went away shaking his head and Karl Siebert sent an inquisitive glance in Arieh's direction. The old woman shouted at her husband: "Mosche, can't you talk like a normal human being? You gentlemen have to forgive us – he's awful! He bends every statement into a question and smoothes out every question into an observation. When he says: 'There weren't any Jews murdered.' – Period! – 'There weren't any gas chambers.' – Period! – , he really means: "Weren't there any Jews murdered?' – Question mark! – 'Weren't there any gas chambers?' – Question mark! Do you understand? He mixes things up, gets them confused."

As in confirmation, Mosche shrugged his shoulders and added: "You understand!" Then: "I get things mixed up?"

She said: "Since he's applied for recognition as a victim, this tick has gotten even worse. He and I, both of us were in camps . . . no one survived from among his family and acquaintances . . ."

The old man reached for a folder, opened it, and pulled out several papers. "I've tried to get compensation? The money doesn't matter to me?" Mosche took out one sheet after another and handed them to Siebert: applications for extensions, petitions for hearings, reports about the causes of his illnesses, letters in which he demands status as victim – countless applications. He had, in awkward language, requested the authorities to kindly confirm the crimes they had once committed, especially those inflicted on him, the very person presently sending them petitions.

The waiter brought the food. But Siebert left the steaming beef broth untouched while he bent over the papers. Gitta tried to calm Mosche down. Then she whispered to Siebert and Bein: "The money has never mattered to him. He wanted nothing beyond a confirmation of the injustice he suffered. He needed proof for our son! An admission of guilt."

"Because of your boy?" Arieh asked.

And Mosche explained: "We're innocent?"

His wife added: "The boy felt responsible for our suffering. He withdrew into a shell and wrapped himself up in self-reproach. We didn't know how to discuss it, how to talk him out of his thoughts. Then Mosche decided to collect the story by going from agency to agency, from office to office and window to window – piece by piece."

Mosche pointed to the documents, shook his head and raised his hands: "I have no right to compensation! No right to any redress! You hear! You see! The authorities have turned down my petitions? I was told the wrong thing at the agency? My petitions were lost? The deadlines missed?"

Bein and Siebert studied Morgenthau's documents. There were psychiatric diagnoses in which the petitioner's fear of confined spaces was described. There were X-ray pictures which clearly showed the curvature of his spine.

His appeals for recognition as a victim had been without success, turned down. He wasn't believed. The findings stated: his afflictions and complaints – the effects of his persecution – the physical problems from that time, were not caused by waiting in hideouts, nor by forced labor nor by beatings in camp.

The old man cried out: "I'm not a victim! I should kill myself? Dani's father is a liar!"

Gitta said only: "He would have turned down any charity. He only endured running from agency to agency and the humiliation in order to prove the persecution to his son. Now it seems like he's trying to haggle with the past and be deceitful. They treated him like a peddler. They always think that a Jew only wants money. But believe me, no Jew can haggle like they can. None of us would dare to bargain down from six million to one, or even zero."

Mosche Morgenthau then hid his face in his hands and sobbed: "Once upon a time there was a boy named Dani?"

Gitta commented: "You have to understand: neither Mosche nor Dani could get over this defeat. The boy couldn't bear seeing his father suffer any longer. He knew that Mosche had gone to the ministries for him. Mosche had a nervous breakdown at the time. He hadn't been able to bring back any proof of his agony. After that Dani disappeared . . ."

Mosche whispered: "I was the one? It was me? I'm guilty?"

After a few moments of silence Arieh asked: "Dani Morgenthau . . . right . . . Your son is Mullemann?"

Gitta leaned back and looked out the window. "Dani left us. He disappeared. We tried to find him, but we didn't know where he was wandering around in his bandages . . . Now that Mullemann has been arrested and charged we can't keep quiet any more."

Later in the interrogation room, the hunched-over Mosche Morgenthau wobbled toward his son and embraced the man covered by bandages. He called out: "Dani, my boy?"

"It was me. I'm the one."

Gitta Morgenthau kissed him on the gauze, hugged him, and asked tearfully: "How you look! Can't you tighten the gauze? You've gotten skinny. Eat something!"

His father promised: "Now we'll come more often?"

That night Siebert wrote the report for Counselor Gmeiner. Arieh Arthur Bein helped him with it. By their arguments they wanted to convince police headquarters, the ministry, and the editors of Mullemann's innocence, but also of the value of his ability and of the usefulness of his talents. In their introduction they established that the bandaged man had not committed any crimes, but only exposed the illegal deeds of others.

The two friends invented "Mullemann." They cloaked him in legend, wove a wreath of heroic stories in which he had forced murderers to surrender and had thwarted the plans of organized crime with his special talent. Karl Siebert and Arieh Bein transformed Mullemann into a genius of criminology.

The most important things we know today about Mullemann really come from that night at the police station.

While Siebert and Bein wrote the report, they succumbed to the magic of their words, and suddenly the sinister apparition turned into a white knight. Siebert and Bein wrote that not only did Mullemann not deserve our condemnation, but that he had earned the respect of the public at large. The report ended with the recommendation that the state should put him under contract.

Dani Morgenthau's name was not mentioned in the dossier. It referred to neither his family nor the beliefs of his ancestors. They withheld their most recent findings. Mullemann, they found, suffered from amnesia. Siebert and Bein were in complete agreement about this decision. "Identity: unknown," Karl Siebert wrote, and when Arieh smiled, his friend the commissioner said: "It's better this way."

The next morning after Counselor Gmeiner had read their account and listened to the commissioner's explanations, he said: "Fantastic, Siebert! Amazing! I knew you wouldn't let me down." He called an international press conference.

The remote area inside the station where Mullemann had lived, was renovated. The man behind the disguise was to have living quarters, a bathroom, and a study. He could live unobserved here in total isolation and work with Karl Siebert. Siebert arranged it so that only Mosche and Gitta Morgenthau were allowed to visit him.

No one found out who this couple was in reality. Siebert always told his colleagues that they were particularly well trained caretakers. He gave the attendants instructions to comply with the requests and instructions of the old couple. The commissioner said to to Mosche Morgenthau: "You can come to see him twice a week."

The old man replied: "Twice? That's fair?"

Although Karl Siebert had recognized Morgenthau's happy agreement, that unintentional question mark echoed in his mind: "Twice? That's fair?" And because of this echo, commissioner Siebert expanded the visitation rights for Mosche and Gitta Morgenthau from two to four times per week.

Morgenthau

Arieh Bein was sitting in the cold, damp kitchen. He had placed the heaters in the rooms where Navah, Jael, and Ruth were in bed. It was quiet in the streets but hardly anyone was at rest. Over night time had begun to move slowly, and the taste in his mouth was bitter from coffee. Arieh's eyes were burning. There was a droning pain underneath the top of his skull. His body seemed bloated and his skin stretched thinly over it. He believed that every one of his steps, his every movement had been slowed down.

Arieh looked out the window. This city had been praised for its *joie de vivre* and seductiveness. It was said that it never slept and now it had waited for days, wide awake, for each of the following attacks. On each morning after, the people ventured out of their homes, went shopping with rings under their eyes, their hands covering their yawns, as if they were coming back from a long-distance flight the night before.

Arieh straightened his writing paper, took the top off his pen and wrote.
"Dear Dani,

I'm not going to call you Mullemann. I'm not going to call you by your pseudonym. My words are not for that famous man, that Mullemann behind whose bandages you're concealed. They're not for the man whose bandages hide you – the man who is the means of your access to others, to their crimes and misdeeds. You are Dani and Morgenthau, my friend.

It's three o'clock in the morning and I can't close my eyes, can't rest. The rockets are going to begin falling again. We put ourselves in airtight rooms and stay on our floor in the apartment. We're protecting ourselves from the gas.

It takes our breath away, although there have not yet been any poisonous gases showered down on us. The fumes of the past find their way through the cracks."

The sirens began to wail. Arieh put down his pen, hurried into the bedroom and woke Navah with a kiss. He stroked Jael's hair until she woke up and put her arms around him. His mother, Ruth, who had come from abroad to be with her family during this time, rushed around still half asleep, bringing thermos bottles with her.

That night he had sealed up all the windows with foil and adhesive tape. Arieh got the phone while Navah looked for the damp towel that was laid in front of the crack under the door. He turned on the radio and television. Ruth slipped the mask on Jael that had been specially made for small children and then they put on their rubber masks. They began to feel a film of perspiration under the synthetic material. The salty moisture irritated their skin.

They turned into ants or cockroaches with snoutlike filters and gigantic glass eyes. They became insects which scarcely moved and breathed with difficulty. Arieh and Navah listened to the voice of the military newscaster.

They could talk beneath the rubber only with great difficulty and facial expressions were impossible. Then came the bang, the impact some distance away and the walls' shaking, the rattling of the window panes. Arieh pressed his thumbnail into the ring finger of the same hand and groped for Navah who had her arm around Jael. Ruth was stroking the little girl's feet.

As soon as the noise died away, Navah read her daughter a story.

After the all clear signal had been given, the phone rang. Leon

Fischer, the elderly family friend, called from abroad and asked in his unique way how they were doing: "Do you have enough to eat? Yes? Shall I send you some pastry?" Arieh assured him that they as well as the refrigerator had survived the attack unharmed.

"Have you heard from Mullemann?"

"Yes," Arieh answered. He sat down at the kitchen table again at five and worked further on the letter. Would it ever reach Dani Morgenthau? Could his words still get through to the person underneath the gauze bindings? An authority in criminology had developed out of that person. Mullemann was celebrated in the press as an expert.

That same night on another continent, the man beneath the bandages sat next to a prisoner awaiting trial. Across from them sat commissioner Karl Siebert. Siebert was bending over the files. Not far from the binder lay a letter that Siebert had written to his friend, Arieh Bein, just a few hours earlier.

The prisoner declared: "Just listen. This bastard – the guy wrapped up – has already admitted everything! Everything! What do you still want from me?"

Siebert handed him a picture: "Do you recognize this woman?"

The prisoner denied it, but Mullemann said: "I saw her, heard her soft 'Don't, please,' before I pressed my thumbs into her throat."

"Yes, into her throat," the other man muttered, cleared his throat and yelled: "There, you heard it, commissioner. He was the one. He did it. It was him."

At that, commissioner Siebert smiled, nodded his head thoughtfully and growled: "Really . . ." Siebert could see the prisoner's fear and believed he was seeing how Mullemann laid bare what had been buried in the man.

He was a Zorro in white. Women sent him love letters and racked their brains over his looks under the dressing. They braided caps for him out of gauze and sent them to him. Masters of *haute couture* designed collections made from bandages. Fathers sent their sons gauze masks for their birthdays. A roller coaster in the amusement park hired barkers in gauze costumes to proclaim and extol its thrills. Two men wrapped themselves in elastic bandages, imitated Mullemann, and claimed to have the same abilities he did.

Foreign governments asked for his help in difficult cases and Mullemann, accompanied by his partner and caretaker commissioner Karl Siebert, traveled to the large metropolises of the world and most of the continents, where they led the investigations to a speedy success. At home he was honored with medals, titles and accolades. His words of appreciation stirred up the public – they moved the women to tears and elicited sighs from their lips. The men nodded in embarrassment, swallowed and their eyes glazed over. Afterwards they spoke only very few words and those in a hoarse voice.

He touched the general feelings of shame and found those words that others lacked, transforming a reticent and embarrassed people into one sincerely moved. He never passed judgment on anyone besides himself.

Some scorned his self-recriminations, agitated against him in the commentaries of the gutter press or in the letters to the editor. He was called presumptuous for warming up "the old stories" again. But his remarks – with clear criticism aimed only at himself – had softened up so many people and were taken to heart so much that he was awarded more and more prizes. A minister, governor, or sometimes a mayor would invite him to the speaker's platform on commemorative occasions and introduce him: "I no longer want to keep you on tenterhooks. You've come to listen to him. Mullemann, if you would." Politicians would gesture grandly as if they wanted to embrace him, but all of them moved aside in the nick of time as the man wrapped in bandages strode toward them. In truth, they were all afraid of direct contact with this man swathed in surgical dressing. They avoided touching him and dared not be left alone with him.

Mullemann trudged up the stairs, went to the microphone and his voice reverberated over the microphone: "Enough of this country's lies and denials. This silence must cease. We must testify and bear witness: I was the one. It was me. I did it." The last syllables faded away in the cheering of the crowd.

The telephone rang around seven in the morning. Before the ring could wake Navah and Ruth, Arieh answered. It was Dani's parents, Gitta and Mosche Morgenthau, calling to express their concern and asking about the victims and damage. Gitta remarked that the reprisals announced by the Israeli government would probably fail to materialize.

Arieh nodded silently into the phone and kept quiet since he was too tired to convey his opinion. He was happy that the army hadn't struck back.

Arieh listened to Gitta's reports. She said: "You should see him, Arieh. He works day and night. Day and night!" She talked about her son and how proud the Morgenthaus were of Dani. Her comfort in this late satisfaction came through clear to Tel-Aviv. "And we always asked ourselves what would become of the boy." For a long time they had believed that Dani wouldn't amount to anything and that Mullemann was a scoundrel. Now late in life, they seemed to have a reason to live, to survive. They basked in his honors. "You should see him," Gitta repeated, "we get to visit him several times a week. Have to sneak through the back door – we can't be recognized. Nobody is supposed to know who we are. But really, we're not complaining. There are worse things . . ."

At times they doubted that Dani had found happiness under the muslin wrappings. Gitta said: "All the trouble with his wrappings and the strain of dealing with felons as well as what he has to go through during the confessions. Just the way it is," she sighed. Intermingled with Gitta's and Mosche's elation was a dissatisfaction and an insatiable need for more and more success and recognition for Mullemann that might offset their discontent.

So they looked after his appearances, hoping he would leave behind the best impressions. In the mirror of his public reputation, they had learned not only to love their son in a new way, but also their own self images as well. They had learned to accept their right to exist.

Gitta recounted: "He works too hard, all bundled up in those bandages which hardly ever get changed. They finally get so shabby hanging down behind him that he has to trudge along with them in tow. And the people he has to come in contact with! Dreadful! He soon has a meeting with a couple that abused a girl and boy and then murdered them. How awful! Mosche and I brought his attention to the case since it seemed like the kind of story just made for him. We're going to fly to meet him today. He's involved in a case abroad again. We want to be with Dani because Mullemann is supposed to receive another honor.

Arieh liked Gitta – this woman with her short, pointed remarks that she let fall from her mouth and sprinkled like pebbles among her listeners. He asked her: "How's Mosche? How's his back?"

"His back? Mosche has a back? Oh, you must mean his hump. Well, excellent as always," Gitta called out. Gitta continued: "He was at the dentist's office yesterday."

"Problems?"

"Mosche? Never," she said loudly and Arieh could hear that her encouraging tone was meant less for him in Israel than for her husband standing next to her: "His dentures are like a chain of pearls!" She paused for a moment and added: "Every tooth has a hole." Arieh laughed.

Before saying good bye, their litany of greetings swung back and forth like a pendulum. "Say hi to Mosche!" – "And you to Navah!" – "Tell Dani I'm going to write him a letter." – "A big fat kiss to the little one." – "And tell Karl Siebert to drop me a line . . ." – "Give my love to your mother."

Gitta had scarcely hung up when such a hubbub of haste and confusion broke out, that the Morgenthaus didn't seem to be leaving for a trip of only a few days but rather seemed to be in flight and running for their lives. Three suitcases were dragged from the closet, the toiletry kits filled, and suits hung on hangars in a garment bag.

In their handbag they took along pudding for Dani, and Gitta was even carrying his favorite soup in a plastic container.

Glancing at the clock, Mosche Morgenthau wailed: "We're going to miss the plane?"

Gitta growled at him: "Just don't get in the way," as Mosche called for the taxi. Three minutes later it arrived and the old man grabbed the suitcases, lifted them one after the other, and hauled them, hump and all, down the stairs. He then scurried back up the stairs to get the garment bag and the handbag and to help his wife. He gasped: "There's a second plane to Berlin?"

Gitta snapped at him: "Don't yell like that!"

As they exchanged a fleeting kiss in the taxi, the driver looked confused and then asked: "Where to?"

Mosche replied: "To the airport?"

The driver looked even more perplexed and said: "But you have to tell me – to the airport?"

"I said, I want to go to the airport?"

Gitta roared: "Mosche! Every time . . . He always talks that way . . . Drive, please, or we'll miss our flight." Mosche Morgenthau's tic – to let every sentence fade away in a doubting tone whether it was a directive, friendly greeting, or a declaration of love and, on the other hand, to anticipate a clearly negative answer in his questions due to his general skepticism – had recently gotten worse day by day.

He put his arm around Gitta, pushed his hump into the upholstery and forced himself to smile. He ignored the screams, the whippings and suppressed what had been overwhelming him with an increasing loud roar just before every departure and trip for the last few months: the detonations, the barking dogs, the screeching of the tracks, the engines' puffing, the crowding and pushing to escape, the struggle for papers . . . The passports! He had forgotten them. He clutched at his chest. There, underneath the coat pocket, the pain flared upwards, burst into flame . . . and the passports, the tickets were nowhere to be found. All was lost. Only the numbness in his fingers cropped up again. They would have to turn around, Mosche thought, but there was no longer enough time to go back and they would miss the plane. At that moment Gitta took hold of the hand on his heart and simply said: "In my pocket. You put them there yourself, Mosche."

She knew his fears, not least because similar fears haunted her dreams and infested her sleep, uninvited, every night. Danek, Marek, and Henryk would knock at the door bringing along to tea the victims as well as some of the executioners dragging their clubs behind them. At times her mother Tonja – Gitta had survived alongside her – looked in. She had passed away twelve years ago. Whenever Gitta Morgenthau's screams jolted her husband from his slumber, he knew that she had just been driven from one of these family celebrations and he put his arm tightly around her until she had fallen back to sleep. Gitta sat in the taxi, raised her eyebrows, and thought about her son wrapped in bandages. She looked out the window into the distance and was glad that she would soon be at his side.

All of a sudden Mosche Morgenthau struck his forehead and called out so loudly that the taxi driver slammed on the brakes: "I forgot the package? You have to stop? There's a pharmacy?" Completely at a loss, the driver tried to stop but the cars behind them began honking and a truck flashed his bright lights at them.

"That's out of the question right now. I can't park here," the taxi driver informed him.

But Mosche Morgenthau, despite the driver's curses, opened the door with cars whizzing past, got out limping, ran to the shop and up to the pharmacist shouting: "You don't have gauze bandages! I need gauze bandages?"

The Morgenthaus had gotten used to bringing along fresh bandaging materials every time they visited their son. They bought him supportive garments, triangular cloths, and sometimes even colored safety pins. Beyond that they once bought him a gauze original created by a French fashion designer since the boy all too seldom wrapped himself in new rolls and had already appeared looking disheveled, slovenly, and dissolute at awards ceremonies. His mother thought this scandalous, something she and Mosche were scarcely able to think about. Mullemann was the pride and only joy of the Morgenthau family. For that reason, it wasn't right that he should look like a ragamuffin. Their child.

In Tel-Aviv Arieh Bein was sipping the coffee he had poured himself. The radio was playing softly, broadcasting a discussion about whether and when the enemies' rockets would be armed with poisonous gas. The neighbor lady with the red lips and blue number on her arm whispered: "German gas." A few old women had suffocated because they had not known how to use their gas masks. An infant had died when his parents had put the balloon-like apparatus over its head without opening up the air valve. A survivor of the gas chambers had succumbed to a heart attack during the first onslaught.

Arieh sat down at the table, rolled himself up in a blanket, and bent his knuckles until they cracked. A shudder of exhaustion ran through his stocky body. He ate a few olives as well as a salad of tomatoes, cucumbers, and curdled milk. Soon he felt a bit better, changed the cartridge in his pen and continued his letter to Dani:

"I've given up my work in the secret service and no longer will track down those deviant elements – criminals and enemies of state – so that they can be killed.

"During the mornings while the war's been going on, I've been helping out in the communal center for senior citizens. It's taken a mammoth internal struggle for me to break with my murderous trade since it seemed for so long to be my vocation and fate.

"I know that Dani Morgenthau can have a clear conscience as long as Mullemann can slip into other people's skins. You're acting out the role of the Jew in rags. Sometimes I ask myself whether you're getting revenge on those criminals or reconciling yourself with them when you confess in their place. Oh Dani, what enthusiasm you put into going after them, into ferreting them out, what zeal you expend in forcing them to confess their crimes, what eagerness, what dedication, what sacrifice! Morgenthau disappears and Mullemann is still there. What theater! It's a script written in your flesh and wound around your body. Your take no responsibility and admit everything.

"I'm putting the masquerades and disguises behind me. There'll be no more pretending, no more gifts to children to coax out of them the best way to kill their father.

"Not to be tied down by the shackles of time like a mummy, to reject all the techniques of preservation, to shed the layers, undo the knots, to go after the knotting together, to feel for the lumps, to unlace and remove the straps: this is the work of memory. Then the Mullemanns of the world throw off the bandages, roll them up again while following where they lead and returning on the paths that they marked out with muslin and find their way out of the labyrinth.

"Sometimes all I see around me is Mullemann. Even myself. Mullemania everywhere. As if all of a sudden entire peoples were running around in compresses and bandages, in bonds and connections, in their full uniform. People in black mourning bands and the tale of their thousand-year legacy. With towels wrapped around their heads and bodies, they yell at each other, get tangled up in conflict and swirl around in a knot of rage.

"It's as if you were sitting in a café in our hometown choosing identities for yourself from the menu. Customers are called by name to the telephone over the loud speaker, but you're always the one who stands up, no matter who is called. The waiter directs you to a phone booth. You go into the booth, pick up the phone and answer the caller. You give out information and make appointments that you never keep; you negotiate agreements that you won't carry out; you pledge your love, promise your loyalty, affirm your friendship, admit your guilt simply in order not to love, never to act and never to keep faith because you fear only one thing: you, your existence, Dani Morgenthau.

"At some point they call a man's name and, once again, you stand up, and a ring closes around you. Police surround you, twist your arm behind your back, put handcuffs on you and tie you up. 'Now we have you,' the officers say and they congratulate themselves on having caught a mass murderer. And even you feel nothing beyond the happiness not to be recognized, not to be identified and found guilty as the person who you are and who you could be."

Arieh Bein paused. He suddenly had doubts about the words he had written. Why should he really slander Dani Morgenthau? Wasn't the disguised man doing meaningful work? He brought criminals to justice with the help of his admissions and, with his

talks, he possibly helped someone in that country where Morgenthau and Arieh had been born to some insight or other. The masses
admired him whenever he was able to establish the guilt of another
criminal, and a few people expressed their appreciation of his confessions quite openly. Should Arieh join those who were abusing
and cursing Mullemann? Wasn't Dani Morgenthau in a dangerous
position anyway? Hadn't Leon Fischer once said to Arieh: "The
Germans look with pessimism to the future, but the Austrians here
look full of optimism into the past."

Arieh took the last sheets of paper he had written on and went
out onto the balcony. He took out a cigarette lighter from his jacket
pocket and lit it, holding the crackling flame to the papers. The
flame ate its way through the pages as they began to twist and curl.
With the writing still vaguely legible, Arieh crushed the blackened
sheets and dumped the ashes into the toilet.

Siebert and Mullemann had worked through the entire night.
First they had discussed the files, then they had sent for the suspect
to be questioned. They had been sitting with the man for hours in
the interrogation room. Rainer Sender denied all of the charges and
merely shrugged his shoulders when his contradictory statements
were pointed out to him. He simply kept quiet in the face of all
objections. An athlete, he kept his tongue buried in his left cheek.
He muttered: "What more do you want from me? The disguised
man has already confessed everything." Sender was afraid of the
man in gauze and his confessions. He no longer wanted to hear
about the murders, about the victims, and the surviving family
members. And, he could hardly remain calm when this wrapped
figure recalled the bloody deeds to his mind. Yet, by no means did
he want to reveal his fear. He sat quietly, feigned composure and
followed Mullemann's descriptions without any noticeable
agitation.

At seven o'clock Berlin time, Sender refused to answer any
more questions and shouted that he, too, had a right to some sleep
and would not take any more abuse. Siebert granted him his
request to be brought back to his cell without the slightest
opposition. He called a guard and the four of them started off

walking through the gray corridor. While the officer walked ahead jangling his keys, Siebert found a few words of comfort for Sender: "Now you have eight hours to rest. I'm tired too. I'll arrange it so that you two won't be disturbed."

"Both of us?" asked Rainer Sender. "Who are you talking about?"

The serial murderer Sender thought he sensed a smile underneath the bandages and believed he saw Mullemann's eyes flashing through the slit as Mullemann spoke: "It's me. Commissioner Siebert is talking about me. We'll just relax a little, won't we Sender? That'll do us good . . ."

Sender grabbed for Siebert's arm and called out: "No!" But the guard took hold of him by the collar and shoved him into the cell. Sender pleaded: "You can't leave me alone with him!"

Siebert smiled and said: "You're making yourself look ridiculous. He's the one who should be afraid of you, not the other way round."

All the while Mullemann was muttering: "It's those images of blood and bodies. The victims' screams . . . I can't get them out of my head."

The two men remained alone. They lay down, but Mullemann kept muttering and talking about the murder scenes that had already been mentioned before during the interrogation: "Blood trickling everywhere, bare flesh under my knifeblade and their whimpering and groaning." Rainer Sender wanted to ask him to stop, to let him go to sleep, but he could do nothing but listen to the descriptions. And suddenly Sender felt he couldn't escape the undertow of these memories.

Sender tried to distract himself, to think of his profession, his wife, but it was impossible. His thoughts accompanied Mullemann's words. He forced himself to press his right ear into the cushions and covered his left ear with a handkerchief. Mullemann's words, however, penetrated to him.

Sender reached for the paper towels on his night table, tore them to shreds and stuffed them in his ears, but Mullemann's voice

didn't seem to get quieter – on the contrary. Now he heard Mullemann's murmuring even more clearly, as if it no longer came from
the bed next to him but from within his own head. Yes, Rainer
Sender thought: he was not following Mullemann's voice but
rather the whispering of the man in bandages was repeating his,
Sender's, most secret thoughts. Sender nearly screamed – pressing
his mouth shut in order not to start bellowing – when he suddenly
realized: Mullemann was already in him, would never leave him.
This faceless ghost – this unrestrained monster whose expressions
lay hidden – had filtered himself into his head. He had moved in,
crept and wriggled his way into the convolutions of his brain and
was lodged there.

As Sender looked at his neighbor with disgust and horror, he
saw his lips moving gently and whispering those syllables which
he, Rainer Sender, simultaneously heard reverberating in his own
skull. Then Sender knew: He had to silence this witness and his
confessions! Only then would the inner echo fade away. Rainer
Sender got up out of bed, a pillow in his hands, and meant to throw
himself on the man in bandages, forcing the pillow down on his
face until Mullemann no longer moved.

He came close to his victim, but then he heard Mullemann: ". . .
and now, alone with you in this cell, I'm going to silence you –
here in this prison in full view of the police – I'm going to throw
myself on top of you, force this pillow down on you until
Mullemann no longer moves . . . "

At that moment, Rainer Sender let out a scream, cut short his
plan, ran to the cell door and cried out: "Open up! I can't stand it
any longer. Let me out! I'll admit everything . . . Everything!"

Karl Siebert opened the door and said: ""Come along, Sender."
After his confessions had been taken as evidence, Siebert said to
Mullemann: "Dani, let's get a little sleep. I can't do any more. This
afternoon you're to receive another prize and your parents are
coming in a few hours. They flew here just so they could feel
proud of their son."

Arieh Bein tried to write Dani Morgenthau a new letter.
Everyone was still asleep in the apartment, but Ruth, his mother,

would soon wake up. She would make breakfast and drive him out of the kitchen and try to convince him to finally go to bed.

"Dear Dani,

I've decided that as soon as this war is over I'm going to Cracow with Leon Fischer. I'm going to the city where both of our families come from. Tonja, Adam, Gitta, Jakob . . . Maybe I'll write you afterwards and tell you about it and about Mullemann, too . . .

"But you have to first pull off those diapers from your wounds, those familial wrappings that your pathetic parents, Gitta and Mosche, bring with them every time they visit you. Undo the bandages, unravel the entanglements.

"Are you afraid? Look in on Sina. Earlier, you were able to escape the bandages at her side . . .

"I know how often she tried to see you, but you were wrapped up in your gauze, caught up in confessing crimes. She's the only one who believes in you and doesn't marvel at Mullemann. . . You should disappear with her, cast off Mullemann and come out of your cocoon. If you decide for Sina, Karl Siebert won't stand in your way. He won't hold you captive. Gitta and Mosche will accept it too.

"Sina will soothe your wounds, loosen the rolls of muslin, stroke your skin, calm your fears, and ease your pain. You won't horrify her with your confessions. But instead, you can enchant her with your confessions of love and excite her with your declarations. Come on, you infant in swaddling clothes, make the move! Sina will hang on your lips, listen to your every word, kiss you and seek you out underneath the bandages. And one day when the time comes and she reveals to you that she's pregnant, then you can utter your incantation, your slogan, your watchword. When she asks you if you'd like to be a father to her child – as she would have it – then you can reply once more with your 'I'm the one.'"

Before Arieh could finish the letter, his mother Ruth came into the kitchen, yawning and shaking her head, and said: "You're at it again. All these letters to Mullemann that you never put in the mail. When are you going to stop this nonsense? You have to quit it! Right now! You have to get some sleep. Now go to bed for a couple of hours and afterwards I'll make you some breakfast."

"Mother, I'm a grown man. Do you want to stick me in the crib again?"

But Ruth took the pen away from him, cleared the paper off the table and said: "Do you know what the difference is between a terrorist and a Yiddish mother?"

"Is there any at all?" Arieh asked.

"Of course, my boy," Ruth declared. "You can negotiate with terrorists."

Arieh Bein crept into where his daughter was sleeping. Jael had curled up and was hugging a teddy bear that was almost bigger than she was. Next to her pillow lay the transparent rubber ball that she had held in front of her face a few months ago. "Just look, Papa. Look through the ball. The whole world is standing on its head." Then Arieh groped his way further into the bedroom, slipped his clothes off and lay down next to Navah. As he cuddled up close to her back, his wife took his hand and placed it on her breast.

At the same time in Berlin, Karl Siebert and a man wrapped entirely in bandages climbed into their beds. At the Tegel airport, Gitta and Mosche Morgenthau's early morning flight was landing and they were eyeing – with fear and trepidation – the luggage carousel looking for their suitcases and boxes of gauze.

Not too much later that morning the art theoretician Sina Mohn awoke in her apartment and, just like every other morning, her eyes lit first of all on a picture that she had acquired a few weeks earlier. The painting was by Otto Toot, an artist totally unknown because of his untimely death. His work was called "Ahasuerus," and Sina Mohn had bought it because it depicted a figure in disguise, a man cloaked from head to foot in gauze. This man stared down every day at the beautiful woman in bed.

She heard her lover of the previous night pulling the shower curtain together, and the water begin to pour down. Sina looked at the picture. She felt miserable and caught in the act. She felt suddenly as if she were cheating on the stranger in the shower with the familiar figure in gauze.

The winter sun reached Sina's bed. She threw the blanket to one side and as she raised herself up, she stretched out her entire body. The she jumped over to the closet, pulled on her robe, pulled it tightly around her and tied the sash firmly. She put marmelade and bread on the table for the guest and called out to him: "Breakfast is in the kitchen!" She than poured herself a cup of coffee and retreated into her study.

Two hours later, a man in a down-filled coat with his hood up and fastened tightly left the prison in Berlin Moabit through a service entrance. His face was hidden under gauze. None of the guards dared asked this famous disguised man for his pass. No one stopped him.

After Mullemann's disappearance had been discovered at noon, the police initiated an extensive search. Karl Siebert's superior was highly agitated when he called Berlin. An embassy attaché hurried to the Moabit prison looking for his countryman Karl Siebert: "But commissioner, can't you possibly think where Mullemann might have headed. Where in the world he might be going?"

The commissioner shrugged his shoulders, thought first of Arieh and right after of Mosche. He then said: "I know who Mulle-mann is? What his name is? I know his parents? No clue . . . "

Karl Siebert turned his back to the man, then around toward the window, looked through the bars into the open spaces and smiled gently.

Afterword
by Francis M. Sharp

Like millions of other Europeans today, the writer and historian Doron Rabinovici is a member of a minority group who makes his home in a country other than where he was born. Three years after his birth in Tel Aviv in 1961, his family left Israel to resettle in Vienna. While Austria and particularly its capital city look back on a long and rich history of Jewish influence, Rabinovici belongs to a Jewish community that has come together there in the wake of the Holocaust. This community today, as the Austrian Federal Press Service reports, "is largely made up of survivors of concentration camps, displaced persons or refugees who only arrived in Austria to begin a new life after 1945, 1956 (Hungary) or 1968 (Czechoslovakia)."

Rabinovici, who retains Israeli citizenship, has been vocal in condemning populist and xenophobic trends in Austrian politics and media. He associates "populist successes" with the "unambiguity of ethnic affiliation" and contrasts the latter with the "babble of voices of various identities" that he hears in his own head. Together with his older and more prominent colleague on the world literary scene, Salman Rushdie, Rabinovici celebrates the immigrant's split allegiance, his hyphenated nationality, the rich-ness of a hybrid identity. In the equation of his own professional self, he rejects summary categorization as a Jewish writer and prefers the less determinate series of elements: a writer and an atheistic Jew with strong ties to Jewish tradition who lives in Austria.

His earliest published essay (1995) begins as a response to a journalist who asked if he would leave Austria in the event that Jörg Haider – the rightwing leader of Austria's "Freedom Party" who has since gained a strong national following with numerous anti-foreigner statements – were to be elected chancellor. Rabinovici's reply shows both a historical appreciation of the question as well as a firm negation of it as his personal response. Refusing to play the part of victim, he underlines the importance of the struggle against such a possibility, a struggle reflected in his

political commentary since the appearance of this essay. Rabinovici's opinions on Haider's electoral appeal and on a variety of
related topics have appeared in editorial pieces in the Viennese
daily, *Der Standard,* since mid-1997.

In May of that year Rabinovici leveled a broadside at the
publisher of the tabloid *Die Krone* whose ostensibly conciliatory
visit to Israel had been canceled at the last minute by the Israelis.
He chides the media mogul for his disingenuous philanthropic and
humanitarian purposes, especially when measured against his
newspaper's history of trivializing Nazi atrocities and reference to
the "so-called Holocaust."[1] Rabinovici's caustic pen has also found
a worthy target in the rightwing extremist views of a regular
contributor to another daily, *Die Presse.* In the belated debate in
Austria about compensation for victims of National Socialism he
finds the contention frivolous and irresponsible that claims against
the former Allies should be given equal weight and labels such
claims a cover for a lingering tie to the past. As one of four
participants in a thematic discussion of Aryanization published by
Der Standard in November 1998, Rabinovici makes a strong case
for a swift response to Jewish demands for compensation. Con-
testing the argument that such demands could call forth renewed
anti-Semitism, he asserts that ignoring them essentially prolongs
an anti-Semitism that has never disappeared.[2]

The Austrian national elections in the fall of 1999 in which
Jörg Haider and his party gained a solid third-place showing were
the occasion for Rabinovici's most strongly worded political
journalism. Reflecting his own "schizoid situation" in the structure
of the essay, the writer born in Tel Aviv engages in a dialogue with
the one living in Vienna. While his Austrian self points out that the

---

[1] "Über das Problem, instant koscher zu werden," *Der Standard* 28/29 May 1997,
33 <http://DerStandard.at/archiv>.

[2] "Wir sind noch nicht im reinen," *Der Standard* 4 November 1998, 2
<http://DerStandard.at/archiv>.

targets of inflammatory political rhetoric were not Jews in this election but other "foreign" elements, his other half clearly detects the tie between Austria's unresolved past, its former anti-Semitism and the new wave of xenophobia. And from the latter's more international standpoint, he warns his adopted country that it runs the risk of being identified with Haider if it defends him. Following the election Rabinovici helped organize a mass demonstration and protest against racism and rightwing extremism that took place on Stephansplatz, Vienna's central square, on November 12.

Prior to the publication of his novel *The Search for M*, Rabinovici published a collection of short stories entitled *Papirnik* in 1994. Like the novel, several of these works incorporate elements of the murder mystery into their characters and structures. Bank robbers, killers, serial murderers, executioners go about their business in a fictional world teeming with unexpected twists and turns of plot, nightmarish events, and identity transformations. A complexly symbolic prologue and epilogue about writing and its perils introduce and close the collection.

One of the stories in particular bears a distinct relationship to Rabinovici's politicized writing. The young Viennese Jew Amos happens by chance to walk past a heated sidewalk discussion taking place in the aftermath of what had been an anti-foreigner demonstration and counter-demonstration. He is unwittingly drawn into an argument that soon splits along two lines: for most, the past has been surmounted, while a few insist that the crimes of this past are ineradicable. When a man shouts at him that he should go to Israel – or New York – if he doesn't like it in Austria, Amos recalls a conversation with the father of one of his classmates, a visiting professor from New York. Professor Rubenstein had dampened his youthful idealism about Israel with stories of certain Jews from Brooklyn – filled with irrational prejudice against blacks – who had emigrated and found in Israel a rationale for their racism in the hatred of Arabs.

In a discussion of the peace process in the Middle East held in April 1999, Rabinovici takes to task just such political factions in Israel that display intolerance of their Arab neighbors. He defends a two-state solution in which both Jews and Arabs enjoy the right of self-determination as the only path to lasting peace in the area and criticizes Netanyahu's intransigence. Nor has the Israeli cultural community in Vienna escaped Rabinovici's public reprimand. When it revoked its permission at the last minute for a congress of homosexuals and lesbians to meet in an inactive synagogue, he underlined their struggle for equal rights as a minority, a minority once condemned in Austria. Supporting his argument with reference to recently legislated anti-discriminatory practices in the Israeli military, Rabinovici pointed out the political dimension of this rejection. Such an act of specific intolerance could only serve to justify and strengthen all intolerance.[3]

For Rabinovici as well as for millions of others living as minority groups within larger contexts, leaving a homeland no longer entails a definitive break with cultural and national roots and a passive assimilation to an adopted home. Identity formation is an ongoing negotiation, a constant transaction sensitive to the changing dissonances and harmonies between the old and the new. A central theme of his novel *The Search for M* is the difficulty of this negotiation for a community of victims, the children of Holocaust survivors. While Rabinovici can claim particular insight into this process he has also begun to play a key part in a renewed dialogue with the non-Jewish majority in Austria. As other Jewish writers have pointed out, there is a need to break the silence and long-simmering resentment, to become what Ruth Klüger called "quarrelsome" and to seek out confrontation. Rabinovici not only seeks out this confrontation directly in his journalism, but indirectly in his fiction as well.

---

[3] "Laßt die Synagoge im Dorf!" *Der Standard* 10 October 1997, 43 <http://DerStandard.at/archiv>.

Ariadne Press
New Titles – 2000

Translations:

The Lighted Windows
By Heimito von Doderer
Translated by John S. Barrett

Stone's Paranoia
By Peter Henisch
Translated by Craig Decker

Pedro II of Brazil
Son of the Habsburg Empress
By Gloria Kaiser
Translated by Lowell A. Bangerter

Odysseus and Penelope
An Ordinary Marriage
By Inge Merkel
Translated by Renate Latimer
Afterword by Gerd K. Schneider

The Search for M
By Doron Rabinovici
Translated and with an Afterword
by Francis Michael Sharp

The Lake
By Gerhard Roth
Translated and with an Afterword
by Michael Winkler

Murder at the Western Wall
By Gerald Szyszkowitz
Translated by Todd C. Hanlin

Brazil
A Land of the Future
By Stefan Zweig
Translated by Lowell A. Bangerter

Studies:

Austria in Literature
Edited by
Donald G. Daviau

Critical Essays on Julian Schutting
Edited by
Harriet Murphy

After Postmodernism
Austrian Literature and Film
in Transition
Edited by Willy Riemer

Autobiography:

Winds of Life
Destinies of a Young Viennese Jew
1938-1958
By Gershon Evan

CPSIA information can be obtained
at www.ICGtesting.com
Printed in the USA
FSHW011911121019
62967FS